RED DAYS
POPULAR MUSIC AND THE ENGLISH COUNTERCULTURE 1965-1975

John Roberts

Red Days: Popular Music and the English Counterculture 1965-1975
John Roberts

ISBN 978-1-57027-364-3

Cover design by Haduhi Szukis
Interior design by Margaret Killjoy

Released by Minor Compositions 2020
Colchester / New York / Port Watson

Minor Compositions is a series of interventions & provocations drawing from autonomous politics, avant-garde aesthetics, and the revolutions of everyday life.
Minor Compositions is an imprint of Autonomedia
www.minorcompositions.info | minorcompositions@gmail.com

Distributed by Autonomedia
PO Box 568 Williamsburgh Station
Brooklyn, NY 11211

www.autonomedia.org
info@autonomedia.org

CONTENTS

Acknowledgments 5

Introduction: English Exceptions 7

1: 'New Folk-Thinking' and the English Pastoral . . . 33

2: Irony and Post-Imperial Deflation 71

3: Feminization and Threnody 111

4: Extensity and the Song-Form 141

Conclusion 183

"Although our songs are frail, they belong to the life we want."
– Friedrich Hölderlin

"We leave unachieved in the summer dusk. There are no maps of moon-
light. Things stand further off. We find peace in the room and don't ask
what won't be answered. We don't know what we see, so there is more
here. More. Here."
– R.F. Langley

ACKNOWLEDGMENTS

This book has been long in the thinking if not in the making; in some sense I've been too close to the material to write about it, too resistant to its charms and affects to make proper use of it. This is because there are, inevitably, philosophically, politically, adolescent passions, resonating in, even coursing, through these materials, and so one should be careful. Yet, in the end one can be too careful, too protective. This book is the outcome.

There are a few scattered people I would like to thank: John Cage, who once, graciously signed a copy of *Finnegan's Wake's* for me after Silvia-Panet Raymond and I had interviewed him, and whose exemplary music and passion have always haunted the things I have most wanted from music, at least when reflection is most needed; the many bands I mention in the book and who I saw at their height such as Henry Cow, Robert Wyatt's Soft Machine and Van Der Graaf Generator; Patrick Wright's *On Living in an Old Country* (1985) a book of forensic magnificence in its dissection of the national spirit under Thatcher and the postpunk settlement, and that has always stayed with me as a guide to the English past and future; the artist Matthew Cornford who I have spent endless hours talking about the incomparable generosity of the 1960s English art school; Marc James Léger and Cayley Sorochan for their insightful comments on the manuscript; to Colin Beckett, Mark Harris, and James Hellings for their support and interest in the project; to Stevphen Shukaitis at Autonomedia for his editorial work and support; and to the artist Chris Riding, whose pre-I-player CD compilation *Mad as a Badger's Armpit: A Partial Gazetteer To The Pastoral Sounds of Old Albion (1965-2004)*, from 2004, uplifted and humoured me, and then coaxed and stirred me into thinking again about what was so transformative about those years; and why England, of all places, in post-imperialist decline, and still mired in a public culture of high-cultural condescension and populist, rebarbative sentiment, could produce so much, with so much intensity.

INTRODUCTION
ENGLISH EXCEPTIONS

BETWEEN 1965 AND 1975 ENGLISH POPULAR CULTURE UNDERWENT AN extraordinary and rapid process of change, particularly in the area of popular music. This history of course is much celebrated, historicized and mined, in an endlessly repeated incantation of what was so special, so transformative, and so creative about the 1960s. Indeed, it was popular music that very much defined and shaped these changes – and changed horizons – as a new kind of popular experience smashed its way through what remained of Tin Pan Alley versification, Edwardian show tunes and 'light entertainment,' and postwar United States-derived crooning and balladeering. And, therefore, popular music, understandably, has come to represent these changes in the popular, more broadly, for good reasons – it opened up an unprecedented space for new kinds of subjective experiences that other cultural forms were unable to accomplish, certainly with the same range of affective power. In addition, in England this is not just about the assimilation of rock 'n' roll as the lingua franca of a new popular cultural exuberance, as if, after Bill Haley in the late 1950s England suddenly 'gets' rock 'n' roll. Rock 'n' roll in the late sixties in

England is soon and comprehensively moved beyond in an act of critical and creative assimilation and displacement. Compare the Beatles *Sgt. Pepper's Lonely Hearts Club Band* (1967) and Van Der Graaf Generator's even more extraordinary *H to He Whom am the Only One* (1970) to Jerry Lee Lewis or Elvis, who by 1965, seems as relevant as Dean Martin. Ironically between 1965 and 1975 popular music in England not only dismantles and ironizes the legacy of light entertainment and Edwardian cultural sentiment (the after-life of which is best exemplified by one of the big hit films of 1968, *Chitty Chitty Bang Bang*),[1] but US rock 'n' roll itself. For every one Ten Years After and Groundhogs paying homage to US guitar-based blues, there were five bands trying to deflate its legacy (The Bonzo Dog Doo Dah Band, early Pink Floyd, Kevin Ayers, Soft Machine), or seeking an exit point into a new reflective, even pastoral space and post-blues jazz dynamic for 'rock' (Van Morrison's *Astral Weeks* (1968), Nick Drake, Sandy Denny, Third Ear Band, Jack Bruce's impressive post-Cream *Songs for a Tailor* (1970), and, of course, The Incredible String Band, who in a sense reverse the process by exiting from rock into folk. Thus, the entry of English folk traditions, as much as jazz, electronic music, nascent noise music, new modernist poetry, and modern-classical atonal forms, all play their part in this shifting panoply of entrances and exits. One might say, then, that the expansion of 'rock culture' (as the defining popular form of the emerging counterculture) is what frames this period, not the arrival and acceptance of rock 'n' roll as a popular form.

The causes and impetus for these changes in the boundaries and meaning of the popular in music during this period are multiple and complex. Of primary importance, however, is the massive and collective entry of the working class and lower middle class after the 1950s into the production and active reception of an industrialized popular culture, in ways that reshape the expectations and horizons of both classes, and the meaning of popular culture itself. This is the defining shift of the period, and it takes various forms across Europe and North America, as young workers and lower middle-class workers and students and intellectuals begin to capture spaces from the post-1950s mass cultural spectacle, that the

---

1   Indeed, at the height of the counterculture, conservative popular taste is awash with nostalgia for Edwardian sentiment, reflected in the revival of interest in the Music Hall song, on the spurious grounds of a lost intimacy between singer and audience, and the passing of the cultivation of 'wit' as opposed to ideas. See for example, Colin MacInnes, *Sweet Saturday Night: Pop Song 1840-1920*, MacGibbon & Kee, London, 1967.

bohemian *marginalité* of jazz, merely dented. In Italy for instance, the rejection by younger workers of the factory system – of boredom and speed-ups and of a narrow PCI/trade-union workerism – finds its expression in an unprecedented revolutionary élan that takes in modernist theatre, film and performance, in a swirling openness to popular culture as an unfolding *gesamtkunstwerk*. Similarly, for young radical workers in Germany, in alliance with students and artists, there is broad identification of creativity with an expanded notion of the popular as event, in which communal living and a modernist dramaturgical spirit predominates. Rainer Werner Fassbinder's early films (1969-72) are exemplary of this shift; notes from this new world of sexual, cultural and political flux. And, of course, in France, post-68 revolutionary workers and students openly identify with a post-bourgeois notion of culture, operating beyond the institution and high-cultural precedent, with the Situationists in the vanguard. In England, however, it is popular music on the whole that drives the same post-literary and performative cultural ambitions and sensibilities. This is not simply because England shares a common language with the US and, as such, becomes the second home of 'rock 'n' roll'; but, rather, because of the weak penetration of avant-garde and revolutionary cultural thinking into public culture and notions of the popular in England after WWII. In England, as Perry Anderson charted famously in 1968 in his essay 'Components of the National Culture' in the *New Left Review* [2] the chronic class hierarchies and intellectual provinciality, and resilient etiolated modernisms of England in the early 1960s, made the European experience of the emerging countercultural, with its dynamic interpenetration of workers' struggles, the new forms of art and theatre and critical theory, less able to hegemonize the radical insurgencies of the English counterculture, even weakening the impact of the revolutionary intersection between art and politics after May 1968. In other words, traditional notions of high-culture (invariably reinforced by a state-driven BBC Reithian paternalism) blocked or severely weakened the lines of communication between the counterculture, worker's experience, and revolutionary theories of art, poetry and dramaturgy. With the exception of Conceptual Art (Art & Language, Keith Arnatt) and Gustav Metzger's auto-destructive events, the new modernist poetry (Basil Bunting's *Briggflatts* [1965] J.H. Prynne, Bob Cobbing, Veronica Forrest-Thomson, and Tom Raworth), and the novels of B.S. Johnson and J.G. Ballard, English high culture, in this period, negotiates a nativist

---

2   Perry Anderson, 'Components of the National Culture, *New Left Review*, No 50, 1968

and 'balanced' place for itself within the new counterculture, in the same way it negotiated a comfortable and 'workable' place for itself inside the European avant-garde in the 1930s, as in the domestication of Surrealism and its channeling into a popular repertoire of enigmatic and comic signs and effects (Bill Brandt, Paul Nash, David Lean's *Great Expectations* [1946], Dylan Thomas, Michael Powell and Emeric Pressburger, the Goons, Peter Blake).[3] Indeed, the new popular music was itself not immune to this BBC lowbrow avant-gardism (*Sgt Pepper*, for all its genuine breakthroughs, is a perfect exemplar of an English homely Surrealism, inculcated in the 1960s though the celebration of Lewis Carroll's *Alice in Wonderland* as a proto-surrealist text, and in the *genteel* absurdisms of Roger McGough and the Liverpool poets).

Popular music, then, given its central position within the Anglo-American cultural industries, finds itself in an unprecedented position: it provides the necessary social dynamic for the pressing countercultural energies from below, that the cultural and political underdeveloped high culture and world of popular entertainment could not provide. Indeed, popular music's *underdetermined* cultural form at the time (popular music had barely been touched by radical and critical sentiment since the 1920s and the days of Bertolt Brecht, Hanns Eisler and Kurt Weill; Bob Dylan recovering some of the spirit of this moment in 1963-64), and its *overdetermined* social form (the fact that it was produced and consumed mostly by the working class), made it extraordinarily rich and flexible space into which, the countercultural energies of young manual and white collar workers and students could flow. In this sense if high culture was not available as a realistic or conceivable site of change for most workers and the lower-middle class, an older popular music culture offered few compensations, given how much it seems to serve the ingrained and repressive interests of their parents, grandparents and teachers. Yet unlike high culture, popular music culture felt *in reach*, particularly since the late 1950s. Thus, whereas writing and performing a play seemed like an impossible, arbitrary and ineffectual way to shift class/cultural relations, opening up the stultifications of popular music in the direction of the counterculture did not; indeed, if young workers felt that they possessed popular music as a sphere of judgement and pleasure, they also felt that it

---

3   The exception being, Jack Clayton's *The Innocents* (1961), scripted by Truman Capote and starring Deborah Kerr, with its atmospheric and sinister echoes of Jean Cocteau's *La Belle at la bête* (1946). Clayton also directed *Room at the Top*, (1959), based on the John Braine novel.

was available to them to change. This is the point where a new generation becomes *producers as a matter of self-definition*; and the rock 'band' becomes the newly primed unit of production, and playing together an act of social solidarity that went well beyond musicianship as such. In fact, one forgets how with the Beatles, in particular, the band becomes a place of learning and shared identity, as opposed to a peripatetic 'work place' whereby managers, promoters, hangers on and advisors, get young musicians to do their bidding. The creative development of the Beatles as a public event is related precisely to the development of the band as a space of group solidarity and learning, irrespective of the personal disputes and difficulties that eventually split the group – and the thousands of groups that followed them recognized this and hoped to emulate it. This is why George Martin is crucial to the success of the Beatles; he helps develop and support this process, as a kind of 'research director.'

After the Beatles, if you're a young musician of ambition, you look at the Platters and Bill Haley's Comets and you think: how these groups are set up to make music are not worthwhile as 'places of learning,' even if they are places where music of some value to the charts might still get made – a crucial difference. Moreover, if you're a young female musician of ambition you also look at these possibilities in a new way. That the 'new band' is still a boy's club is undeniable; the remaking of the popular is for the music business always about a strict sexual division of musical labour, and the production of the 'female fan' above all else, irrespective of the direction and content of the music. Even at the high point of the counterculture in England the music business is still being driven by a certain male camaraderie and assumptions about rock, old and new, as the domain of an irreducible masculine energy. Yet, it is the 'new band' certainly, post the Beatles, that incorporates women musicians – albeit mostly singers – into the working life of the band, laying the ground for the female singer or female singer-song writer who fronts her own group (Joni Mitchell, Sandy Denny, Janis Joplin, Gilli Smyth). The process is terribly uneven and women's contribution as musicians at the time is subject to attack and ridicule, particularly when they threaten symbolic castration (think of the condemnation of Yoko Ono when she 'joins' the Beatles as Lennon's occasional collaborator), nevertheless, the new 'band-form' opens out a space for women musicians that is irreversible, as women demand a stake in how the new popular musics frame the languages of 'freedom' and 'liberation' and 'sexual identity.'

So, we should not underestimate the dynamic character of what the 'new band' meant for a new generation of musicians, negotiating a space between an older popular culture and the expectations of a new one. This means that post the Beatles a critical choice was offered to young working class and lower-middle class musicians: what are my ambitions worth? How serious can they be? This is not to inflate the intellectual judgements and expectations of this generation of young musicians raw and uncertain as they were, but, rather, to recognize this as a real moment of transformative autodidacticism in the working class's and lower-middle-class's remaking of the popular in the 1960s: popular music, was seen, largely for the first time, as a place where ideas and workers' own intellectual identity could be explored, even if the primary drive and dominant narrative was to 'entertain,' and further, even if the pressures of the business were always there to compromise these intellectual and creative ambitions. In other words, the 'new band' circa 1966 (as opposed to the vocal group or knock-about ensemble or 'rock show band,' such as The Shadows or Swinging Blue Jeans) was equivalent in certain respects to the experimental 'artists group' or even workshop training provided by a bourgeois academy. Without acknowledging this shift in expectation one cannot understand the huge investment that working class and lower-middle class musicians make in the production and reception of a new popular music from the 1960s; on the one hand, it obviously produces a moment of sensuous and transgressive rupture from the old cultures of sentiment, a moment of hedonism – without doubt – yet on the other hand, it defines a space for heterodox intellectual exploration and invention, that defies the received place of the 'untrained' musician, and as such defines popular music as a social and collectivizing force. Frank Zappa and the Mothers of Invention in the US, working under very different countercultural and class conditions than the new 'rock' in England in the late sixties, are exemplary of this shift, even if Zappa has little sympathy for counterculture politics, reflected in his 'parallel' career as writer of cynical pastiches of rock songs, as we will discuss later; nevertheless Zappa's *Hot Rats* (1969) is definitional of a new ambition for rock that extends the band-form into the spirit of the collective, offering 'rock' post *Sgt. Pepper* (before English progressive rock of the early 1970s) a certain gravitas and spatial range borrowed from jazz, but without any of the melancholic defeat of jazz after be-bop.

Thus the prestige of a received high culture and the creaking timbers of an older popular music culture (of languid sentiment and sanguine lovesickness and tired priapic 1950s 'rock 'n' roll) were soon pushed aside in the mid-1960s given that neither were able to hold back the new cultural demands of a younger generation of workers, who had absolutely no stake in the old social reference points and markers of imperialist and class deference, that the high culture and the old popular culture still peddled, either aggressively or nostalgically. This truly is a cultural revolution from below; and, certainly in England this had much to do with the impact of 1944 Butler Education Act, as many working class and lower-middle class students passed into higher education for the first time, benefitting from the expansion of higher education in art and the humanities. Thus, even if the lines of communication between the new European counterculture and the new art and workers' struggles did not open up a radical countercultural space itself – of note, that is – nevertheless, the advent of the new music and the counterculture in the mid-sixties in England was not possible without this accumulative impact of new educational opportunities from below. Thus, the very simple idea of 'seeing' the notion of a band as a possible space of learning and self-transformation and participation is inseparable from this, for it is in the very act of seeing what rock music might be, that is produced through exposure to the counterculture.

Pete Townsend, Ray Davies and David Bowie are very precise about this moment of interpolation: the band is the staging of a creative process that is potentially infinite, and as such being in a band, for their generation at least, once working class energy and experience began to remake the popular, felt like being at the centre of the world. One cannot imagine any young working class man or woman, at their place of work, or elsewhere for that matter, saying anything like that with the same degree of confidence 30 years before. Popular music in England, then, from 1965-1975, certainly takes on some of the classic characteristics of a counter-hegemonic insurgence, insofar as working class participation in the remaking of popular culture and the making of a counterculture provided a collective and liberatory moment of dissociation between workers' identity *as* workers and workers' experience and identity outside of the workplace; a radical shift in subjectivity. And, as a result, the very symbolic order of working class experience shifts in England, as the increased visibility of rock bands as the vanguard of working class creativity displaces the subaltern visions of saluting squaddies, and mute or comic factory workers from British films from the decades of imperialist decline, or clumsy ingrates and idiots from popular radio comedy shows.

In this respect we might say the new educational opportunities prepared young workers for the new counterculture. The entry of workers and the lower-middle class, in sizeable numbers, into (some) universities and colleges gave students the intellectual tools and resources and reference points to remake popular music in their own interests. This is why the creative space for a new popular culture did not happen overnight, nor was it simply an explosion of youthful energy let loose by the postwar growth in wages – the usual and comforting narrative. Rather, it was the release of incremental coming together of new forms of working class self-representation and ambition and lower-middle class ambition – formed by the new educational opportunities – into negotiation, alliance and conflict with bourgeois cultural achievement and values, that is, with non-instrumental (abstract) ideas and systematic forms of knowledge. In other words, the counter-hegemonic insurgency of the period is not simply the re-assertion of 'working class identity' under the aegis of a new popular culture made available by the new media technologies, but of an *unprecedented creative exchange between the working class and the lower middle class and the class that has economic and administrative power*. This is the crux of the extraordinary achievements of the period 1965-1975 in England: capital and the culture industry are compelled to give the new music space on its own counter-hegemonic terms as a 'popular movement' from below. One can talk cynically, like Manfredo Tafuri in *Architecture and Utopia* in 1973,[4] therefore, about how accommodating the culture industry was in its use of popular music's place in the counter-culture – indeed how *simpatico* counterculture and culture industry were in the end, given the eventual dissociation of the new popular music from revolutionary culture by 1974; the primary function of the countercul-ture being to instigate a new regime of consumer desire – or, one can talk more profitably like Michael Denning, in his work on the Cultural Front in the US in the 1930s,[5] about these years in England as representing a comparable shift, albeit brief, in cultural power, as the working class (in alliance with the lower-middle class) reorganize the pleasures and terms of engagement of the popular. The palpable superiority of the latter po-sition derives then from the fact that the remaking of the popular in this period is the transformative outcome of collective self-representa-tion and self-education as it meets a bourgeois culture in retreat or on

---

4   Manfredo Tafuri, *Architecture and Utopia: Design and Capitalist Development* [1973], translated by Barbara Luigia La Penta, MIT Press, Cambridge Mass., and London, 1976

5   Michael Denning, *The Cultural Front*, Verso, London and New York, 1997

the defensive. And this is why the institutional conditions of the new educational settlement are so crucial to this impetus and vision. For, above all else, it is the art school in England where much of the primary transformative work gets done, as working class, lower-middle class and middle-class students, mix freely as creative equals, in contrast to the experience of working class and lower-middle class students elsewhere in the educational system, particularly outside of the art and humanities in Oxbridge and the red bricks. The crucial point here, therefore, is the art school in England, after the 1944 Education Act, is one of the key conduits and support mechanisms for the counterculture in its early years, becoming in a small way unofficial 'academies' or 'conservatoires' for a new generation of rock musicians, or if one wants to be less grand: rehearsal rooms.

There are two reasons the art school becomes so crucial to this shaping of the counterculture in England in this way: firstly the new educational changes allowed students to attend art school with few academic qualifications (enfranchising large numbers of working class students) and, secondly, as a quirk of pre-war state provision for art and mostly design, England had a huge number of independent art schools that offered a large number of students around the country the opportunity to go to a local college to complete a Foundation art course in order to discover what aspects of visual practice they might want to pursue.[6] In this respect, unlike, Germany or France or the USA, by the early 1960s, there was an extensive and informal state network of creative entry points into higher education that many working class and lower-middle class students were able to benefit from (that, in short, were inclusive), and that, consequently, had a real transformative impact on lives. Admittedly, many of these regional art schools in the 1960s were not particularly interested in the vicissitudes of contemporary art – indeed many were opposed to it and were still negotiating early modernism in a grizzled and uninformed way – but that in a sense didn't matter for many students, for in the light of the overall liberal character of the art school and its unwillingness to impose anything like a regime of study, whatever tutors may have said in the studio about 'contemporary art' was actually secondary to the

---

6   For a discussion of the call from improvement in the teaching of art and design from within the 'progressive' fraction of the British bourgeoisie in the 1830s, and the rise of the English Art & Design School, see Andrew Hemingway, *Landscape Between Ideology and Aesthetic: Marxist Essays on British Art and Art Theory, 1750-1850*, Haymarket Books, Chicago, 2017

real opportunity the school offered for students to meet other people, and experience the demands of artistic ambition and auto-didacticism in a sympathetic setting. In this way the art school became – for those who took the opportunity – an informal meeting ground for the new counterculture, politics and emerging music (at some level John Lennon, Townsend, Bowie, Davies, Eric Clapton, Brian Eno all testify to this, in various ways, and with various emphases). Thus, if the 'new band' houses a new spirit of collective creativity, the art school houses the 'new band.'

However, to say the art school had a powerful influence in this respect, does not thereby mean that it *defined* the contours of the English counterculture or shaped its overall direction; there were far more budding rock musicians outside the art school system as were in it, far more young musicians on provincial housing estates and in forgotten corners of small towns; similarly, for all its confluence of ideas, and openness to cross-disciplinary ideas, art schools in the 1960s were not alternate universities in any strict sense; and as such the transformation of art student into thinking rock musician, or musician into rock musician was largely a post-theoretical affair; a huge number of writers, musicians and intellectuals and leading artists may have tutored part-time in art schools, and many contributed to a countercultural agenda during this period, but the art school was not producing 'countercultural cadres' to order.

These conflicted horizons of the English counterculture and the new art school are no better illustrated by the Hornsey School of Art sit-in – which lasted for six weeks – in May 1968. Referred to casually as England's own Paris May 1968, it was actually far from it, reflecting the particular localized character of the English's counterculture's relationship to the European avant-garde, revolutionary political thought and the counterculture. Like the student uprisings in Nanterre which started as a dispute about academic conditions and freedoms, the 24-hour strike at Hornsey (May 28) began with a frustration with the poor working conditions for students and a range of disciplinary measures imposed on student movements, yet, the students' later pedagogic demands were far from suasive or coherent, at least in relation to the radical cultural expectations of the time. Thus, on the one hand, the students called for the egalitarian dropping of *all* entry qualifications (it was at the time just 5 O-Levels) on the basis that the study of art was a special (non-academic case), and therefore did not require formal methods of assessment as did other subjects; but, on the other hand, the students' struggle for disciplinary autonomy collapsed into, and indeed was framed by, a conservative anti-intellectualism that fell in line with the worst aspects of countercultural 'spontaneitism' of the period. In this respect, underlying the students' demands was a regressive resistance to art's increasing place in post-artisanal intellectual division of labour, represented by the rise of minimalism and the emerging conceptual art and the need for different sets of artistic and critical skills. Indeed, the initial disciplinary and pedagogic demands of the students were intellectually unexacting, seeking a strengthening of the old atelier system (perpetuated by still active defenders of Abstract Expressionism). This in turn was reflected, as the sit-in unfolded, in the students' defence of the special creative dispensations of art and the independent art school, against the impending subsumption of Hornsey and other art schools in the UK under the new 'open access' Polytechnic system, and its concern to drive out some of the ingrained intuivistic mechanisms of conservative fine art education. The Hornsey sit-in, therefore, represents a perfect snapshot of the English counterculture and the art school: it sets out to protect what is unusual, vital and compelling about the post-war English art school, yet, relies on mostly provincial arguments to do so, reflecting the wider ad hoc, links between revolutionary politics and new avant-garde cultural practices and the transformation of the popular in England during the period.[7]

Nevertheless, what is unprecedented and remarkable, is that the 1960s pre-Polytechnic art school and the art school between 1970 and 1975 *does more than it offers*, that is, art students having arrived to study art don't necessarily make art and no one is particularly worried. In the academy schools in the 1930s that would have been incomprehensible, and a clear sign for the student to be disciplined or removed (and for the middle class student a source of shame). In the 1960s, it was seen, rather, as an opportunity for the student to do other things, even if not making any art at all would have more than likely still meant you failed the course. The difference, then, is that by the mid-1960s art education, for all its immanent resistance to what passes for the contemporary, can see the value in treating 'art' as a process that can take in all kinds of heterodox activities. Using the art school as a jumping off point for a career in music, or as a place where thinking as opposed to the production of objects (conceptual art, passim), is done, is therefore tolerated. And this

---

7   For a discussion of the Hornsey sit-in and the English art school, see Lisa Tickner, *Hornsey 1968: The Art School Revolution*, Frances Lincoln, London 2008, and Nick Wright, 'What happened at Hornsey on 28 May 1968,' available at http://21centurymanifesto.wordpress.com/2012/05/28what-happened-at-hornsey-on-28-may-1968/

in turn, produces a training of sorts for those working class art students who do become rock musicians, and those working class art students who find their place in some creative capacity in the counterculture: a training in critical values that takes seriously what the 'untrained' might contribute or aspire to. In other words, the art school offered working class and lower-middle class students space to *fail creatively* without malicious judgement, and this is decisively important in contributing to the subjective shifts in class agency that contribute to the remaking of the popular in the 1960s. The art school, consequently, offers working class and lower-middle class students an enabling link to a space of production in which the expression of *their* ideas and their connection to processual thinking has merit; and these ideas, in turn, as the interdependent values of the new rock musician, become the new means of evaluation of what a rock 'band' is or can do; and this begins to have wide influence. This is why progressive rock bands in 1970 (such as Van der Graaf Generator, Soft Machine, King Crimson and Comus) are not formed simply out of 'musical partnerships' (as free-floating jazz musicians might have done in the 1950s), but out of a new sense of the band as a place where the ideals of the counterculture can be processed and negotiated and therefore where *concepts* and *projects* might be hatched without preconceptions. In other words, progressive rock in the wake of the profound influence of the Beatles' *Sgt. Pepper*, is more than a place where rock music 'goes to school'; it is, rather, one of the key points where the 'use values' of popular music undergo an unprecedented critical expansion, fluidity and destabilization. Crucially, then, these use values are at odds with both the received assumptions about working class and lower-middle class musicians' expectations, and the presumptions of popular taste, as popular culture assimilates a new hybridity and curiosity that stretches repertoire, instrumentation and the narrow conventions of the song-form.

Thus, if only something like four percent of the adult population in Britain at the time went onto higher education, a sizeable minority of the working class and lower middle class from this larger minority of students did go onto art school, the art school becoming an unprecedented meeting ground for new ideas and values. The point, therefore, is that this making manifest of working class and lower-middle class creativity – albeit confined to a domain that most workers, certainly older workers knew little about – was an important point of attraction for most young workers not in higher education and unfamiliar with expanded notions of creativity espoused by some of the art schools and new cultural theorists. Consequently, we need to be clear that by 1966-67 these shifts in

educational provision and cultural allegiance in effect produce a generational rift between the older language of class (of family ties, trade union
consciousness, and Workingmen's Clubs) and the dissonant and heterodox values of the modernist counterculture, raising the expectations and
confidence of young workers as a result. That, these expectations are not
shared by older workers is, of course, a source of severe political tension
as the counterculture in Britain becomes the seedbed for the New Left
(young radical workers in alliance with the radical lower-middle class), as
opposed to being an ally of the old class politics (wage struggles). Indeed,
this rift lays down a pattern of political realignment that defines the increasing readjustment of a corporate and industrialized working class
identity to that of the worker as consumer. Yet, whatever wider processes
of class re-composition are at play in the counterculture and the remaking of popular music between 1965 and 1975, there is no disputing the
fact that the decade's counter-insurgency is made under the sign of the
Red Decade, as opposed to simply 'liberal' inclusion. To obviate this, play
it down, stress the fundamental asymmetry between music and politics,
music and class assertion, or diminish the politics of the counterculture
as such, is to disaggregate the massive collective transformation in consciousness and values that actually occurred; a radical transvaluation of
what a reflective life and working life might sound and look like outside
of the nuclear family, factory and office.

David Widgery talked in *Oz* in 1973 about the counterculture as "trans-
mitting a mood of indiscipline to young people of all classes."[8] I would
be far more specific: it transmitted *techniques* of indiscipline, or 'techniques of negation,' specifically through popular music. This is why I
am loath here to talk just about working class 'resistance,' still one of
the mainstays of the study of popular music within cultural studies and
popular musicology.[9] What is at stake in *Red Days*, is not simply working class 'resistance,' but more exactly *working class and cross class
creativity*. Popular music under capitalism produces microcultural and
informal forms of resistance continuously; in a sense the music industry

---

8   David Widgery, *Oz*, No 45, 1973. For a more openly critical view of the counter-
     culture, see Widgery, 'Let's Have a Party,' *Oz* No 42, May/June, 1972: "You can't
     think your way out of capitalism. Those who make the revolution in a commune
     or a bookshop or a rock band end up turning the treadmill of their own desires in a
     self-deflecting attempt at totalization." p26

9   See for example, Marek Korczynski, *Songs of the Factory: Pop Music, Culture &
     Resistance,* Cornell University Press, Ithaca and London, 2014

demands it. These can be described as communities of resistive-listening or rituals of disorder. However, popular culture rarely produces an upsurge in working class creativity as part of a social transformation in values. The late sixties and the early seventies did so, through an unprecedented process of *collective and productive indiscipline*, as definitions of the popular unmoored themselves from the condescending judgements of post-1950s high culture, the chronic sentiment of the old popular culture, and the conformist rock 'n' roll seeking to displace it. The remaking of the popular, therefore, between 1965 and 1975, is more than a revision of popular taste; it is, rather, the demolition of old cultural allegiances and habits, as cultural forces inside and outside of music (the belated legacy of Dada and Surrealism, modernist poetry, post-tonal and non-Western musics,), shatter the assumption of popular music as the home for passive adolescent identifications or 'unthought' passion and escape. And these forces, cultural, political and educative, *re*-resource the popular through the release of the critical energy of young working class and lower middle-class musicians and listeners determined to remake the culture in their own name. For example, the song-form is opened up to an extraordinary range of literary, artistic and high-cultural transformations, that brings performance, staging, new instrumentation, and the radical extensity words and music, into new kinds of alignment (viz: the opening up of the song-form *outside* of the dance-hall traditions of blues/rock). This in turn produces new kinds of listeners, with new musical and social expectations, given the pressure the counterculture brings to bear on the self-identity of *all* musicians at the time, ensconced within their own class identities, racialized and gendered traditions and generic musical domains. In other words, it is through this intersectoral re-alignment of form and tradition, that new techniques of indisciplinarity and the remaking of the popular are produced.

Yet, even so, we need to be careful about where, and by whom and under what conditions these techniques of indiscipline took place, for they are certainly not uniform. This is because the counterculture was not one thing; there was the counterculture of the 'swinging sixties' centred on London and a small charmed circle of the aristocratic, privileged and well connected, close in spirit to late 19th century Symbolists in its élite indifference even antagonism to the production of a new culture from below or new claims on popular music; there was the counterculture of synaesthetic *ambience*, drugs and environmental affects and stimulation, of fashion and casual sexual encounters, of hanging out at the Arts Lab in Covent Garden, largely a play area for the middle class; and there was the counterculture of popular music as a place of utopian impulses and critical identities for the young working class and lower middle-class across the country intent on remaking the popular in its own projected image; a place where making music or attending to those making music, seriously, is determined by the notion of what the counterculture might be as an egalitarian cultural force. None of these domains are wholly separate: the counterculture was an alienating and fascinating elite club and 'sorority,' a middle-class playground and newly sexualized domain of the everyday, *and* a transformative encounter with bourgeois and modernist culture; and each young person negotiated these domains, depending on class, gender, race, sexuality, history and cultural needs.

But what expressly defines the techniques of indiscipline here? What is, indeed, captured by the general effects of this indiscipline? Is it, to reiterate, the libertarian expansion of consumption, of a newly individuated hedonism, as Tarfuri would claim of the counterculture? Or, does it, facilitate, rather, in unprecedented ways, the negation of a bourgeois culture that hitherto had allowed little or no place for the (emergent and unformed) creative techniques of the dominated? In these terms, the question of technique – who possesses it and to what ends and under what conditions – is always a social and collective question. So, what defines the techniques of indiscipline, here, is less the recalibration of popular taste for new markets, than a radical convergence between the production of new social use values in music – new subjective spaces and modes of attention – and collective experience. The making of music attends the making of new social relations that presuppose, a wider dissociation from prevailing social forms and ideologies. Hence one of the key musical determinates of techniques of indisciplinarity in the late sixties in England is the emergent intersection between heterodox nativist English musical traditions (folk music and choral music, in particular) and European modernisms as part of the post-Empire critique of the racism and xenophobia of English monoculture, and the delimited sense of the social use values of music this produces. In this light, there is a wonderful photo of Gong that accompanies their 1971 album *Camembert Electrique*, in which the band, dressed in their quasi-medieval togs and Romano 'countercultural' *haute couture* and are lined up in front of their farm house/studio in Sens in rural France. Daevid Allen who is standing confidently and determinately in the middle in his blue tights and furry boots is holding a long staff, their great drummer Pip Pyle in his calf length black and silver boots (who was to soon join Hatfield and the North) is peering down solicitously at his young stepson (Sam Wyatt, Robert Wyatt's son);

to the left of Pyle, looking like rather dashing Spanish spies from the Napoleonic wars, are the saxophonist Didier Malherbe in baggy flowing shirt and the bassist Christian Tritsch in riding breeches, and to the right of Pyle and Allen, both turning away from the group, are Venux De Luxe ('Switch Doctor') in his knee length leopard skin print waistcoat and the singer Gilli Smyth (*Mother*, 1978) in a gorgeous floor length brocaded dress. One part a company roll call from a Middle Earth inspired rock panto and one part a sylvan vision out of Edward Carpenter, the scene carries with it all the pathos of failed counterculturalist ruralism and spiritualist hokum (poignantly underwritten by the sight of a forlorn rabbit in a hutch in a line of empty hutches, neglected or dead). Yet, it touches – if lightly – on a spirit of communization that occurs and reoccurs in many forms and guises, creative and absurd throughout the period, as popular music rethinks the terms of its social reach. For this is also an image of the 'band' as commune (as opposed simply to the collective), as a family without Families and as such a more explicit presentation of the concept of the band after the Beatles, as a site for musical and social experimentation. In the same year the album was released David Cooper published *The Death of the Family*, in the spirit of what he was later to call in *The Grammar of Living* (1974), a "revolt against first world values;"[10] something of this haunts this photograph, in which the extended band as 'ideal' family, stands against the unrealizable nuclear family of industrial capitalism, and the insidious families of an exclusionary high culture and a self-loving and sentimental postwar popular culture. Without recognizing this spirit of communization, there are simply 'rock bands' and 'festivals,' crowds and parties, bad trips and 'dropping out,' freaks and straights.

Thus, this was a generation, in all its heterogeneity, delusions and conflicted desires, whose thinking was produced at the intersection between an emancipatory language on the other side of wage labour, workerism, and the nuclear family, and the pleasures of musical and artistic creativity in process; that this should be called 'hedonism' is an insult, therefore, to the huge labour of affective and somatic and intellectual transformation (of voice, tone, song structure and performance; of instrumentation; of musical use values and music as collective experience) that young musicians put in place, and that, drew towards it, irrepressibly, in turn, other transformative experiences, knowledges and practices. But there is a moot and oft mentioned point that needs addressing. The English

---

10 David Cooper, *The Grammar of Living*, Allen Lane, London, 1974, p3

counterculture was not revolutionary, even if it was made in revolutionary times and with revolutionary materials. And when the old left chastised it as such in 1968 at the height of the students' movement and after it was right; you cannot organize a revolution from the side of a stage, or in a squat, or from a tent in a field or a rural retreat in France (unless, that is, you're fronting up a monstrous regiment of workers and the plebeian righteous). Indeed, once, the political and social expectations for cultural change dissolved, and as such no longer appeared supportable, musical expectations and horizons became narrowed, subjecting the possible links between new use values in music and new collective experience to constraint and eventual foreclosure. And so, we should not be surprised about the fate of the counterculture after 1974.

By 1975-76, after the political downturn, the counterculture – certainly what remained of it at the English summer festivals – had become a galumphing caravanserai of Edenists, tricksters, herbalists, Tofuism and recidivist Blues-band bores, that haboured a lower-middle class anarchist line of least resistance, in which 'rock' stood against the world in a dreary inflation of the Romantic mythos of the outsider; some of the bands continued (like Gong), but, there was no framing culture and set of expectations to renew what was being lost; and the music became awful in a softening of earlier glories. Even Henry Cow, the best of the best, could only stick it for a few years more, unable to survive financially, and eventually losing their way like everyone else. In this sense, the counterculture had been defeated, outrun by events, as the new inventories of market realism and popular entertainment began to reassert themselves in a grievous backsliding against the sublimities and extemporizations of the late sixties, particularly once the political expectations of the counterculture began to be talked of as a 'failed experiment' in the music industry, and as such as an increasing burden on the marketing of new and adolescent desires.

Let us recall: by 1979, with the election of Margaret Thatcher and the Tory Party in Britain, the family had again become the redoubt of (racist) patriotism, waged-labour and conservative paternalism and a bolt hole from public culture, shifting notions of the popular into highly defensive modes. Indeed, the identification of the popular with openness, non-instrumentality and the challenges of the non-generic were resisted, certainly in popular music, as the pursuit of new listeners was channeled through the recovery and adaptation of old rock formats and hackneyed pop and rock 'n' roll habits and signifiers. In an ordinary sense, then, countercultural 'rock culture' simply didn't know what to do under these circumstances, given that the exoteric politics and economic conditions and cultural reference points that had helped produce it were no longer available to keep things flowing, whether musicians and audience directly paid attention to these things or not. No wonder punk seemed like an incendiary attack of realism, as the would-be radical vanguard of these 'new-old' formats. For it appeared to get the musicians to look up again from their amps and keyboards to what had been borne from the end of the counterculture, certainly in the England of the mid-1970s: a world in grey, dark ruins. But one should not confuse realism here with capacity. Punk was realism without extended capacity, and as much a victim of circumstances as were the bands left hanging at the end of the counterculture.[11] Thus for all its localized interventions and reinventions punk could not compete with the affective and somatic and intellectual challenges of its immediate predecessors in any comparable fashion; and this is its unfailing limit (and even embarrassment) in relation to the glorious achievements of the 1960s and early 1970s, as its own brief countercultural moment splutters in and out of focus, to burn out, not in a great conflagration, but in a beer drenched squib, somewhere in Kentish Town, followed by the familiar howlings of betrayal and sell out. Punk, saddeningly, was a *Grand Guignol*, faux-anarchist remaking of the Edwardian music hall and the crapulent rhetorics of old school rock n' roll's priapic transgression of Mummy and Daddy's 'straight culture' (viz: the New York Dolls). Indeed, forget its sonic disruptions, what it did more than anything else was to help to forge a revived marriage – with Johnny Rotten as a pumped up Tommy Steele – of working class experience with the 'lumpen picturesque,' which continues to infect the representation of working class life and experience in English popular culture today, from the post-punk squalidness of the TV series *Shameless*

---

11 I'm very hard on punk in this book (when I briefly discuss it, that is), because punk divorced negation from technique, contributing to, and pre-empting, the proletarianization of cultural capacity that now ravages the working class (and 'surplus populations') culturally on a global scale. (See Bernard Stiegler, *The Re-Enchantment of the World: The Value of Spirit Against Industrial Populism*, translated by Trevor Arthur, Bloomsbury, London, 2014, and Bernard Stiegler, *Symbolic Misery, Vol. 1: The Hyperindustrial Epoch*, translated by Barnaby Norman, Polity Press, Cambridge, 2014). The nostalgia for punk is baffling, then, if only to underline how the monetized memory of popular music is increasingly tied into the wan and picturesque imagery of 'transgression.' For a discussion of these tensions around punk, see Pete Dale, *Popular Music and the Politics of Novelty*, Bloomsbury, London, 2016

(Channel 4) to the 'anti-globalization' nostalgic Anglo-hedonism of Jez Butterworth's play *Jerusalem* (2009). And let's be honest The Clash didn't escape this fate either. Yet, in the end, perhaps not so strangely, the vision of Rotten as a stage-turn is precisely that: a stage act, that reveals behind the curtain an unambiguous revulsion against rock itself. As Lydon was to say in 1980 after forming PiL:

> The Pistols finished rock'n'roll. That was the last
> rock'n'roll band. It is all over…We don't consider
> ourselves rock and roll at all. Rock and roll is shit
> and it has to be cancelled. It's vile, it's gone on for
> 25 years, it's dismal. A granddad dance, and I'm not
> interested in it.[12]

In fact, after the break-up of the Sex Pistols, Lydon offered his vocal services to Can (who at that point contained two ex-students of Karlheinz Stockhausen). In a sense Lydon's fury against conventional rock hides an old-school working class auto-didacticism and moral distaste for falling for the old ideological traps. In this Lydon's musical ambition is tied less to Tom Wolfe's *The Electric Kool-Acid Test* (1968), than to Richard Hoggart's *The Uses of Literacy* (1957): don't waste your energy on shit; don't assume that the would-be freedoms of rock are anything, but oppressive; rock is for schmucks and dullards (hello AC/DC!) and punk a debilitating sop to working class creativity: a negation not of the music that preceded it, but a rage against the destruction of the radical culture that produced it; dimwits like Sid Vicious never got that. So, one would want to say that the Sex Pistols lack of capacity, at least, had a good solid intellectual base to it! As, Malcolm McLaren, fueled by Situationist horizons, hoped. Indeed the marginal irony of this 'becoming punk' as the exorcism of rock was that Rotten knew what was worth listening to and what counted in 1973 and 1974, mostly progressive rock; Can certainly, Amon Düül 11, but also Van Der Graaf Generator who were a significant influence on Lydon, in particular Peter Hammill's post-Van Der Graaf Generator, *Nadir's Big Chance* (1975), the first English 'pre-punk' punk album, with its tight song-formats, guitar distortion and driving $\frac{4}{4}$ time signatures. Listen to Hammill's voice on 'Birthday Special' and his uplift on 'I': a dead ringer for Rotten on 'Anarchy in the UK' (1977). Yet, in many ways *Nadir's Big Chance* is a no less a regressive move than punk (the creation of rock 'n' roll snapshots, with rock 'n' roll whoops to boot,

---

12   Mark Cooper, 'Lydon the Exorcist,' *Record Mirror*, March 29th 1980.

accompanied by companionable soft-rock meanderings, removing all evidence of the extended and even operatic spatiality, sci-fi imaginary, and powerful crepuscular shading of the early Van Der Graaf Generator albums). Nevertheless, it is perfectly in keeping with the growing antipathy and intolerance to the intermediated spaces of the 'high' and 'low' in the best new music and progressive rock of the previous five years, as the record companies were no longer willing to support such bands, as the cultural and political landscape changes irrevocably.

1975-1976, then, is a real cut-off point for a post-rock 'n' roll sensibility, as the post-war boom, the Red Decade, the radical legacy of the counterculture, come to a crushing end. Punk is the gurning, retro-Edwardian music hall, anaclitic, revolutionary-in-a-counter-revolutionary guise substitute for this. And, whatever energy it released (and the extended participation of women in popular music), was not matched by the cross-class creativity and encounters with modernism of the previous years, as musical acuity was now defined by the empty signifiers of working class stylism and 'rebellion,' the bane of all rock music post rock's cataclysmic birth; a 'shock-stylism' that has more in common these days with right-wing US outrider 'survivalism' and US Republicanism and its imperialist 'Rock the Casbah' pugilism, than it does with the complex and heterodox musical communities of the late 1960s English counterculture. This is not to deny the extensive reinvigoration of the popular song-form in late 1970s and 1980s Britain after punk. In Britain from 1977-78 the chart pop song underwent an undeniable creative reinvention from New Order to David Sylvian's Japan, to Mark Stewart and the Pop Group and Green Gartside's Scritti Politti, as the attenuated political legacy of the counterculture, found its expression in a renewed investment on the part of working class and lower-middle class musicians in defining and defending the song-form as a space for heterodox social identities and sensibilities. Elvis Costello's achievement in this respect is enormous, as is Robert Wyatt's legacy after the 1970s, whose version of Costello's and Clive Langer's 'Shipbuilding' (1983), is a defining moment in this post-punk and post-countercultural settlement, and one of the great songs and performances of the period, just as are the sonorities of Liz Fraser of The Cocteau Twins, who manage to wrest a wondrous and newly indeterminate space for the song-form in the same period as the music industry begins to renew its pact with Tin Pan Alley under the economies of scale of neo-liberal accounting.

But the defence of the traditional song-form and the reinvention of 'rock 'n' roll' as antidote to modernism's transfiguration of popular music, is not what the late sixties and early seventies imagined alone for a newly ambitious and extended popular culture, and for the expansion of working class creativity. Indeed, one forgets what was at stake more generally for many of the working class and lower-middle class musicians who had been to art school or come under the sway of those who had been and told the tale: the re-making of popular music as a cultural activity was to be in the *spirit* of (modernist) artistic practice; and as such, music and musical collaboration, its staging and production, was on the one hand to find some working connection to visualization, performance, and dramaturgy, and on the other hand, some living and exploratory connection to non-rock and post-rock forms; thus if the song-form was absolutely central to the counterculture – as this book contends – it was not because it stood for continuity with the past, but because it offered an *underexplored space of experimentation*, and as such spatial extension (beyond verse-chorus-verse) into new forms of scenic, non-rock accompaniment. Townsend and Bowie, and later Mark E. Smith and the Fall, clearly understood this, but particularly Bowie, defining a distinct dramaturgical and later neo-avant-garde space – or aura – for his work in the late 1970s; similarly Eno in 1976, after Roxy Music, with his usual alacrity, pulls, some of the more interesting bits of 1970s German 'progressive' electronica into the orbit of a new post-rock space, as a bridging exercise between the fast disappearing progressive ethos and the new world of 'prepared' electronic (synthesized) soundscapes and later computer-based music, in his collaboration with Harmonia (Dieter Moebius, Hans Joachim Roedelius and Michael Rother [*Tracks and Traces*]). In typical Eno fashion, in 1976 he calls them "the world's most important rock group" (sleeve notes *Tracks and Traces*). However, we might say, rather, that this hyperbole is evidence of the strain of the counterculture in retreat, inasmuch as Eno celebrates technological novelty in music as a passkey to the future (his recurring mistake in his own radical positioning within the counterculture). One might say, then, that given Bowie's and Eno's respective histories and position in the market they had the wherewithal, unlike most musicians of their generation, to redefine – or at least, reconnect – with some of the formal and spatial ambitions of progressive rock. But of course, this is as much a holding operation, as it is a reinvention of the music of the art school; after *Low* (1977) and *Lodger* (1979) Bowie, 'restablizes' his career and makes his own significant contribution to the reinvention of the song-form in the 1980s ('Ashes to Ashes' (1980) and 'Fashion' (1980)); and Eno, moves more and more into production, indeed, song production. What connection their musics had with the broad political and creative class dynamic dynamics of the countercultural remaking of the popular is long gone. Here we might say, the countercultural is less the remaking of the popular, than the reassertion of 'genre' as the plural definition of musical style and ambition; the beginning of a wholly new world of inventories and their intellectual commodities.

Of course, I'm not the first to defend the socially and musically pre-figurative character of the English counterculture. Rob Young, for example, does a fine job in *Electric Eden* (2011) of excavating the English pastoral lines of descent of the counterculture, showing how closely connected were the notions of folk tradition and what I call 'new folk-thinking' (Chapter 2), to the new spirit of literary and musical hybridity; Jonathan Green, likewise, offers a nuanced, capacious and non-cynical account of the utopian longings of the English sixties counterculture, *All Dressed Up: The Sixties and the Counterculture*, (1998).[13] But *Red Days* does what most other books on the English counterculture do not do: locate these musical and literary changes within popular music firmly within this radical counter-insurgency and the internal re-composition of class and cultural relations: that is, those trained/untrained skills and attributes that produced a huge shift in modes of engagement, cognitive attention, and cultural allegiances from below. The book, therefore, in its decisive shift away from the 'resistance' model of popular music studies and cultural studies, highlights that largely for the first time, working class and lower middle musician and listeners had a direct say in the production of meaning, without facing the condescending judgements of those with cultural power. This is why the focus of this book is on techniques of in-discipline as part of an emancipatory emphasis on cross-class and post-generic creativity, under, the umbrella of what I define, more specifically, as the deflationary and radical impact of modernist *poiesis* in England in the sixties – England's own Weimar and US Cultural Front. This is why much of the book is taken up with the discussion of the expansion of the song-form during the counterculture and its aftermath. The literary, formal and musicological reworking of the popular song-form is one of the great and abiding achievements of popular music's expansion of these 'techniques of indisciplinarity' during the period, insofar as it is one of

---

13   Rob Young *Electric Eden*, Faber and Faber, London, 2011, Jonathan Green, *All Dressed Up: The Sixties and the Counterculture*, Pimlico, London, 1998. See also Jonathan Green, *Days in the Life: Voices from the English Underground 1961-1971*, Pimlico, London, 1998

the means by which, new musics and *politics* and new communities of listeners are sustained.

So, this book is in no sense a 'completist' history of progressive rock in England between 1965-1975. Rather my purpose is to single out those bands and singers who represent the shifts, expectations and horizons that define the radical transformations in the 'popular' that I outline. As such some music has to fall by the wayside, even those musics in the early 1970s that are fighting for their own space in Britain during this period, and which come loosely into the late orbit of the counterculture, such as ska and reggae. Indeed, in this light, we need to make a distinction between the general impact of (American) black modernism on jazz and popular music in this period (the assimilation of jazz into popular music post-John Coltrane and post-Ornette Coleman) and the specific influence of England-domiciled black modernist musicians, in jazz and dub reggae, on the new post-generic topology that I defend. The impact of this contribution falls outside of my time frame.[14]

Hence, just as this book is not a sociology of resistance through music, nor is it an exhaustive account of the English counterculture. Rather, it is an invitation to think again about the unparalleled character of the transformation from below of the popular and popular music in England during a brief period of counter-hegemonic insurgence, in the face of a capitalist culture today in grievous and ugly decline. In this respect, for all its recollective and redemptive qualities, the book provides a set of political, cultural and philosophic interrogations of the *possibilities and limits* of popular creativity under capitalism. Hence the distance it takes from 'resistance' per se and the emphasis it places on emancipatory

---

14   Thus, important dub albums by Augustus Pablo, *King Tubby Meets Rockers Uptown* (1976) and *East of the River Nile* (1977) establish their modernist influence in Britain *after* the counterculture, particularly in the early 1980s (Lydon's PiL for instance). Similarly, influential London-domiciled black jazz modernists such as Joe Harriott (who played with Ian Carr and Jimmy Page) and who died in 1973 and his colleague Shake Keane (who left the UK in 1966), have only the most fleeting impact on the new music and the English counterculture. Furthermore, black jazz virtuosity and the jazz *solo*, (irrespective of who is playing) is part of the problem for the new post-generic landscape of the popular; jazz may provide an expanded sense of 'space' for a good deal of the new musical hybridities (Sun Ra for example), but the most exacting progressive rock is antagonistic to instrumental improvisation as a mark of expressive value.

technique. This is why, in contrast to the school of self-authenticating masculine 'rock purism,' it situates English progressive rock within the broader achievements of the late 1960s and early 1970s, as opposed to its usual marginalization as a tributary influence on the period. And, as such, it is the post-generic space of progressive rock as a destabilizing horizon within popular music that is crucial to the book's overall claims. Progressive rock is the loose space into which and out of which a large number of musicians and musics pass during 1968-1975, in an attempt to reorganize the collective pleasures, political affects, and formal intensities and extensities of a post-rock popular music. In these terms it is worthy of high consideration. Indeed, the musical and political sequence between 1965-1975 we have been discussing, of which progressive rock plays a key part – and which England and to a lesser extent the US plays the dominant role – is period of cultural transformation of world historical importance. The counterculture insurgence – but particularly the counterculture in England – fundamentally changed how popular music operated under capitalism capturing for millions those moments of self-critical reflection and pleasurable immersion as a movement of the (sceptical) 'common spectator and reader' that early Romanticism so prized, and yet so feared was lost to reaction and sentiment in the years of post-Thermidor repression after the French Revolution. In this the English counterculture produces a transformative space of producer and audience that identified popular music and its social effects as critically, not just, distractingly affecting; that is, it produced 'listeners' as opposed to 'consumers.' This is why the new communities of producers and listeners after 1968, were able, in the spirit of the popular theatre and song of Weimar in the 1920s, to bend the popular into invigorating experimental and pleasurable shapes, particular in and around progressive rock, in its basic assumption that 'experiment' and the popular, could be, if not the same thing, at least concordant. One might say, accordingly, that progressive rock is the general name, not just for the new and varied post-rock musics of the period, but for an *intense conjunction* of the popular and the 'experiment,' of new kinds of songs, of new instrumentalizations, of new affective musicalities, that defines the great sweep of the popular from below during this period. Indeed, contrary, to the received view of progressive rock as extending popular music beyond the song-form (particularly through jazz rock), I argue, that what distinguishes the best of progressive rock is its continuation and development of the innovative moves being made in the new folk and post-rock re-functioning of the song: indeed, this is where its claims to experimentation most vividly lie, insofar as the best of progressive rock distinguishes itself from jazz, as a critical claim on hybridization.[15] In this, progressive rock continues the subsumption of the most ambitious of popular songs in the late sixties and seventies under the demands of musical hybridization and modernist *poiesis*. However, this does not mean that everything within the counter-culture that is of note was moving towards the achievements of (some) progressive rock; progressive rock is not the secret telos of the 1960s/early 1970s counterculture. Yet, progressive rock does represent a kind of open working space that derives from all the achievements that went before it, redefining in the process what preceded it, and, therefore, an encapsu-lation of the potentialities and possibilities of the period. In this respect a Hegelian spirit drifts through these pages. Firstly, one needs to see the integral shape of the musics produced between 1965-1975 (their inter-nal development, mutualities, discontinuities/continuities and local ne-gations) and secondly, overall, against the broad sweep of contemporary cultural post-class amnesia, one needs to acknowledge the world histori-cal character of the remaking of the popular during this period, in which progressive rock played its part. This was a period in which millions, as listeners and participants, helped create a popular music and counter-culture that was not just 'staffed' and serviced by the creative efforts of working class and lower middle class musicians, but actually shaped and defined by them in the interests of transforming the historical exclusions and icy and condescending hierarchies of bourgeois culture; and as such, if this period throws up moments of communization ('communization effects') as a result, it is because these moments are intimately connected to a music in the making that is open to all.

As a result, this book, unquestionably, is more than a book about what music counts or doesn't count from the late sixties and early seventies. I

---

15   I do not feel much sympathy for the term as such; any term 'progressive,' is bound to come with all kinds of compromises and let downs. Accordingly, progressive rock has its own academic and stylistic aporias like any form of music; it has its high points, and advanced moments and sequences, and its dismal lows; its peaks and strange byways. Indeed, I have no interest in much instrumental-based and sym-phonic progressive rock, which misreads the demands of hybridization and modern-ist *poiesis*, as a need to 'complexify' rock through adventitious forms of musicianship (Genesis, Yes, ELP, Gentle Giant, Gnidrolog, and more mannerist [non-English] epigones such as Hands and Eloy). Most of this music's post-genericity is pleonastic and feebly eclectic. This is the abject musicological mistake Edward Macan makes in *Rocking the Classics: English Progressive Rock and the Counter-culture*, Oxford University Press, Oxford and New York, 1997.

do this work of course, but I do more, for doing more means that the judgements I make about this period are at least parsed by the social and political forces that *moved* the work, and moved the work along formally, cognitively, culturally. This, in turn, does not mean that everything countercultural of note in late 1960s England was good and everything that was good counterculturally is now of note, just as we should be clear – as a kind of ready reckoner – that the good work that survives and now defines what is best about the period (an incomparable range of songs; some progressive rock) didn't last long and had little sense of itself holding open a place for itself in the world; indeed, for those working class and lower middle class musicians involved it must have felt like the world had opened up invitingly like a flower – as it did: this is not hyperbole or sentiment – but then closed just as quickly, as if there had been a secret time limit, as if someone was counting the 'English experiment' down month by month in a boardroom somewhere, until then one morning in 1975 time was called, the end of an era – as it was – and nothing was quite the same again.

With this brief analysis and conspectus, let us, move forward then. In the following, I want to look in detail at what these new kinds of songs, new forms of instrumentalization and new musical affects, and sonorities, mean in terms of their localized conditions of production. With what musical, cultural and political materials did musicians and their supporters remake the popular (and such vocalization, song structure and the meaning of musicianship) from the mid-sixties to the early seventies? What was left behind, what was given value and credence? What social and political valences – techniques of indisciplinarity – entered this musicianship to change 'voice,' 'song' and 'instrumentalization'? This will make the book as much an excursus about England, Empire, English identity and Englishness, as about popular musics beyond the inherited vernaculars of rock 'n' roll. For, the remaking of the popular between 1965-1975 in England is as much about the remaking of 'Englishness' as it is about sloughing off the crusted remnants of rock lore and its commodified palpitations; indeed, one defines the other. Thus, just as 'post-imperial ironization,' 'feminization,' and 'the pastoral,' will be key signifiers in understanding the early years of the Red Decade, progressive rock's embrace of Europeanized notions of formal extensity, will be a key signifier for its end years.

CHAPTER 1
'NEW FOLK-THINKING' AND THE ENGLISH PASTORAL

ON THE 17ᵀᴴ OF SEPTEMBER 1965, A 23 YEARS OLD PAUL SIMON IS WAIT-
ing on Liverpool Lime Street station for a train to take him to Hull to
play at the Watersons' folk club, at the Old Blue Bell Pub. He's been on
a long and tiring tour in England, up and down the whole length of the
country, but is looking forward to visiting the Watersons club, run by
the sisters and brother group, who had just released the widely-acclaimed
Frost and Fire: A Calendar of Ritual and Magic Songs. Simon had already
seen a lot of the country on his travels, certainly more than most visitors
and tourists from the US, and probably far more than most natives in
the 1960s. By this time, he had also played with practically everyone
on the folk scene in London and elsewhere and perhaps felt that he was
now well-schooled in the range of folk musics doing the rounds and all
the petty power struggles that accompanied them. Perhaps he was also

feeling quite pleased with himself, having got through all this and such a long tour, living on nothing and sleeping on floors; many of the gigs were good, he had already had experience as a producer, on the American singer Jackson C. Frank's eponymous album (1965), recorded in the CBS studios in London, and he still had more gigs to come. It had been hard, but he had accomplished something. Yet sitting on a bench, his guitar resting by his side, and looking up at the grimy high vaulted Victorian architecture of Lime Street station, perhaps whatever good thoughts he was having about the tour and his long English sojourn, were perhaps beginning to be offset by other less sanguine, more confusing thoughts. Having just played in the city of the Beatles and seen up close what the Beatles and pop music had become, and what it meant for all music, perhaps the idea of a folk revival in England began to seem less compelling, even slightly bewildering. Perhaps, in fact, the folk revival was an illusion. Perhaps, indeed, he was having second thoughts about England claiming to support a folk renaissance. Where had the pastoral and rural upsurge in popular music actually come from? The Watersons were hardly country people or tied to the countryside. And where was it all going, and with whom? Traditional musicians with attachments to long held folk traditions, didn't seem to be much in evidence in Grimsby or Portsmouth, and certainly in London for that matter. There was a lot of folk music about but not many 'folks.'

But perhaps, as he reflected on the conflict between the English Woody Guthrieists spear-headed by Ewan McColl and Peggy Seeger and the rustic and romantic troubadours back in London, that's precisely it: maybe the folk revival, has nothing to do with the popular musics of rural England at all, or with songs about the actual, living and breathing countryside and its labours, with good husbandry, haymaking, of good and bad harvests, milking cows and getting tractors and dray horses to the field, of harsh winters and summer frolicking, of debts, subsidies and bankruptcies; of bad land owners, and impoverished labourers and hill farmers; of the loss of good land and the steady drip, drip of depopulation and boredom; perhaps it was just a dream of Arcadia, of folk music as a conjuring up of an imagined England, that was no different in its idealizations and imaginings than any number of past and long forgotten imaginings that stretch back to the Anglo-Saxon dream of pre-Norman England. Perhaps, really, the English folk revival, that promised so much as an elemental opening out to the riches of the English rural past, was simply a snapshot from the heart of the city, of self-preoccupied longing formed from the constraints and disappointments of a grey and dismal postwar metropolis. Perhaps chasing the authentic voices and songs and traditions of folk was nothing more than that: making life in the city a little more comforting, and therefore, finding an active connection to those who labour in the countryside, and know it as a working landscape would have to wait, indeed, perhaps wait forever. And perhaps this is the unspoken truth of the fear that it is all an illusion: there is no *folk* music to speak of; this revival is not a living tradition, because it is first and foremost a music of alienated urbanism, of heightened false memories called up by cold and dark city-dwellers hugging close to an invented tradition of the pastoral and rustic; and perhaps that's why it's so hard to be part of this would-be revival and so hard to feel it's going anywhere, and why it feels easier as a 'folk' musician in the end to have urban attachments rather than rustic ones, because such attachments feel richer and forward looking. And, in turn, perhaps this why it is easier to say that the city is where folk music should find its home, or least a place to rest its head, for the city is where we always seem to be heading from one gig to the next, and where people, who love folk music and wish it well, have a living connection to it.

These thoughts are only conjectures and speculations; there is no record of Simon having felt any of this on Lime Street station on the 17th of September 1965. But, in a spirit, of implicative reconstruction, these thoughts do point to the tensions and pressures that Simon later said he felt, along with many other 'folk' musicians of the period, faced with the shifting and drifting allegiances of the folk 'revival' in England in 1964-65. Indeed, there appeared to be a fundamental cognitive dissonance between what got played and said in the folk clubs up and down the country, and the reality of the grey and dismal landscapes of early 1960s industrial England. The reinvention of folk music as a living tradition looked more and more like an enchanted enclave, as opposed to an actual reconfiguration of the relations between country and city, in which the non-professional working class rustic singer and musician, might at last, have a stake in a new culture; a New England. It is no surprise, therefore, when Simon returns to the US, and widespread success as a singer-songwriter with Art Garfunkel, that the peripatetic vision of the folk singer, moving in empathy with his or her surroundings, should be thoroughly urbanist. In those early songs of Simon, the folk singer becomes expressly the urban traveller, producing one genuine masterpiece, 'America' (1966) with its deep longing not for 'home,' precisely, but for a place for the singer/musician in industrial culture that offers the same sense of expressive continuity and grounding in tradition that folk music (or the memory of folk music) promised. That this continuity is an impossibility, is, of course, what defines the dialectic of modernity; and, as such, more prosaically, the profane and commodified history of rock 'n' roll after the Beatles. The folk revival in England hoped for a home against the depredations of urbanism and capital, yet found only a displaced mimetic encounter with the urban that it mistook for an escape from the urban and capital itself.

Yet, if there is no folk *revival* in England, nevertheless, folk music in its highly-mediated way plays an important role in the countercultural insurgence, that is to gather force from 1966-67. Folk music and folk-thinking may not shift the locus of cultural production from city to country, but it opens up the emerging rock culture to experiences and identities, and mythic resources, that defy the narrow parameters of 'popular entertainment' and the old rock 'n' roll. The dreaming of a new England through folk, therefore, maybe based on the misrepresentation of real-world conditions, but it is also, indeed as a result of this process, a rich and shifting confluence of ideas and ideals – of techniques of negation – that profoundly shift the subjective conditions of popular music and popular culture. This is because the failure to stabilize folk as a traditional or authentic set of forms and values paves the way for the exact opposite: the inter-musical and hybrid stretching of the folk song and folk instrumentation into new domains and spaces, that opens tradition and the tropes of authenticity to scrutiny. Yet this is not folk music 'giving up,' so to speak, being forced blandly to submit itself to 'rock' or electronic music generally, in order to curry relevance or popularity. On the contrary, the inheritance or reworking of tradition can be seen as both an opening up of what is defined as tradition, and, as such, an opening up of tradition to the present. This is why folk music *asked questions* of itself and of the emergence of the new rock music and counterculture.

This, however, is not what the 'trad' folkies wanted, or deemed appropriate to what they saw as the long-term struggle that folk music was engaged in against capital and the new commercial musics. Ewan MacColl and Peggy Seeger favoured a tight repertoire (based on *bona fide* musical precedents), 'authentic' performances (invariably unaccompanied singing; no guitars) and a certain preference for songs of struggle and labour. This milieu was quite small, but it had a good deal of influence in the folk clubs, certainly up until 1964 when Simon was planning his return to the US. And part of its allure or strength (particularly in the late 1950s) was the notion that the new rock 'n' roll wouldn't last, and that,

the working class would see that they had far more in common as producers and consumers with the rich and extensive legacy of English folk,
than the new commercial musics. It gave them a voice and a history that
was incomparable. This kind of thinking was at the core of the thinking
on culture in the British Communist Party (of which MacColl was a
member) and on the left of the British Labour party. This was based on
a number of factors.

Folk music and folk culture were grounded in the lives and achievements
of the rural and urban working class; it was a music in which the working
class were skilled 'masters' and historians of their own musical achievements; it was a music that held up a continuous light to past political
struggles and collective experience; and it was a music produced largely
'outside' of the market, that is, mainly for local audiences, providing one
of the few remaining links to an older independent and diffuse working
class culture, now suffering the relentless onslaught of commercialization. The Communist Party and the left of the Labour Party thus saw
folk as a music *of* the people, that had the residual capacity to take on
the cultural crisis of capitalism; a music able to invoke, evoke, recall
and intervene, 'heal' even. This is why a figure like Hamish Henderson
(1919-2002), CP member, early Gramscian and translator of Gramsci,
folksong collector, friend of E.P. Thompson and Raymond Williams
at Cambridge, is particularly representative of this moment in the late
1950s and early 1960s.[16] Folk music is held, as it was for MacColl and
Seeger, to express the active and latent interests of the rural and urban
working class. Henderson was less of a purist than MacColl when it came
to this; yet both saw folk music as possessing an integral relationship to
the defence of an independent working class culture. In an interview in
1987 Henderson quotes Gramsci to these ends:

> Really, the most suggestive remark of Gramsci's
> about folksong – the most pregnant insight – is in
> his fifth prison notebook. (There were 33 altogeth-
> er). This is how it goes: 'What distinguishes folksong
> in the context of a nation and its culture, is neither

16   Timothy Neat, *Hamish Henderson: A Biography. Vol 1- The Making of the Poet (1919-
      1953)*, Polygon, Edinburgh, 2007. For a discussion of E.P. Thompson and Raymond
      Williams and the cultural debate on the left in the 1950s and 1960s, see Tom Steele,
      *The Emergence of Culture Studies 1945-65: Cultural Politics, Adult Education and the
      English Question*, Lawrence & Wishart, London, 1997

the artistic fact nor the historic origin; it is a separate and distinct way of conceiving the world and life, as opposed to that of 'official' society.'[17]

But, of course, this is a fantasy, as much as the folk revival itself was; or rather, whatever counter-hegemonic content folk might have possessed at this time, it was not able to break through the dominant 'expressive' understanding of class relations that shaped so much of the left and folk club debates on folk music during this period, reflecting the broader crisis around class, representation and (cultural) technique. That is, the debate on folk music in England suffered from the same problems in which the debate on class and representation was itself mired in the postwar period: the neo-Stalinist (Second International) and old social democratic notion that it was the job of a progressive culture to represent the experience and history of workers *as* workers. This would then secure the symbolic and cultural space to fight for socialism. But what this invariably produced, as either a self-conscious virtue or unconscious outcome, was a delimitation of worker's language, identity and cultural ambitions – what the early Marx called, pejoratively, the domination of 'class interest' over workers' needs, that is, the interest that fails to move class struggle beyond the working class's immediate relation to capital.[18] In other words, the 'expressive' model of class relations produced and reproduced workers as workers, as opposed to the production of workers engaged in struggle against their received (and oppressive) identity as workers, whether the former was framed within an expressly counter-hegemonic model or not. One even sees signs of this crisis in the early 1950s, in a book like CP militant Bob Darke's 'resignation memoir,' *The Communist Technique in Britain* (1952).[19] In a series of reflections on the diminution of working class creativity in the Party, he reminds the reader that aesthetic judgements, cultural attainments, and the superfluities and spontaneities of everyday life, always had to be subordinated to the relentless drive of political work and recruitment.

---

17   Hamish Henderson interviewed by Jennie Renton, *Textualities*, http://textualities. net/jennie-renton/hamish-henderson-interview). See, Antonio Gramsci, *Selections From Cultural Writings*, Lawrence & Wishart, eds, David Forgacs and Geoffrey Nowell-Smith, translated by William Boelhower, London, 1985

18   Karl Marx and Frederick Engels, *The German Ideology*, Karl Marx and Frederick Engels, *The Collected Works*, Vol 5, Lawrence & Wishart, London, 1976

19   Bob Darke, *The Communist Technique in Britain*, Penguin, Harmondsworth, 1952.

Thus, traditional folk music, for all its good intentions (and real achievements), played an unfortunate conservative role in the early 1960s, confronted as it was with the beginning of a mass revolt of workers from their identity as workers, which, of course, eventually found its heightened expression in the Paris évènements of 1968 and Italy in the early 1970s, and in the first systematic historical account of this gap between class identity and class experience in Jacques Rancière's magnificent (post-1968) recovery of the intellectual and artistic 'inner' lives of early 19th century French workers, *La nuit des prolétaires*.[20] In England in 1964-65 such cultural resistance was not codified as a resistance to a received class identity as such, yet nevertheless, there was a generalized resistance by young workers to their parents' unexamined class assumptions, whether conservative or radical. This is where the techniques of indiscipline later find a subjective and creative home. And this is why traditional folk music definitions of authenticity, language and history, couldn't hold the cultural line in any shape or form. On the contrary, singing unaccompanied, 'banning' guitars, inviting young workers (and lower-middle class white collar workers) to participate in the recovery and extension of a 'grand tradition,' just appeared, opaque and arbitrary, antiquarian even, and therefore at odds with any truly emancipatory transformation of culture from below and the remaking of the popular, that pop music *and* guitars seemed to offer. Moreover, it threw into relief the managerial and performed nature of the current folk revival, echoing the earlier and solidly middle class revival of English folk music pursued by Cecil Sharp and his colleagues and followers, who took it upon themselves to represent the 'best' of the Anglo rural labouring 'other' to a musically educated middle class audience.[21] MacColl (Scottish), Seeger (American) and Henderson (Scottish), were operating essentially as archivists of working class tradition, rather than as co-producers with rural and urban workers of a new music, in which, as a result – irrespective of the politics of MacColl, Seeger and Henderson, and other singers and archivists who were involved – power accrued to the act of representation itself and to those doing the representing.

---

20   Jacques Rancière, *La nuit des prolétaires*, Librairie, Arthème Fayard, Paris 1981. See also Carolyn Steedman, *An Everyday Life of the English Working Class,* Cambridge University Press, Cambridge, 2013

21   Cecil J. Sharp, ed., *One Hundred English Folk Songs: For Medium Voice* [1916], Dover, New York, 1976

This is why in the end the folk revival seemed less like the archivisation of a living subaltern culture, and more like the capture of ghosts and phantoms; things trembling on the edge of cognition and understanding. And crucially, therefore, removing guitars and non-standard arrangements of songs from the repertoire in order to maintain quality and rigour, technique was reduced to the *recovery of the authenticated remnants of tradition*. This is crucial in understanding the impact of pop music and the parallel emergence of a new folk music more broadly (after 1966). The drive to hold the traditional 'ideological line' robbed folk music's participation in a new realm of subjective engagement and affects – a new realm of popular techniques – despite everything this music wanted and hoped for. A good indication of this is Ewan MacColl's work with the remarkable producer, writer and editor Charles Parker for BBC radio – that Rob Young discusses so well in *Electric Eden* – that uses the narrative drive of traditional folk-thinking and the song-form to memorialize and investigate the lives of different workers, insofar as it concretizes the question of technique as fundamentally a social one. There is no doubt these sound works (for example *Song of a Road*, 1959, *Singing the Fishing*, 1960), involving field recordings, voice-over, traditional folk musics, especially composed songs and natural sound, are in certain respects original, enlivening, even indebted to a certain avant-garde *esprit*, pulling folk-thinking in a new, possible multimedia direction. MacColl called them 'radio ballads.' Yet, despite their formal achievements and attempt to produce a new set of musical and aural techniques identifiable with a new folk-thinking, what is striking about this work is how easily the folk musician and folk music appear caught up in a kind ethnographic trap of memorialization, that ultimately plays to the radical sentiment of a middle class audience ('this is what workers do and sound like') as opposed to capturing the energies and imagination of young musicians themselves. Asking young working class musicians and young listeners of folk to commit themselves to the task of *representing* a tradition in this ethnographic way, whether dressed up in avant-garde clothes or not, is still an ethnographic act, that in a way forces musicians and listeners to be archivists of their own class experience, before they are producers of their own lives and a new culture. This is the great dividing line in the early 1960s that the folk revival plays an inadvertent if important role in foregrounding: *what are those techniques of indiscipline that can open a productive and creative space between class experience and class identity?*

Traditional folk music, then, couldn't provide those techniques of indiscipline, because, folk was too in thrall firstly, to a defensive and identitary transmission of class, and secondly, to the ethnographic trap of music seeing tradition as an act of class resistance. In a different register, therefore, the inability of folk music to hegemonize a new sense, or possibility, of the popular, lies in its failure to provide enough resources for what J.B. Priestley in the English cultural 'brow' wars of the early 1930s, and still ringing in everyone's ears in the late 1950s, called 'broadbrow' art.[22]

In response to sniping from Virginia Woolf about writers like himself and Arnold Bennett being horribly middle-brow, Priestly, thinking of the broad popular appeal of writers such as Charles Dickens and William Thackeray, talked instead of the need for a 'broadbrow' art as a narrative art of high and complex ambition, as opposed to the clichéd notion of middlebrow literature as being mean, narrow and sentimental in scope, an opinion promulgated by Woolf and T.S. Eliot and the Bloomsbury Group. He called for the common reader and spectator to bring their critical faculties and capacity for discrimination to bear on all cultural forms and practices, popular and modernist. MacColl and Henderson's view of folk music as a popular music of ambition captures some of this spirit of 'broadbrow.' But if millions still read Dickens and Thackeray, few (workers) wanted to listen to folk music, or take their cultural identity from it, however it was conceived or presented; indeed, when workers did take notice it just felt regressive, and, in its way, peculiarly 'highbrow' (even, in some instances, quite learned). A better candidate for the category of broadbrow, then, would, in fact, be pop and rock music, given their perceived openness to change. For pop and rock provided what seemed like, in the circumstances at least, the best opportunity to create a new range of song-forms as markers of new experiences and post-ethnographic working-class identities. Highbrow, lowbrow, middlebrow and broadbrow, of course, are all highly dubious categories and provide little real connection to the dynamics of cultural division and hierarchy, given their essential pejorativeness. But Priestley does touch on something that will be central to Marxist cultural studies in the late 1970s and 1980s: that the popular is *produced*, and therefore open to the conflicts and struggles of social experience. It can just as easily produce the critique of sentiment as evoke sentiment itself, in all its dreary finery. The perception, accordingly, that pop and rock offer a new domain of technique through a range of song-forms and varied instrumentalization is crucial to defining a new space of indiscipline from below. This is why technique isn't simply about musicianship here – about access to guitars, and electric amplification, so

---

22   J.B. Priestley 'To a highbrow,' *John O' London's* 3 Dec, 1932, p354.

to speak – it also captures the idea of pop and rock as space where show-ing and telling – storytelling; narrativization; self-assertion – can provide a genuinely new world of subjectivization, *despite the pressure of commer-cialization and the prevailing sentiment of the old popular culture*. In this sense, pop and rock become the testing ground for the interface between musical form, subjectivity and class indiscipline; and, as the countercul-ture unfolds this meeting becomes an incendiary mix.

But if traditional folk music is left behind in the early 1960s, folk-thinking and the rural and pastoral as places of imagined Englishness and radical and nonconformist passions and identifications are not. Thus, if there is mass investment in the new popular musics, nevertheless, traditional folk music in England in the early 1960s retains a pull and influence out of all proportion to its actual social constituency. This is because, folk-thinking as opposed to traditional folk-music itself, retains a certain radical allure that is able to connect the remaking of the popular with a conception of the 'people' not beholden to the workplace and the mass sentiment of the old industrial popular culture. That is, folk-thinking – the pleasures of landscape and rural life, the 'truths' of ancient tradition, pagan reli-gion and ritual, non-materialist values, and primitive communist visions – becomes, in its distance from the realities of waged labour, a mythic and imaginary resource for a growing disenchantment with industrial life, enforced consumerism and widespread moral piety; an emancipa-tory 'carrying stream' to borrow a term of Henderson's. Hence, the new folk music after 1966 (Incredible String Band, Sandy Denny, Shirley and Dolly Collins, John Renbourn, Bert Jansch and Fairport Convention), far from being a revival or extension of tradition in MacColl's under-standing, in a sense, takes a radical leap *over* traditional folk's local and nativist assumptions in order to connect with this wider set of spiritual and universalizing concerns; the English rural landscape becomes 'Deep England,'[23] and 'Deep England' becomes the metaphysical home of all that the city, industrialization, and capital has no care for, or only cares for as a source of cheap labour.

This presages a new modern folk culture, therefore, quite different from the one imagined by MacColl and Seeger: a culture of pastoral and pagan enchantment and enrichment that lends itself, on the one hand, abstract-ly to utopian visions and, on the other, more pragmatically to an actual revolution in values; the countryside – its lore, its legends, its myths, its

---

23   Patrick Wright, *On Living in an Old Country*, Verso, London and New York, 1985

stories, its skills, crafts and beauty – is held to be a place from which musicians can learn and gain sustenance from in their struggle against both an alienating high culture and an old popular culture, as much as a place, conventionally, to travel to in their imagination for ideas.

The 20th century obsession with lost Englishness, 'Deep England,' Visions of Albion, of course plays its part in this process of reflection, as it did in the 1930s and the 1940s, when the Depression, the ravages of industrialization in the North of England, and the rise of fascism in Europe, allowed writers and musicians to again recover the English landscape and rural custom as a source of long standing resistance to the depredations and abstractions of modernity (if not modernity itself). Visions of old Albion recall England to the longevity of her beauty and harmonious and closely worked fields and vales. Thus, Priestley's *English Journey* of 1934 is a classic of this new folk-thinking. It doesn't avoid the realities of 1930s Depression England and the immiseration of the North – indeed seeks them out – and despises the easy conflation made between a love of the English countryside and little Englanderism, yet it takes most of its pleasures from rural vistas, as if keenly aware of what industrialization takes away from the glories of the English pastoral, even one shorn of the comforts of nostalgia. "We might have been journeying through the England of the poets, a country made out of men's visions," he declares as he arrives in the Cotswolds.[24] In this, it echoes the more overtly pastoral and nostalgic post-Edwardian English journey of H.V. Morton, *In Search of England* in 1927, which on its final page recalls the reader, like Priestley on his last page, to the intimacy between a sense of home (perversely London in the fog for Priestley) and the familiar comforts and contours of the English landscape:

> I went out into the churchyard where the green
> stones nodded together, and I took a handful of
> earth and felt it crumble and run through my fin-
> gers, thinking that as one English field lies against
> another there is something left in the world for a
> man to love.[25]

---

24   J.B. Priestley, *English Journey*, Heineman in association with Victor Gollancz, London, 1934, p50

25   H.V. Morton, *In Search of England*, Methuen, London, 1927, p280

But, if these are undoubtedly beautiful words – written in order to conjure a benign patriotism of place – both books fail to address the growing crisis in the English countryside itself. It will take a very different kind of book and a very different kind of author to point this out. In 1940 Vita Sackville-West published *Country Notes in War Time*, a collection of short pieces on country life from the *New Statesman and Nation*. Ensconced in the Kent countryside during the Phony War (1939-40) Sackville-West's writing on farm life, bulb growing, wild flowers, the vagaries of the weather, and her immediate landscape, is deceptively pastoral and comforting – a Bloomsbury version of the *Dalesman*. Yet for all its exquisite charms and attention to crop maintenance and husbandry it is also haunted by a terrible sadness and loneliness, as if Sackville-West is fighting to wrest a sense of meaning from the countryside and rural life. This admittedly has something to do with the extraordinary circumstances of her time there (the book ends with sirens and the beginning of the Battle of Britain in the skies above), and the reflection on her own class privileges, as a 'gentlewoman' farmer and gardener 'out of time' with the war, but more, importantly, derives from the encroaching material realities of country life and the rural economy alike. That is, her sadness and loneliness seem less a personal crisis, than a social one. As she says:

> Unthinking, I had begun to feel that life must
> revolve round country matters, and that to divorce
> the Englishman from his fields and cotes was to
> bring spiritual death upon him. I know better now.
> It seems that with a miserable 7 per cent. we have
> the smallest agricultural population in the world. It
> seems also that during the last eighteen years three
> hundred thousand men have deserted the land..."[26]

Loneliness, then, is less an individuated state here, more a collective one, indeed, an unavoidable condition of an increasingly depopulated landscape. Quite simply rural England feels 'deserted' – despite the arrival of land-girls, evacuees from London, and returnee aristocrats and writers. This sense of a countryside stilled by depopulation is barely visible in Morton and Priestley, despite the increasing visibility of depopulation in the rural economy at the end of the 1920s. This is precisely because at some level countryside and city still seem to be in balance culturally, the

---

26 Vita Sackville-West, "Yeoman Calling,' *Country Notes in War Time*, Hogarth Press, London, 1940, p17

pleasure and drawbacks of one, contrasting with the pleasures and draw-backs of the other in a process of negotiated adjustment. Here, though, the absence of a populous and living countryside reveals a deeper and growing sense of evacuation: the loss of the English countryside as a place where labour on the land and the imaginary horizons of rural living fit together. As she says in a striking aside late one evening on her rounds, reflecting on the arrival of a group of land-girls and boys evacuated from London, sleeping in the local village:

> The place I love; the country I love; the boys I love.
> I wander around, and towards midnight discover
> that the only black-out I notice is the black-out of
> my soul. So deep grief and sorrow that they are not
> expressible in words. [27]

Morton and Priestley may muster pity in the English countryside, but not grief like this; as if in a Romantic conjuration, Sackville-West, recon-nects landscape to the highest of emotions.

Country Notes in Wartime, therefore, hints at the kind of countryside and rural life that the folk revival will find in the late 1950s and the new folk-thinking and emergent counterculture will certainly find in the mid-1960s: a landscape largely without people and event; a landscape of a relatively small number of rural workers locked away on big farms, many amalgamated from smaller farms; a landscape of silent and invisi-ble efficiency. Indeed, the recurring impression of the new generation of folk and folk-rock musicians as they venture into the countryside in the late sixties (in order to 'get things together,' rehearse and compose or eke out a living from rural living) is that 'no one is around.' Traffic, Vashti Bunyan, Incredible String Band, the Strawbs, and Fairport Convention are all firstly, excited, then bewildered then challenged by this sense of rural emptiness. By 1970 the total figure of agricultural workers in Britain was less than 350,000 and many of these were casual and season-al; only 28 per cent of farms in the South East, for example, employed full-time labour.[28] But paradoxically this is why the new folk-thinking achieves the resonance and reach that it does; the England that they find is one amenable to all kinds of projections, utopian or otherwise,

---

27 Ibid, p16

28 B.A. Holderness, *British Agriculture since 1945*, Manchester University Press, Manchester, 1985

that reopens the contracting countryside and rural life to the suppressed and untapped riches of ancient and spiritual lore and native storytelling. Two things emerge from this. Firstly, a folk music that discards the trappings of traditional instrumentation and repertoire – MacColl's ethnographic trap – a folk music that broadens its range and musicality; and secondly – which reflects back on and channels these ambitions – the pursuit of a folk-thinking that disconnects Englishness from nation and state. Whereas at some level Morton and Priestley, and even the socialist programme of MacColl, were attached to a late Edwardian pursuit and defence of a national-popular rebuilding, the new countercultural folk-thinking sense of Englishness, the English countryside and English folk music is defiantly post-national and post-statist in its sense of what English folk music might mean in its expansion beyond unthinking traditionalism. That is, far, from the new countercultural folk music being an escape *into* the countryside as an escape into a *restitutive* Englishness, the new folk music invests the imagined emptiness of English rural life (its obvious signs of depopulation), and the instability of folk tradition, with an englobalizing spirit of the local; English folk music breaks onto the brightly lit uplands of an inclusive 'folk spirit.' In 1959, Pete Seeger the brother of Peggy Seeger is already noticing this, but with little sympathy:

> a new problem looms, to threaten disaster. Today's citizens who love folk music are being thrown in contact with not one or two or three, but dozens and hundreds of traditions. Which to follow?... for good or bad, young people today who like folk music are combining various traditions together at a faster rate than the world has ever seen before. Some hybrids flourish so like weeds, that one fears for the very existence of other forms, just as the English sparrow has driven other birds from our parks. (Sleeve notes to *Nonesuch and Other Folk Tunes*, Folkways LP, 1959).

Seeger has no objection to the flourishing of other 'national traditions' as a global family of folk musics; however, like MacColl, hybridity in itself is perceived as a threat to the local and the subaltern class integrity of a given national folk music. The class identity of folk music – that Gramscian-Hendersonian 'distinctiveness' – becomes secondary to an indiscriminate musicality.

Thus, in these first shoots of folk hybridity and given the universalizing push of the new music into the open plains of this new Englishness, we see the beginnings of a popular 'folk indiscipline' that the counter-culture will reshape to its mostly urban needs by the end of the sixties. This indiscipline of folk hybridity is no more evident than in the work of Davy Graham and The Incredible String Band (Robin Williamson, Mike Heron) in the mid-1960s, whose debt to non-Western musics and to the use of non-standard modal tunings is crucial to this sense of possibility. Graham introduces Arabic, West Indian, Greek and Moroccan sonorities and timbres and willowy lines into his guitar playing and song repertoire (*The Guitar Player*, 1963, *Folk, Blues and Beyond*, 1964), just as the Incredible String Band, draw on a range of non-Anglo-American instruments and global musical references and melismatic vocalization, to produce their own range of song-forms that initially seem to offer a certain deference to Anglo-American tradition, yet on closer inspection, sound quite unlike anything anyone else is writing and recording during this period, such as the melismatic 'Iron Stone' a droning Gaelic ballad that switches into a raga, and the wonderful, plaintive 'The Circle is Unbroken,' with its use of whistle and Irish harp and echoes of plainsong and lament and ancient tabernacle. Melismatic vocalization, accordingly, is particularly pertinent here. For it is melismatic singing – holding down one syllable while moving through several notes – that is common to ancient Middle Eastern, African, Indian, and Balkan, folk musics and to Gregorian chanting; non-standard vocalization and open song-forms combine. Both 'Iron Stone' and the 'The Circle is Unbroken' are collected on The Incredible String Band's 1968 album *The Big Huge*, which, along with its companion record, *Wee Tam*, and the richly melismatic *The Hangman's Beautiful Daughter* ('Waltz of the New Moon' and 'There is a Green Crown') released in the same year, makes clear that folk-thinking cannot be contained by anything so presumptuous as a national tradition that might lay claim to its unofficial character by holding tenaciously onto its local character. As Robin Williamson says in an interview in 2001 discussing this period:

> I wanted to have a go at a number of different
> things. It struck me that you could write a sponta-
> neous, free-form lyric, a la Jack Kerouac. And then
> you could link it up with spontaneous free-form
> music, drawn from the various regions of the world.
> So you have like an Indian bit, a Spanish bit, a
> light opera bit, and you could use all those things

like tonal colors, and have a bit of a go on various
instruments and so on…So I suppose that in a way,
more than folk-rock, what I was trying to do then
was try to open up the whole subject of folk music
into a different, and wider, sphere. Not necessarily a
rock sphere, but more of a sort of literary and world
music sphere. In fact, the term "global village" was
first coined by a New York reporter to describe an
Incredible String Band concert in the '60s.[29]

Williamson's voice, indeed, never seems to rest within a definite idiom,
yet is one of the most distinctive of the period, resistant as it is to any
of the clichés of traditional folk and rock delivery. There is of course
an added irony here to this proto-hybridity, that, in a crucial sense, defines these shifting allegiances and spaces around Englishness, nation and
state; namely that, the indisciplinarity that produces the great upsurge
of new English folk-thinking, and the new England, is largely the work
of Scottish musicians moving south. Davy Graham, Robin Williamson,
Mike Heron, Bert Jansch, Donovan Leitch, Jack Bruce, John Martyn
all have Scottish parentage. So, if all these musicians are invested in the
opening up of a localized English folk revival, they do so, armed with a
highly-attuned sensitivity to the problems of Scottish folk music's own
conservative embeddedness in the rhetorics of nation-building and the
national-popular. In moving south, they may bring a Gaelic sensibility,
and familiarity with the rich legacy of Scottish rural and urban folk musics, but this is not attached to the genealogical lines and nationalist fer-
vour of a Henderson. Thus, these musicians, emerging from the Scottish
borders, produce a music precisely disruptive of borders, Scottish and
English; a post-nationalist folk-thinking, Yet, obviously 1960s England
is not a post-nationalist political space, far from it. To work as a Scottish
musician within the traditions of English folk music, no matter how hybridized, is to feel a very different set of historical and political perspec-
tives and cultural lineaments at work; a Scottish *nationalism*; an English
imperialism.

Yet, the new English folk music and its promise of a New England is not
the reality of the England of the 1960s. It is, rather, an imaginary zone

---

29 Robin Williamson interviewed Richard Unterberger, *Perfect Sound Forever*, 2003,
    http://www.furious.com/perfect/robinwilliamson.html).

through which all might pass and settle. This is what defines the ruralism of the new English folk music: not a rural Edwardian nostalgia attached to the trumpery of Empire, but a place of ancient settlement and fealty in which (however implausible) all tribes lived in concord with the land.

But why is England so amenable a place for this myth? Why is the notion of a New England for the counterculture able to detach itself from an old and imperial England? There are a number of reasons. Firstly: the ease with which rural depopulation from the late 1930s onwards is able to link up with the hegemonic legacy of Southern English pastoralism to create, not an anti-modernist ruralism exactly, but certainly a place in which the critique of industrialism (if not capitalism as such) could take a hold, *despite depopulation being a consequence of the spread of abstract labour and the increased industrialization of the countryside*; secondly: the availability of cheap land and disused agricultural property in order to effect a 'return to the land' based on realistic forms of productive self-sufficiency and the rebuilding of derelict plots and buildings for new habitation – a return that significantly was far more than Arcadian in outlook – as in the work of John Seymour (*Fat of the Land*, [1961] and *Self-Sufficiency* [1973])[30]; thirdly: the sense of England as self-contained geographical entity, with few extreme or abrupt shifts in geology, landscape and weather – an 'hospitable' terrain linked by wood and forest and pathway – that stretches from the legend of Robin Hood to William Morris down to Roger Deakin's "dream of greenwood liberty" today [31] (who was a Seymourite 'land returner' himself in the early 1970s); fourthly: the idea of the habitable and even walkable spaces of the non-agricultural English countryside as a patchwork and extendable 'garden'; and fifthly: the increasing availability, irrespective of its conservative cultural anti-modernism, of the rich and interconnected legacies of folk music in England and Britain, as analyzed in A.L. Lloyd's, *Folk Music in England* (1967).[32] All these 'returns to' draw on the available utopian motifs of a long-standing pastoralism within the dominant, Arcadian conservative tradition, but all resist, at some level, the pre-modern English nationalism that accompanies this Arcadian pastoralism, that so dominated H.V.

---

30   John Seymour, *Fat of the Land*, Faber & Faber, London, 1961 and *Self-Sufficiency*, Faber & Faber, London 1973

31   Roger Deakin, *Wildwood: A Journey Through Trees*, Hamish Hamilton, London, 2007, pxii

32   A.L. Lloyd, *Folk Music in England*, Lawrence & Wishart, London, 1967

Morton's *In Search of England,* and to a certain extent inflected Priestley's *English Journey.*

In these terms the new folk music and the new folk-thinking allow the English pastoral and English rural tradition to open up a sylvan 'Englishness' to traditions, histories, forms and experiences, not contained or re-channeled by this dominant conservatism. A cultural and syntactic rupture occurs. English pastoralism becomes a source of radical *discontinuity* with capitalism and imperialism, and not simply the place where imperialism and capital and the alienations of urban life come to heal themselves; or where English nationalism comes to think best of itself. This does not mean the comforting sense of the countryside as a retreat or haven, or place of repose stops. The countryside is, of course, not the city, and therefore because it is not the city it continues to be a place of obvious reparation against the alienations of urban life. But, it is also the place where reparation produces other ways of thinking and doing in imaginary continuity with ways of being and doing long before cities; and therefore, it produces ways of thinking and being that might redefine the notion that the city is the only or primary home of emancipatory thought and practice. In this respect, the shift is from thinking of the countryside in imagination as a place of repose or solace to a place of *work* (of practical and ideological reconstruction), that refines the meaning of labour-power in city and countryside alike. This work of reconstruction, then, is not simply a question of letting nature 'speak,' of giving space to ecological thinking in the conventional sense: that is inviting the countryside to tell the city how to organize its affairs better. But, rather, a question of expanding those techniques of well-being that capital and its adversaries are unable to provide in the city, indeed, that are destroyed in the city. And this is why the emptying out of the imperial and hegemonic reservoir of Southern pastoral tropes in the late 1960s, is largely to do with this question of ideological labour. All the new practical forms of rural 'entryism' and folk-thinking from below from the early 1960s, on the back of the widespread depopulation of the countryside, make it increasingly difficult for the hegemonic pastoralism to impose, in its usual self-flattering ways, an image of rural life as existing in a kind eventless, benign and even continuity with the ancient past. When, for instance, Ronald Blythe talks in 1969 in *Akenfield: Portrait of an English Village* [33] about the brutal reality of agricultural labour and tedium of most village life, he places the final nail in the coffin of Morton's and

---

33   Ronald Blythe, *Akenfield: Portrait of an English Village*, Delta, London, 1969

Arthur Bryant (*Makers of the Realm* [1953])[34] and Ernest Barker's (*The Character of England* [1947]),[35] postwar inflation of enchanted rural vistas. Consequently, by the late 1960s, with the increasing takeover of diffuse forms of agricultural skill and craftsmanship by abstract labour, this link between the image of a passive rural proletariat and a holding conservative pastoralism can no longer do its ideological work so efficiently. This is why the Incredible String Band can enter this traditionally alienating cultural domain and make it their own in the name of their new musical hybridity, without feeling the full and alienating weight of a conservative English pastoralism. For 'Englishness' as it comes to be ideologically repositioned by the counterculture and the 'return to the land' opens up this sense of the English pastoral and rural identity as a *construct*, as *work in progress,* that, in turn, many musicians can enter and claim for their own, particularly when this New England is itself part of an emergent, if unfocused, anti-imperialist historicizing. Something of this is also derived from W.G. Hoskins,' influential *The Making of the English Landscape* (1955), reprinted in 1970, who sees the English landscape as an evolving and shifting palimpsest: "most of England is a thousand years old, and in a walk of a few miles one would touch nearly every century in that long stretch of time." [36] Similarly, as Oliver Rackham stresses, there have been no areas of England untouched by human presence or labour since the Iron Age. Since this period every part of England has had an owner or has been maintained communally.[37] Indeed, even in the days of the Domesday Book (1086) England, as M.M. Postan argues, was an 'old country': "in general there were about as many settled places in 1086 as at the end of the eighteenth century."[38]

More concretely, then, for musicians the English landscape is a kind of 'work in progress' that Scots, Welsh and Northern Irish can contribute to without losing their own identities, despite the bitter legacy of English imperialism. For, paradoxically, it is the very underdetermined character of this emergent rural 'Englishness,' within the overarching span of British national and conservative urban cultures, which allows musicians

---

34   Arthur Bryant, *Makers of the Realm*, Collins, London, 1953

35   Ernest Barker, *The Character of England*, Greenwood Press, London, 1947

36   W.G. Hoskins, *The Making of the English Landscape* [1955], Penguin, Harmondsworth, 1970, p303

37   Oliver Rackham, *Woodlands*, Harper Collins, London, 2006

38   M.M. Postan, *The Medieval Economy & Society: An Economic History of Britain in the Middle Ages*, Penguin, Harmondsworth, 1975, p18.

who have arrived from the borders at the centre to dispense with those national and provincial attachments that hitherto had prevented them from pursuing a new hybridity. This is why under-determination here takes on a progressive character. And, at the centre of this, ironically, is the character of the pastoral myth itself, for its real and imagined enchantment – the labour of centuries – enables the idea of the English countryside as a habitable and fertile place – despite depopulation, despite rural tedium, despite rural poverty and low wages – to flourish. So, what the English countryside loses in terms of extremes of geology and climate, of Romantic sublimity and enticing fear, along with the realities of rural life, it makes up in terms of a powerful image of nature 'husbanded' and accordingly, open philosophically, culturally and historically to a universalizing spirit: namely: this is what the countryside might provide for all if country and city respoke the wheels of labour.

Thus, it is precisely the continuous link between the Southern pastoral myth and the largely homogenous (domesticated) character of the Southern English landscape that makes the English countryside inhabitable imaginatively for a new generation of musicians, intent on producing an industrialized and modern folk music. The very absence of geographical and climatic extremes allows a hybrid folk-thinking to put down roots. This is in contrast, therefore, to the other and border geographies of the British Isles with their predominant barrenness, colder climes and relatively unhusbanded sparseness. Yet, this is not to diminish the affective qualities of other landscapes, but, rather to say, that as regional and 'unstable' landscapes, and landscapes and folk traditions in conflict with the hegemon of the Southern English pastoral, they were not available for countercultural appropriation in the same ways and to the same ends, particularly given the power of the dominant Anglo-American popular culture. Under-determination, then – the generalized notion of the English countryside as canopied greenwood and sylvan 'hold-out' – is the condition for English folk-thinking to become the channel through which other folk musics flow. Thus, if, on the one hand, the new folk music owes its initial drive to the Scottish and Gaelic folk revival, on the other hand, it owes its living continuity outside of any clash of parochialisms, to the multi-accented continuities of the English pastoral. 'The Circle is Unbroken,' contains some inimitable lines from Robin Williamson on this score:

> Now over the skyline I see you're travelling.
> Brothers from all time gathering here.

Come let us build the ship of the future.
In an ancient pattern that journeys far.
Come let us set sail for the always island.
Through seas of leaving to the summer stars.

Indeed, these lines could be written about, and for, the other, great achievement of the new folk hybridity of the late 1960s: *Astral Weeks*, by Van Morrison (1968). Given its emergence, like *Big Tam* and *Wee Huge*, from the British borders, and as such given its strong connections to place ('Cypress Avenue,' Belfast), one might have imagined the album being titled, certainly a couple of years before, as *Belfast Days*, or *Belfast Visions*. But in 1968 this would have seemed too much like regional assertion and accordingly too parochial for the times: thus, Morrison, goes for something grander, something spectral, something imposingly abstract, that captures the new folk-thinking: a title in which the crossing of borders is given an expressly transcendental and spiritual dimension. And, indeed, the music reflects and rises to this ambition. *Astral Weeks*, may not draw directly on the new folk *in fine*, or even the Incredible String Band's global eclecticism, yet it does have a gliding, lilting plangency, that gives the scattish, jazz sonorities of Morrison's voice, as it dips and weaves in tandem with the acoustic instrumentation the cadences of an unprecedented jazz pastoralism, in which the 'song of experience' is divined from out of new and attenuated shapes. Indeed, these pastoral and open shapes are derived from a striking amalgam of jazz talents: Jay Berliner on guitar (who had played with Charlie Mingus), Richard Davis, bass (who had played with Eric Dolphy), Connie Kay on drums (who had been the drummer in the Modern Jazz quartet), Warren Smith Jr., percussion and vibraphone (who had played with Miles Davis and the American folk band, Pearls Before Swine) and John Payne on flute and soprano saxophone. Here then is a kind of jazz-folk indiscipline, that draws on the affective lightness of jazz extemporization, but subjects it to the lyrical sweep of the poet-songwriter; the overwhelming, feeling for me, still, is as if Morrison is singing *plein-air* to the skies, and we, following his painterly trails, are lying on our backs in a field somewhere close by. In fact, this is where The Incredible String Band and Morrison differ quiet sharply from the Beatles in their move away from standard rock and blues and Tin Pan Alley: for one of the defining features of the new hybridity of folk after traditional rock 'n' roll, is its potential space for drift and modernist *poiesis*, that is, its capacity to capture not only the fluidity and 'wandering' character of jazz, but also *poetry's intimacy with the song-form itself*. And this is why the new folk music in England is very particular in its assimilation of Bob Dylan into its cross-border fertilizations and encroachments.

Dylan of course from 1965 on, stands as a colossus behind the early dissident and rebel attachment of the new folk to the emerging counterculture. His music is the focal point through which all the new countercultural politics and dissonant modernist cultural values converge. But whereas the Beatles continued to feel a residual sympathy for his move from folk into rock (particularly Lennon) as the advent and high point of a new urban literateness in song writing, The Incredible String Band and Van Morrison focus principally on the *bardic uplift* his songs release or reconnect with; the release of folk from folksinesss *into folk poetics*. In other words, the new folk-thinking of The Incredible String Band and *Astral Weeks* are far more concerned with the convergence of modern and pre-modern poetic sources in Dylan's early songs and the new folk moves, than with his residual ties to the protest song tradition and singer-songwriter as tribune. What focuses their attention is how the new open folk song is able to encompass non-standard forms of versification (and its melismatic possibilities), and as such, transform the song-form from the usual verse-verse-chorus structure, into one in which sound and free-form poetic invocation converge. *Astral Weeks* completely jettisons verse-chorus structure in this way ('Sweet Thing'). And this is where the split from Guthrie-MacColl-Henderson traditionalism is most pronounced: the new folk song-form, embraces oblique poetic word play or mood, or free-form allusions, to create a folk-thinking that sings the spirit of a freedom from city alienation and industrialized habits and constraints back into alignment with ancient fields or futural pastoral vistas. In this way, bardic uplift and pastoral evocations, certainly in Morrison and The Incredible String Band, redefine the singer-songwriter as poet and vector of literary tradition, in a way that refuses to make any worthwhile distinction between the poem and poetic tradition and the popular song itself. Indeed, Morrison invokes W.B. Yeats and William Blake and the English Romantic landscape poetic tradition, in order to make clear that folk music has other points of entry, points that don't necessarily need to go through the standard folk-song itself. As a consequence, national cultures that enter this poeticized non-standard space of the song-form reemerge transformed. *Astral Weeks* is shaped by its Northern Irish cadences and inflections, but is irreducible to them.

This convergence, post-Bob Dylan, of song-form with poetic versification, in turn, produces what will define one of the key signposts of countercultural post-ethnographic class identity of the folk singer after 1965: namely, the folk singer who identifies with the radical subjectivity of the poet, as opposed to the singer who subjects his or her radical poetic skills to 'collective struggle,' a 'political movement,' or to social reportage. Thus, if the countercultural opens the popular to the post-literary, it also, refines the literary in the interests of the popular. This is why, of course, Dylan is the seminal figure at this juncture, insofar as he bridges these older demands within the 1940s and 1950s American folk tradition, drawing on Guthrie's 'movementist' folk, but investing its confrontational élan and anger with a lyrical inventiveness, that pushes the song's folk-thinking four squarely into the orbit of Beat poetry and eventually into the urbanist dynamic of rock.

Thus, in 1964 in an interview with Nat Hentoff in *The New Yorker*, clearly haunted by the Beat revolution, Dylan talks openly about no longer wanting to "write *for* people anymore,"[39] just as he had dismissed politics in music as "trivial"[40] a year earlier in New York, at the Emergency Civil Liberties Committee dinner, where he was given the Tom Paine Award. One might want to contest that the Beat poets, such as Allen Ginsberg, no longer wanted to write *for* the 'people,'[41] just as Dylan hardly holds to these sentiments after 1965 (the magnificent 'Hurricane' in 1975), nevertheless, this seeming break with the legacy of Guthrie and the activist tradition, covers a vast and complex history, that has a determining effect on why the new folk music takes the (bardic) forms that it does in the US and England after 1965. In other words, Dylan's views here point to a fundamental reorientation in the subjective stance of the singer-songwriter, insofar as it shifts the traditional relationship between the folk singer as 'I' and 'we': the 'I' as 'we' of Dylan is no longer the 'I' as 'we' of the workers' movement or the 'people.' But in separating the 'I' as 'we' from the people, Dylan is not thereby *denying* the importance of the folk singer's subjective mediation between the 'I' as 'we' and the people. Rather, as with Jean-Luc Godard, in the early 1970s at the height of his Maoist involvement with the Dziga Vertov Group, Dylan did not

39 Bob Dylan interviewed by Nat Hentoff, *The New Yorker*, Vol 40, No 36, 1964, p65

40 Quoted in Robert Shelton, *No Direction Home: The Life and Music of Bob Dylan*, Da Capo Press, New York, 1997, p200. For photographs of the award ceremony, and Dylan's later reflections on Guthrie and the folk 'protest' movement, see *No Direction Home: Bob Dylan*, directed by Martin Scorsese, 2005

41 Allen Ginsberg, 'September on Jessore Road,' *The Fall of America: Poems of These States, 1965-1971*, City Lights, San Francisco, 1972

want to be identified as a representative *of* the people, in order that he might retain some 'modernist'-like autonomy as an artist. It is into this gap, therefore, between the artist and his or her constituency that the bardic and modernist *poiesis* enters into the new folk music after 1964 as a kind of kind of anti-ethnographic distancing device. The question of not writing for people as a representative *of* the people, then, is less a conservative withdrawal from politics as such, than a move against the received identification between folk music and certain received class identities and cultural expectations (certainly on the part of working class or lower-middle class singers and musicians). And this, of course, is where the new folk music begins to stake out its difference from the old left, particularly in England, in the late 1950s. Folk music in its range of vocal and instrumental possibilities is far more – and far more politically – than its traditional allegiances would assume, even if this means folk music finding a compromised place in the market.

But if the new folk music led by Dylan is post-ethnographic these concerns about representation and identity, of course, cover harsher and unforgiving realities for all those involved culturally on the left. When Dylan talks about the triviality of politics in music, he is hiding, through a thin bravado, the unmitigated trauma experienced by the left and folk music in the US during the late 1950s under Cold War conditions. We need to understand, consequently, that the post-ethnographic stance is double coded. On the one hand, the old folk music, had reached a dead-end particularly in its overt commercial forms and, therefore, needed to be creatively displaced, but, on the other hand, the idea of speaking *for* the people, *for* the working class, was likely to get you castigated as a dupe for the CPUSA, and in some instances even gaoled, or certainly prevented from touring and recording. Standing behind the ethnographic shift in the USA, then, are two major forces: the tectonic shift in class relations (the 'completed' industrial assimilation of rural workers in the US and the West generally; the increasing dislocation between urban class experience and received class identity under the new consumerism), that was in the process of weakening and then pathologizing the links between collective class identity and the idea of the people; and the renewed attack by capital on the left after the progressive interregnum of the 1930s, in an attempt to destroy the alliance between left social democracy and Communism (exemplified by the hubris of McCarthyism and the Manichean insurgencies of the Cold War), as US imperialism reorganizes its global alliances in the fight against the 'threat of World Communism.' Faced with these forces, folk music – the music *of* the left – finds itself mostly destroyed in its old heartlands and centres of influence, as the right realized how (relatively) successful activist folk music had been in stepping around the ideological constraints of the mass media. Thus, in order to understand Dylan's throwaway comments and the rise of the bardic (steeped in both new and pre-modern poetic voices) we need to look more closely at this fundamental shift in the USA. For in doing so we will be able to get a clearer picture of why new folk-thinking takes on the forms that it does in England, and the relationship between the new folk and the old left.

Key to this conjuncture overall and to the emergence of the new folk in England after Dylan is the legacy of Woody Guthrie. MacColl, Peggy Seeger, and Henderson, are, in a way, despite their various local interests and concerns, producing political footnotes to Guthrie's achievement. And we should not underestimate this achievement in order to make the crisis of the old folk music easier to comprehend.

From the late 1930s to the mid-1950s, with the onset of Huntington's disease, Guthrie produced an astonishing and unprecedented range of songs, reaching according to a number of estimates, to well over a thousand. These cover an enormous variety of subjects, individuals and events, largely detached from rustic themes: Adolf Hitler, Henry Wallace, the nuclear industry, Franklin D. Roosevelt and Cuthbert Olson, Eleanor Roosevelt, Hanns Eisler, Hooverville, the Dust Bowl drought, the labour martyr Harry Simms, Jesus, the Peekskill fascist attacks in 1949, the Ham and Eggs initiative (pension relief), the celebrated Red Army super sniper Lyudmila Pavlichenko, land ownership, Isaac Woodard, the black WWII veteran blinded by police, Columbia River and the Grand Coulee Dam project, the attack on Pearl Harbour, wage slavery, ballad singing, union politics, the anti-fascist Second Front, skid row, the death of the union organizer Mario Russo, the execution of the anarchists Nicola Sacco and Bartolomeo Vanzetti in 1927, Stetson Kennedy, Rosa Lee Ingram, the American Federation of Labour, the sinking of the convey escort ship the *Reuben James* in 1941, John Doe, vigilante men, the Nazi torturer Ilse Koch, the lynching of Laura and Lawrence Nelson in 1911, deportees, the Ludlow Massacre in 1914, and Chiang Kai-shek – to name but a few. Indeed, this variety is matched by a particular kind of intellectual energy, that derived from extraordinarily disciplined and ambitious powers of research, analysis and synthesis, that puts us in mind less of the folk tradition, as it was in the early 1930s, than Soviet reportage and the early avant-garde. As he says in *Bound For Glory* (1943):

> I never did make up many songs about the cow trails
> or the moon skipping through the sky, but at first
> it was funny songs of what's all wrong, and how it
> turned out good or bad. Then I got a little braver
> and made up songs telling what I thought was wrong
> and how to make it right, songs what everybody in
> that country was thinking…my eyes has been my
> camera taking pictures of the world. [42]

In the early 1940s, for instance, Guthrie is recommending singer song-writers that they should read Carey McWilliams's *Factories in the Field* (1939)[43] the first systematic and highly influential account of the corporate takeover of agriculture in the US, and the crisis of the agricultural worker, in the wake of the widespread despoliation of the land for short-term profits. In a letter to Pete Seeger in 1941 Guthrie calls on song-writers to mine the book for material, in particular the question of soil erosion, in order for it to be transformed into songs and skits:

> soil is caused to decay through replanting the same
> crop too much, and not enough attention to dif-
> ferent scientific ways of curing the land. Right now
> the right to vote in the south is more important.
> Next to that and union organizing, I think Soil
> Erosion, Rotten Everything, is very good material
> for a show.[44]

The comparison here with Bertolt Brecht is perhaps not fortuitous. For Guthrie like Brecht, through the highpoint of cultural leftism between 1935-45, takes it as axiomatic that the responsibility of the cultural activist is to transfigure the abstractions and concepts of political theory into popular and long-living forms of solidarity and engagement, creating a social landscape of struggles present and past that people can orientate themselves through in the production of a *shared tradition from*

---

42 Woody Guthrie, *Bound For Glory* [1943], Penguin, Harmondsworth, 2004, p178 & p295

43 Carey McWilliams, *Factories in the Field* [1939], University of California Press, Berkeley and Los Angeles, 2000. McWilliams had good literary connections, he was close friends with the novelist John Fante.

44 Woody Guthrie, Letter to Pete Seeger, quoted in Will Kaufman, *Woody Guthrie: American Radical*, University of Illinois Press, Champaign, 2011, p60.

below. This Brechtian-type passage from concept and learning to companionable and politically affecting song, is also evident in the ambitious Columbia River and Coulee Dam Project song cycle, which, in celebrating the achievement of the building of the dam (1933-41), establishes, as its backdrop, the crisis of the New Deal for workers ('Grand Coulee Dam,' 'The Biggest Thing Man Has Ever Done'). As he says, in a list of topics he sends to the singer Millard Lampell in 1941, his job overall in the song cycle is to make purposeful and revealing connections between the demise of the New Deal and the new war economy and the continuing crisis of agriculture:

> 1. The draft. 2. Higher wages in big towns. 3. Defense Booms. 4. But farm wages are so low that farmers can't attract workers to the fields. 5. Lots of big industrial workers, etc., are going by the 1000's into the crops, but still not enough. 6. Big aluminium and light metal industries opening up around here every day drains the farms of workers. 7. Guarded freights and patrolled highways make it harder for field workers to travel. 8. Vigilantes and hired thugs have discouraged workers who travel – and fake contractors and crop racketeers have won the hate and the distrust of the farming people.[45]

The received impression of Guthrie, then, as either an Okie indigenist, always on hand to spontaneously compose a few hokey verses for every occasion – which he was genuinely capable of doing with wit and vibrancy – or a singer of quick-fire agitprop, is belied by this structured, interdependent, and concept-rich approach. Indeed, a few years earlier he had called on the CPUSA aligned Alamancs (who he had been working with) and other musicians to *modernize* the folk song and folk repertoire. In this he is no less Brechtian in his insistence on the mutability of popular forms.

> Our job aint so much to go way back into history, that's already been done, and we caint spare the time to do it all over again. Our job is Here & now, Today. This week. This month. This year. But we've got to try and include a Timeless Element in our

---

45   Woody Guthrie, Letter to Millard Lampell, Kaufman, op cit, p61

songs. Something that will not tomorrow be gone with the wind.[46]

But by the early 1950s these ambitions had stopped in their tracks by a Cold War Administration that was determined to finally break what remained of the 1930-40s Cultural Front and counter-insurgency, leaving Guthrie's reputation as a figure of the modernizing left, so to speak, in abeyance. Thus, with the onset of Huntington's disease Guthrie's gradual physical deterioration as a musician provides a poignant bodily expression of this ideological 'freezing.' Yet, this isn't a story simply of missed opportunities and connections or personal decline. This is also a story about the revolutionary's relationship to the left, and the Communist Party at the Midnight of the Century in the late 1950s, the period, when all the old assurances begin to unravel. Guthrie and Brecht are both revolutionaries *aligned* with the Communist Party (although some say Guthrie was in fact a member of the CPUSA), in ways that register in a similar fashion that terrible ambiguity about both being *of* the Party and its steady critic so common to artists and musicians in or around the CP in the 1950s. But by 1956-7 – certainly after the Soviet invasion of Hungary and Nikita Khrushchev's revelations – this ambiguity is stretched to breaking point on both sides, as the party feigns a new openness on the one hand, and yet redraws the boundaries of dialogue with the left on the other, in its increasing attack on modernism, heterodox cultural thinking, and most importantly, revolutionary practice and theory itself. Guthrie and Brecht's revolutionism and identification with power from below, becomes, if not an embarrassment or superfluous to the Party under the terms of the new East-West détente, then something to be academicized or merely alluded to by the Party when the circumstances require; like many artists left over from the radical thirties, Guthrie and Brecht by the mid-1950s are sometimes revered (and occasionally 'called') but not exactly 'wanted.' For instance, Guthrie by 1947-48 was experiencing the chill wind of anticommunism in his relationship to the workers' movement as the majority of the big unions (the Congress of Industrial Organizations, the National Maritime Union, and United Auto Workers) – all previously CPUSA led or influenced – severed their links with the CPUSA (under state pressure) and passed draconian anticommunist legislation, just as his relationship to revolutionary politics was being put in severe jeopardy with the political weakening of the CPUSA itself. After the Party's social democratic reconstitution as the Communist Political Association (CPA)

---

46 Woody Guthrie, Letter to the Alamancs, 1941, Kaufman, ibid, p77

in 1944 under Earl Browder, it then dissolves and resurrects itself as the old CPUSA, but, this is in name only, and points to a wider political malaise. Ostensibly the Party has thrown in the towel and become an organization of capitalist state power, demoralizing industrial militants and cultural activists alike. Similarly, Brecht's last plays written in the GDR before his death in 1956, fail to find an audience in the country, largely because the Party is uncomfortable with their revolutionary rhetoric (*The Days of the Commune*) and anti-bureaucratic tone (*Turandot or the Whitewashers' Congress*) after the workers' uprising in Berlin and in Hungary. Indeed, there is an assumption on the part of the authorities that *The Days of the Commune* is unambiguously 'counterrevolutionary' given the attention it gives to the ideologically deceptive character of the revolutionary process, holding, as it does, an oblique light up to the revolution from above in the Stalinist GDR. Thus, Brecht has the worker Pierre Langevin say as part of a lengthy exchange on revolutionary violence and workers' power: "in this struggle the hands not bloodstained are the hands chopped off."[47] The implication being, here, that the hands in question are not those simply of the vacillating (and merciful) Communards faced with hard choices about who lives and who dies, but all those revolutionaries, who, confronted with the 'good intentions' or assurances of their friends and enemies, are prepared to accept them in good faith, enabling the reactionaries to regroup and retain or reclaim power. Despite giving his support to the GDR regime, Brecht knows that he is part of a struggle and tradition that has had its hands chopped off when it has made alliance with its seeming friends and with its enemies. The air of despondency in *The Days of the Commune* then is both palpable and deceptive. The play clearly stages the inevitable (the impending massacre of the Communards), but it also, presents revolutionary politics as movement *through* defeat, in despite of defeat. And of course, if the Party is willing to accept the pathos of the defeat of the Communards, it is certainly not prepared to give any room to it as an allegory of the present state of the workers' movement. However, if Brecht is philosophically astute and valiant enough to think revolutionary politics as movement through defeat, beyond his own sense of measure and localized possibilities, this is nevertheless a dialectics of the coffin. And consequently, for those on the left opposed to Stalinism after 1956, there is fundamental distinction to be made between the movement of revolutionary politics

---

47 Bertolt Brecht, *The Days of the Commune*, in *Brecht: Collected Plays Eight*, edited and introduced by Tom Kuhn and David Constantine, Bloomsbury Methuen, London, 2004, p111

through defeat *inside* Stalinism, and the movement of revolutionary politics through defeat *outside* of it. And this is why by the late 1950s and early 1960s the old left appears *only* to be a narrative of reactionary defeat, in which the old Communist Parties are identified as having given up the ghost. This, in turn, explains why the early folk revival in England appears to its critics to be culturally compromised or academic. Because it is tainted by the wrong kind of response to the wrong kind of defeat, the idea that the prevailing cultural conditions for the left could be improved by writing more and 'better' activist folk songs – as Guthrie himself was insisting in the late 1940s and early 1950s – or by getting the 'tone' and 'content' and traditional attributes right, as in MacColl and Peggy Seeger, appeared risible to those who truly wanted to modernize folk-thinking and create a new culture – a counterculture – of the left.

Dylan, then, is the progressive figure that fills this void; a figure formed by the defeats of the old left, and the legacy of Woody Guthrie, but untroubled or untrammelled by those defeats and the class sentiment of the ethnographic trap. Hence his deeply ambiguous identity as a new kind of folk singer who thinks politics in music is "trivial": a singer, who, draws on the rich social detail and anger of Guthrie's modern folk songs, yet who seeks another kind of indiscipline, through poetry's rejection of the traditional folksong's commonplace lyricism. In these terms the subjective shift to modernist *poiesis* and the bardic that I have identified in relation to the singer's mediation between 'I' and 'we' finds its expression through a very different reading of the ballad tradition that Guthrie made his own, and that brings Dylan's writing closer to the 'prophetic' ballad tradition than it does to social reportage, as is also the case in The Incredible String Band and Van Morrison. That is, if Dylan, at one level, draws on a folkcentric ballad tradition out of Guthrie – as a means of connecting social details to the recollection or commemoration of a particular life or event – on another level, this standard move, nonetheless, is subject to a general dis-alignment between his radical persona and bardic identity and 'collective struggle,' (such as 'Desolation Row' [1967]), a split obviously that is quite alien to Guthrie. This is not because the bardic allows Dylan to inflate 'I' over 'we,' but, rather, recalibrate what 'we' might actually mean given the realities of the Cold War. In order to do this he draws on another ballad tradition – a premodern poetry – that certainly shares in the spirit of the popular song with Guthrie, but, whose sense of the popular and the inclusive is quite different: the mocking and sardonic 'lowlife' ballads of François Villon.

If Guthrie helps produce the critical space for Dylan, the 15th century Villon is the poet that helps redefine the meaning of a post-ethnographic 'we' after the Cold War and the new folk-thinking out of Beat poetry. This does not make him the poet of the counterculture or the new folk music itself, or even the antiquarian patron saint of the Beats, but it does make him a key reference point in understanding the new subjective conditions of folk music and the incipient counterculture, as poetic tradition opens up song-form, vocalization and the self-identity of the singer-songwriter. As D.B. Wyndham Lewis (no relation) says in his audacious and erudite book on Villon, *François Villon: A Documented Survey* (1928): in Villon's poetry, in its

> rich tumult, its vivid colour, its cruelties and gener-
> osities and riotings and obscenities and crimes and
> dirt and splendor and prevailing largesse…in its
> strange pathos and preoccupation with Death, in all
> this there is mixed the brawl of the streets and the
> laughing loud song of taverns.[48]

Little of this of course is alien to Guthrie's world of roustabouts, hobos, farmhands, wranglers, dust panners, Skid Row skidders, drunks and gulls, with perhaps the exception of Villon's casual obscenities and boasting of criminal adventures; yet, Villon provides something more, something touched by madness and intoxication: an imaginative register in which the poet and the demi-monde of the tavern share a divers world in which all are welcome; a heightened democracy of pleasure and disgruntlement. Villon's 'we,' then, is not any more open and capacious than Guthrie's, but, at its very heart, it runs against, and celebrates a freedom *from* labour, and those who are prepared to defy the sanctity of 'good order,' in contrast, to Guthrie's intense commitment to the dignity of labour as a restitution of the honour of the 'working man and woman,' and the relentless communist commitment to making sense of what seems senseless. Thus, what is striking about Villon's socially (or asocially) precocious poetry is its interweaving spirit of discord and passion, and as such its capacity to create a 'we' outside of the proprieties of state and church, a 'we' of the rabble (despite Villon's own intermittent mortified and sorrowful genuflection in front of King and Mary after escaping gaol and the hangman's noose). It is no little surprise, therefore,

---

48   D.B. Wyndham Lewis, *François Villon: A Documented Survey*, preface Hilaire Belloc, Sheed & Ward, London, 1928, p9

how appealing this might appear as a poetic voice for a new generation in the 1950s, when, the contours of a new 'we' are coming into being inside and outside the old left. Acting in the spirit of Villon is to allow poetry a place in the dramas and passions of everyday life, enabling the poet the freedom to roam, in the manner of the old troubadour; a poetry that takes adventure as the measure of its alacrity. The irony is, however, that Villon was the least troubadour-like of all medieval poets; he loathed the countryside, he loathed the poetry of swains and shepherds, he loathed courtly poets and protocol, he loathed traveling, and he loathed the very idea of writing about anything but his beloved Paris and the denizens of his favourite taverns and brothels.

> Ie suis paillart, la paillarde me suit.
> Lequel vault mieulx? Chascun bien s'entresuit.
> L'ung vault autre; c'est a mau rat mau chat.
> Ordure amons, ordure nous assuit;
> Nous deffuyons onneur, il nous deffuit,
> En ce bordeau ou tenons nostre estat.

"I am a lecher, and my whore dogs me. Which of us is the better? We are two of a kind, and equally worth. Bad cat, bad rat. We love the dregs, and the dregs pursue us. We fly honour, and honour flies from us, in this brothel where we drive our trade," ('Ballade De La Grosse Margot' ['Ballade of Fat Margot']). [49] Indeed, he was the most urbanist of poets in a 15th century French tradition that prized the idealizations of pastoral love and lore, or the self-imposed austerity of rustic simplicity. "Mais quoy que soit du laboureux mestier/Il n'est tresor que vivre a son aise. Whatever the life of the hardworking rustic/the best treasure of all is living in ease."[50] Yet it is the image of the poet on the country road, derived from the Villonesque translation of the poet into the inveterate wanderer, that will define the Beat Generation (Jack Kerouac obviously, but also Ginsberg's relentless wanderlust propheticism), and that will retrospectively define Guthrie as the singer of the roads and rails, East to West, North to South, city and plains. But if Guthrie was indeed a wayfarer, Guthrie's reputation eventually became caught up in the wings of this (misleading) Villonesque poetics of flight, quite out of keeping with the exigencies of his new communist folk-thinking: learn, learn, learn; let

---

49 Francois Villon, 'Ballade of Fat Margot,' in D.B. Wyndam, op cit, pp269-70

50 François Villon, 'The Testament,' *Poems*, translated David Georgi, Northwestern University Press, Evanston, Illinois, 2013, p127

nothing human be alien to you as singer and songwriter; there is always something to be gained from every situation.

Yet in the end it is the concocted Villonesque image of the troubadour that will serve Dylan's self-identity well, and also secure Guthrie's transition into the counterculture and into the minstrelism of (some of) the new folk. Interestingly the writer Lee Hays recalls, having being asked by a young man how Guthrie was doing when the singer was in hospital being treated for Huntingdon's: What interests you about Woody? Hays inquires: "Woody represents freedom, the ability to just pick up and go and not be responsible to any living soul, absolute freedom," says the young man. [51] Of course, as we have seen, this was the very opposite of the truth and the truth of a modern folk music imagined by Guthrie and his comrades; Guthrie was incredibly disciplined as a writer and performer, and after the early 1930s, saw himself as creatively beholden to struggles greater than his own particular self-identity as an itinerant songsmith. Yet, it is this image, through Dylan, that will be passed onto the counterculture, allowing the bardic and the prophetic to provide the space for new song-forms, new instrumentations and a new 'we,' a 'we' of non-labouring bodies at the expense of, learn, learn, learn.

Villon, therefore, is a complex figure to assimilate and define in relation to both the new folk music and the new poetry. His resistance, even antagonism, to the labouring body and the body of traditional religious piety is attractive to folk singers, modernist poets and countercultural revolutionaries alike, all seeking new techniques of indiscipline and infelicity. Indeed, between the early 1920s and 1960s Villon is fought over; in the 1920s by the modernists, Ezra Pound and Basil Bunting ('Villon,' 1925),[52] as the precursor of a secular modernist sensibility (the Joycean particulars of the 'day'), revived in William Carlos Williams' introduction to *The Complete Works of François Villon* in 1960,[53] and then reassessed in John Fox's *The Poetry of Villon*, in 1962,[54] and then also on the left in the 1930s, in Brecht's identification of the poet as a materialist ally

---

51 Lee Hays, *Sing Out, Warning! Sing Out Love: The Writings of Lee Hays*, edited by Robert S. Koppelman, University of Massachusetts Press, Amherst, 2004, p150

52 Basil Bunting, 'Villon' (1925), in *The Complete Poems*, associate editor Richard Caddel, Oxford University Press, Oxford, 1994

53 *The Complete Works of François Villon*, translated by Anthony Bonner, introduced by William Carlos Williams, Bantam Books, New York, 1960

54 John Fox, *The Poetry of Villon*, Thomas Nelson & Sons, Edinburgh, 1962

of his notion of '*plumpes denken*'; and in the 1960s, also on the left, as an anti-Stalinist revolutionary voice of the non-labouring body, as in the GDR singer Wolf Biermann's 'Ballade auf den Dichter François Villon' (1968),[55] and, in Tristan Tzara's research on the poems in the 1950s as the voice of 'le petit peuple' and as a 'secret store' of mysterious word puzzles and anagrams.[56] Indeed, the 1960s were Villon's in the US and Britain, primed as his work had been already by the widespread impact of Dylan Thomas' bardic modernism. Caedmon Records' 1952 recording in Steinway Hall, New York (re-issued 1964) of Thomas reading from his poems, 'A Child's Christmas in Wales,' 'Fern Hill' 'In the White Giant's Thigh,' 'Ballad of the Long-Legged Bait,' and his homage to Rimbaud's 'Drunken Boat,' 'Do Not Go Gentle into That Good Night,' was a huge influence on the bardism of the Beats. Thus, it is perhaps no surprise that Dylan begins his career – even before he left Minneapolis for New York – by composing his own music to Villon's ballads, as if to see how their energy, prurience, and social dissonances might sound in modern folk idiom, open to jazz.

> I didn't start writing poetry until I was out of high
> school. I was 18 or so when I discovered Ginsberg,
> Gary Snyder, Phillip Whalen, Frank O'Hara, and

---

55 From the album *Chausseestrause 131*(1968). First stanza:

Mein großer Bruder Franz Villon
wohnt bei mir mit auf Zimmer.
Wenn Leute bei mir schnüffeln gehn,
versteckt Villon sich immer.
Dann drückt er sich im in' Kleiderschrank mit einer Flasche Wein
und wartet, bis die Luft rein ist
Die Luft ist nie ganz rein.

(My elder brother Frank Villon lives with me as my lodger.
When people come to case the joint Villon the artful dodger
hides in the closet solaced with the wine he loves the most
and waits until the coast is clear but it's an unclear coast).

Translation: Eric Bentley

56 See, Daniel Heller-Roazen, *Dark Tongues: The Art of Rogues and Riddlers*, Zone Books, New York, 2013, and Marius Hentea, *Ta Ta Dada: The Real Life and Celestial Adventures of Tristan Tzara*, MIT Press, Cambridge Mass., 2014

> those guys. Then I went back and started reading the
> French guys, Rimbaud and François Villon; I started
> putting tunes to their poems. There used to be a folk
> music scene and jazz clubs just about every place.
> The two scenes were very much connected where the
> poets would read to a small combo, so I was close up
> to that for a while. My songs were influenced not so
> much by poetry on the page by poetry being recited
> by the poets who recited poems with jazz bands.[57]

So, if it is relatively easy to ascribe a place to Villon in the new folk's
bardic shift, it is far harder to place exactly where he fits within the new
folk-thinking as a whole, given how little of his writing and his character
connects to anything approaching the rustic or pastoral. But perhaps this
isn't the point, as I have stressed in my comments on the surprisingly an-
ti-rustic nature of the early 'folk revival' in England. The new folk music
in the US may have been captivated by the richness of indigenous rural
popular musics (Hillbilly, gospel and blues), and of lives beyond the metropolis, and Guthrie may have devoted much of his early career to Dust
Bowl themes and the conditions of agricultural workers, but this didn't
amount to rurally *focused* culture; so when folk found an urban audience
and a political *raison d'etre* coast to coast in the early 1950s its themes and
interests became invariably urban out of expediency, even if it spoke with
regional accents. This is why there is little direct rural hold over Dylan's
imagination, and why new politicized folk music in the US after Guthrie
sees rural life as essentially industrialized and the problems and concerns
of rural workers and residents as continuous with urban workers and residents; there is no reimagining of the great plains, great Northern moun-
tains and valleys, or the Southern swamps as the 'countryside' as a 'hold
out' against capital, and therefore, little place for folk music as a version
of a Whitmanesque American pastoral, even if Walt Whitman himself is
regularly evoked by singer songwriters as another missing link between
the poem and song, *poiesis* and politics, people and the American landscape outside of the metropolis. In 1945 Henry Miller, for instance, pub-
lishes a vehement attack on American industrial culture (*Air Conditioned
Nightmare*),[58] but it is hardly an invocation of the restitutive power of the
rural landscape; perhaps the work that comes nearest to this is, in fact,

57 Bob Dylan interviewed by Scott Cohen, 'Bob Dylan Not Like a Rolling Stone,'
   Spin, Vol 1, No 8, December 1985
58 Henry Miller, *Air Conditioned Nightmare*, New Directions, New York, 1945

visual, Ansel Adams's photographs from the 1940s of Yosemite National Park, but these photographs are far from pastoral or rustic for all their intense, high definition natural beauty. Villon, then, at the beginning of the new folk music and the counterculture, is above all else – certainly in Dylan – a key reference point for a new bardic uplift and not a gateway through to the pastoral and the charms of the countryside. And this, in turn, is what is passed onto English folk music in the early 1960s, finding its own way out of self-delimiting folk tradition, a voice that invites the non-labouring body into a 'we' that speaks musically and culturally with multiple voices.

The Incredible String Band and Morrison's *Astral Weeks*, then, presides over an imaginary landscape or landscapes, in which, the singer sings of 'I' as 'we' as a countercultural community in the making, in which the melismatic delivery of certain songs is matched by the flow and drift of the music. This is not the end of the presence of traditional folk song or traditional singing within the English counterculture – Pentangle, John Renbourn, Anne Briggs, Martin Carthy, Bert Jansch, Steeleye Span, Fairport Convention all draw on a traditional repertoire and song-forms – but, it does point to a transformative threshold, in which the new folk music, new modes of enunciation from below, and the indisciplinary horizons of the counterculture find a mutual space of articulation. And this is why the 'remaking' of the English landscape is so crucial to this moment of interconnection and exchange: it is the pleasing and self-contained, historically layered and mythically embedded, green-canopied and richly husbanded space of the English pastoral that offers the new folk music the space to explore these interconnections. Dylan's bardic uplift, consequently, may have little direct purchase on shaping the pastoral themes of the new English folk itself, but it certainly puts in place by the mid-1960s the possibility of a new folk song that could be equal in word and music to the growing invitation of popular music overall, to embrace many voices and many forms of instrumentation. The Incredible String Band and Van Morrison, and John Martyn (*Solid Air*, 1973) certainly hear this call.

The bardic, therefore, is what moves the folk song away from folk to folk poetics, and from rock into jazz, premodern musics, and classical forms, producing an unprecedented confluence of traditions. In a kind of unacknowledged debt to the old folk and MacColl and the Communist Party's (un-nuanced) critique of rock 'n' roll, the new folk realizes it had to sideline rock (if not defeat it) in order to open out the emerging counterculture to the riches of local, premodern and modern forms, that rock was determined to repress or destroy. One can see the influence of the bardic on song-form almost immediately after the first wave of the new folk, and the impact of *Astral Weeks*, in Van der Graaf Generator's, 'Refugees' (1970) from *The Least We Can Do Is Wave to Each Other* (1970). One of the great songs of the period, it points exactly to the confluence of voices that the new folk enables, yet one would be hard pressed to say it had any connection to the folk tradition new or old at all. Indeed, its spatiality and enunciative mode is choral; yet the bardic out of Dylan after Anglo-American modernism after Villon is unmistakable, in Peter Hammill's plaintive, almost sopranic voice, with its strange but beautiful modulations set against Hugh Banton's church-like organ and the massed background voices; just as *Astral Weeks* sounds nothing like Woody Guthrie or Dylan, Hammill sounds nothing like Morrison, or anyone else at the time for that matter. Ostensibly a song about the time Hammill spent sharing a flat with his friends Mike McLean and the actress Susan Penhaligon, its majestic sweep and melancholic allure invites us to read its lamentations and recollections as a farewell and coda to the 1960s itself. We might say, then, this is the new English folk-thinking in action; a song, that invites a new world or worlds into the popular. But before we discuss the formal connections between the new folk-thinking and progressive rock in any detail (Chapter 4) we need to reflect on those other resources and forces which contribute to the remaking of the popular and the emergence of the counterculture. For if the techniques of class indiscipline of the counterculture are incomprehensible without the destabilization of the affections of urban life and routines of wage-labour which folk-thinking provides, folk-thinking itself is incomprehensible without the broad anti-imperialism of the time, as younger working class and lower middle classes musicians, artists and activists, seek to destroy the last vestiges of connection between, Empire, Englishness and the popular. That this process will prove, in many respects, to be a comic and sardonic enterprise, invites for further consideration other unofficial definitions and images of 'Englishness.'

CHAPTER 2
IRONY AND POST-IMPERIAL DEFLATION

I<small>F THE</small> S<small>OUTHERN</small> E<small>NGLISH PASTORAL IN THE</small> 1960<small>S IS A MULTI-ACCENT</small>-ed and weakly imperialist zone, this also is largely because of the demilitarized character of postwar social life and public life in England. When conscription ended in 1960, it completed a process of the demilitarization of the everyday that found its popular expression in the embrace of civic and suburban values, as opposed to the popular glorification of metropolitan, royal and state power, even if the Royal family suffered little in the way of public opprobrium for its dalliances with fascism in the 1930s. This in turn had much to do with the hangover from the democratic glow from WWII, which continued well into the 1950s, despite the two Tory victories in that decade (1951 and 1955), in an extraordinary reversal of Labour's 146 seat 1945 majority, as Labour was stymied by its introduction of rationing and austerity economic policies and the exigencies of rebuilding a bombed Britain. For many ordinary serving soldiers who were unwavering in their understanding of the anti-fascist

character of the war, the British army felt closer to a vast democratic militia, than it did to an imperialist army, and so, on demobilization many
of these soldiers felt the struggle against fascism was also by definition a
struggle for democracy at home and inside the army itself; indeed, during
the war, for soldiers and radical officers alike, the political regressiveness
of sections of the officer corps was a constant reminder of the wider nature of the struggle. As Peter J. Conradi reveals in his biography of Frank
Thompson (the elder brother of E.P. Thompson), who served as an officer in the Middle Eastern campaign before being executed by fascists
in Bulgaria whilst working for the Special Operations Executive (SOE),
Thompson, would fume against

> the semi-literate officers who think every Jew a cad
> best off underground, and every striker deserving
> to be shot: he was as indignant as if he were a Jew
> or striker himself. He rants against the ruling-class
> English – finished as world leaders, tired dishon-
> est, moral cowards without imagination, who had
> lost all capacity for idealism or adventure, enjoying
> second-rate pleasures. He raged against his fellow
> officers.[59]

This is one of the reasons why the Churchillian imperial rhetoric is so
comprehensively defeated in the polls after the war. Churchill and his
ruling class fraction assumed that the victory over fascism was a resound-
ing affirmation of old England and the status quo ante, even the Deep
England of Morton, Byrant and Barker. That there is a partial restitution
of this conservative vision under the two Tory victories and American-
led Cold War, does not alter the fact that the de-militarization of public
life in England in the late 1950s still remains attached notionally to the
democratic record and transformations of the war years, whether mythically and patriotically sustained or not. This is because the actuality of
the war was never an abstraction, even for the majority back home who
didn't fight in Europe and the Far East; the war on the homefront served
to define the lives and experience of all. Indeed, the war released the 'free
spirit' of the people, as J.B. Priestley valiantly describes it in *Out of the
People* in 1941.[60] As John Baxendale says in *Priestley's England* (2007):

---

59 Peter J. Conradi, *A Very English Hero: The Making of Frank Thompson*, Bloomsbury
    London, 2012, p233-34
60 J.B. Priestley, *Out of the People*, Collins/Heinemann, London, 1941.

"[This 'free spirit'] had broken down distinctions of class and emphasized what we all had in common. It had dragged us out of the sterility of the prewar world."[61]

Thus, with the open acceleration of the US-Soviet arms race in the early 1950s there was a large minority on the left and in the centre still committed to the residual anti-militarism of the postwar settlement, and who felt affronted by both the Tories and Labour's support of a new Western militarism by stealth. This is the political constituency that will form the social base (and ecumenical intellectual breadth) for the rapid growth of the Campaign for Nuclear Disarmament (CND) in the late 1950s. CND is the point where the anti-militarism of the war years, finds a renewed purpose, and even philosophical validation, in a new popular culture of dissent that sees the Tory and official Labour line on the atomic bomb as a betrayal of the democratic and progressive 'militia spirit.' In turn, it seeks to reconnect national identity to an experience of 'Englishness' that defines itself in accord with the small-scale and localized, rather than the centralized, statist, unaccountable and plutocratic vision of the new post-war Britain being built by the Tories and Labour in a shared drive towards technological renewal. One version of this of course is a sleepy or cantankerous withdrawal from modernity and the popular, favoured by new and old Tories, and liberal nostalgists alike, another version, however, is an identification of the small-scale and localized with a spirit of quiet self-sufficiency and pragmatic creativity, an 'Englishness' that finds solace and strength in irony and making do and getting by, and that, despite the militaristic threat of the Cold War state, sees a productive place for itself in the newly industrializing world of the popular and the common.

These anti-militaristic, sceptical and pragmatic values are not class specific, but they certainly find a social consistency in the working class and lower middle class, particularly on the Labour left, in defiance of the rationalizations and patrician expertise of the upper-middle class Executive and a public culture of demonstrable abstraction and privilege. Something of these values is expressed in the distinction George Orwell makes in 1945 in 'Notes on Nationalism' between 'patriotism' and 'nationalism.' Patriotism is a

---

61   John Baxendale, *Priestley's England: J.B.Priestley and English Culture,* Manchester University Press, Manchester, 2007, p155

devotion to a particular place and a particular way
of life, which one believes to be the best in the
world but has no wish to force upon other people…
Nationalism, on the other hand, is inseparable from
the desire for power. [62]

CND politics, then – and in particular the CND marches to Aldermaston
– are briefly the channel through which these plebeian values find a
public, even carnivalesque, form in the late 1950s, enabling a dissonant
'Englishness' to connect to a wider disenchantment with the overbearing
assumptions of a 'modernizing' but deeply reactionary order. Thus, if the
link between the small-scale and the local and anti-militarism, provides,
a well-worn path to rural and pastoral values as a vision of a world beyond the Big State (which of course draws on conservative post-armorial
visions of a Deep England restored), it also releases a flood of dissenting
and deflationary sentiment, that has its sights on the myths and mon-
uments of Old England and imperialist and Edwardian nostalgia. The
early 1960s, consequently, are charged by an overwhelming, desire on
the part of the young manual and white-collar workers and educated
sections of the middle class to finally dismantle the stage machinery and
fustian retinue of Empire, still draped over Britain and England's public rituals and their fading attachment to imperial global influence. The
Coronation of Queen Elizabeth II in 1953 is the last gasp of that imperial décor and clamour. This is why the 'folk revival' and the new rock
and pop are so transformative. In their initial modes of creative disorder,
they provide a focus for various forms of non-deferentiality and dissent
that mock the idea that the future might be much like the present and
the past, and that, therefore, the future was in good hands. Thus even if
CND marchers, on the whole, were not those to be found at rock 'n' roll
gigs at the Leeds Empire and Hammersmith Palais (something that the
film *That Kind of Girl* [1963], makes play with; a young working class
CND activist has to be taught the twist by a beautiful Austrian au pair),
both marchers and rock 'n' roll audiences did share a certain set of expectations: that being young no longer meant waiting in line to be like one's
parents. Obviously youthful independence, distrust and distaste for one's
elders do not begin in the 1950s; modernity and youth are entangled
from the 18th century on, if not before; Goethe's *The Sorrows of Young*

---

62   George Orwell, 'Notes on Nationalism,' *Decline of the English Murder and other
      essays*, Penguin, Harmondsworth, 1975, p156

Werther (1774)[63] stages a disappointment with the present as much as a Gene Vincent concert. [64]

However, in the late 1950s generational needs and desires pass beyond localized questions of educated taste within the bourgeoisie to open up the very claims of parental and public control across all classes. This is why the later counterculture is such a rupture: it draws on the local, small-scale, deflationary and non-deferential values of this period, to produce an extraordinary shift in class expectations, in which the relations between action, pleasure and identity begin to mean something quite different for those who were used to being spoken *to* and spoken *for*. Crisis and decline of Empire, then, is an opportunity to dismantle the symbols and attachments of a ruling and patrician culture that, in Orwell's sense, conjoined 'reason' with 'tradition,' and 'tradition' with submission to nation and state power. Certainly, for the young there is mocking ridicule of imperial language and authority, of deference to church and state, and revulsion at the racist exploitation of the colonies. The origins of the English counterculture lie in this shift, a turning of 'England' away from the legacy of colonial conquest and exploitation as the defining transformation of the age. If this sounds implausibly inflated, one should not forget the magnitude of the post-colonial transformation globally after 1945. The end of the British Empire was not just about the loss of entrepôt trade and the contraction of primary raw material markets, in a kind of benevolent hand over of power, but a massive reordering of the lives and destinies of hundreds of millions, that of necessity broke the racial hierarchy of the imperial bond, and, therefore, immediately heightened sensitivities in England to the reality of these global changes. As Michael Barrett Brown was to say in 1963 in *After Imperialism* – a major contribution on the left, at the time, to the political economy of Empire:

> In 1945, something like 780 million people, more than a third of the people of the world lived in the colonial possessions of the imperial powers. Most of them lived in Britain's Indian Empire; but Britain ruled nearly 200 million people in colonies outside

---

63   Johan Wolfgang von Goethe, *The Sorrows of Young Werther*, translated with an introduction and notes by Michael Hulse, Penguin Books, London 1989

64   For a discussion of the continuity between Romanticism, German Idealism, and the adolescent passions of rock culture, see, Tristan Garcia, *The Life Intense: A Modern Obsession*, Edinburgh University Press, Edinburgh, 2018

of the sub-continent of India, and there were the same number of in aggregate in the French, Dutch, Belgian and Portuguese colonies… The wildest enthusiast for colonial liberation could scarcely have dared in 1945 to hope that, within, fifteen years, all but a few million of these people would have freed them themselves from subject status.[65]

But, if Empire – at a distance – is open to challenge and rejection, the racism of the colonial legacy sets the wider terms of post-colonial and extra-European immigration into Britain in the 1950s, repositioning England as a place of narrow and *selective* immigration from the ex-colonies, intent as England is on managing and retaining its monocultural identity as the post-colonial flow of immigration unfolds. From the late 1940s the government is determined to limit the permanent settlement of working class 'coloured' immigrants (initially Indian *Lascars* [sailors], West Africans and West Indians), even if they have British passports. This is why one should be careful about assuming that the *Empire Windrush* emigration (June 1948) represents the beginning of a new liberal de-colonial immigration process. The *Windrush* exodus of 492 black immigrants from the Caribbean on a journey from Australia via, Mexico, Cuba and Bermuda to England is framed by a succession of restrictive immigration legislation that makes the entry of the *Windrush* immigrants into Britain the exception to the general rule. Much of this restrictive legislation is based on the fact that the Colonial Office and Inter-Departmental Committee on Coloured People believed that the English people may be able accept de-colonialization in the abstract, but not if it threatened the social integrity of a monocultural England. As the Trinidadian novelist Sam Selvon highlights – the great chronicler of the lives of the first *Windrush* generation and the unfolding crisis of English monoculturalism – England in the 1950s is in a state of 'shock' that de-colonialization has actual implications on its own doorstep. "So Galahad talking to the colour Black, as if is a person, telling it that is not he who causing botheration in the place, but Black, who is worthless thing for making trouble all about,"[66] (*The Lonely Londoners*, 1956). Indeed, this "botheration," turns nasty, as public policy and anti-immigration legislation, transformed racism against the new immigrants into a 'colour problem.'

---

65   Michael Barrett Brown *After Imperialism*, Merlin, London, 1963, p190

66   Sam Selvon, *The Lonely Londoners* [1956], Penguin Books, London, 2006, p77

As fear was encouraged by white racists, politicians
saw the solution to the 'colour problem' in a ban
or severe restriction of black immigration from the
Commonwealth countries…one public opinion poll
showed that 75 per cent of those questioned were in
favour of [immigration] control.[67]

The Colonial Office trod very carefully, then, secure in the legal precedents
of what they were doing. In fact, the restrictive climate on immigration
was hardly new, contrary to popular opinion today. Britain's 'exemplary'
record on immigration, transmigration and settlement is a very partial
and limited one. During the war 500,000-600,000 case files were pend-
ing with the main refugee Jewish organization, with only 80,000 eventually admitted, with thousands of these refugees also interned as 'enemy
aliens.'[68] Furthermore, directly after the war many Holocaust survivors
were turned away from Britain on the grounds of their would-be socially
destabilizing character (read: poor, unskilled and Eastern European).

Something of this moral panic around social destabilization is also evident
in the Hungarian immigration crisis of 1956, after the Soviet invasion of
Hungary. Even though the Immigration office acknowledged that allowing Hungarian refugees into the country would be in the best interests
of British foreign policy (at the height of the Cold War), the government
was overwhelmingly ambivalent about who was worthy of entry, fearing
'communist' influence, for many exiles were dissident communists and
radicals. In the end Britain accepted just 22,000 of 200,000 refugees, on
temporary permits. And once the immediate duty of care diminished,

the Hungarian refugees in Britain were treated
increasingly as problematic aliens who were encouraged to disperse and find work (for men,
largely as coal miners) or to re-emigrate to North
America. Eventually one third would move on or
return home.[69]

---

67 Ron Ramdin, *The Making of The Black Working Class in Britain* [1987], Verso,
London and New York, 2017, p227

68 Tony Kushner, *The Battle of Britishness: Migrant Journeys 1685 to the Present*,
Manchester University Press, Manchester, 2012

69 Kushner, ibid, p78

Similarly, after WWI war the "quarter of a million Belgian refugees, including…children, were quickly and unceremoniously returned home by the British state."[70] This restrictionism, then, accompanies, even shapes, the post-Empire adjustment and deflation of imperial grandeur in the 1950s and 1960s. If England has lost an Empire yet gained a Commonwealth, this does not mean England now sees itself thereby as a host to its former subject peoples. The restrictionism continues with the blatantly discriminatory Commonwealth Immigrants Act in 1962. It is no surprise, therefore, that into this weakening imperial space rushes a revival of an early modern Anglo theme: namely that the distinctiveness of Britain (but specifically the English) lies in the fact that Britain is home to an 'island race'; it is England's long maintained 'insularity' as an island people, a people or peoples of the seas, that has secured its 'racial,' historical and cultural identity. The idea of the British as an 'island people,' was particularly influential before WWI at the height of late imperial hubris, best represented by H.J. Mackinder's popular *Britain and the British Seas* (1902),[71] which raised the Union Jack over (a narrow) English exceptionalism. In the 1950s and 1960s, post the initial intake of commonwealth immigrants this becomes a self-congratulating celebration of 'cultural integration.' Bourgeois social science is, in the renewed spirit of Walter Bagehot, keen to emphasize the English people's integration into a largely monocultural polity as the basis for parliamentary continuity. As Richard Rose was to say in 1965 as the first great waves of the counterculture were to transform England:

> What is most impressive in contemporary England
> is the amount of agreement on basic political
> attitudes…The great implicit major premise of the
> English political culture would seem to be that all
> necessary and desirable changes can be assimilated
> into the existing political system.[72]

Exceptionalism, then, retains, some of its force, and consequently, it is not unsurprising that its would-be allure is mixed in with the residual democratic militia spirit in the late 1950s and 1960s, creating a tense encounter between Orwell's patriotism of place (its defence and maintenance) and an aggressive (English) nationalist self-identity that Tories

---

70   Kushner, ibid, p124

71   H.J. Mackinder *Britain and the British Seas*, Heinemann, London, 1902

72   Richard Rose, *Politics in England*, Faber & Faber, London, 1965, pp55 & 57.

and official Labour agree, needs to be remade and strengthened under Cold War and post-colonial conditions. As such, there is something of the non-martial aspects of this isolationism of place, in the folk revival and re-articulation of the symbols and myths of the Southern English pastoral in the 1960s. The vales, woods, and fields of Southern England, remain a space apart – indeed a secret realm to be revealed through patient experiential work – of long honed beauty, local knowledge and communal village practices, that contribute to the distinctiveness of English history and culture.

The utopianism of the late sixties folk-thinking carries with it the legacy of this exceptionalism and isolationism. It would be historically delimiting to think otherwise, as if to suggest nothing remained of the Edwardian ideology of an 'island people' in its imaginings. Yet, we should be careful not to define the remaking of the English Southern Pastoral as *solely* a defensive move, as if folk-thinking was an unconscious conservative adaptation to these post-Empire conditions; the recovery of an Anglo 'race memory.' On the contrary, as I have stressed, 1960s folk-thinkings' remaking of the Southern pastoral, is one of the key insurgent openings that allows a progressive and post-nationalist cultural politics to help clear away the debris of Empire, and, is thus inseparable from the radical claims of the earlier folk revival and, in particular, the post-imperialist claims of Scottish musicians on this heritage. Pastoral exceptionalism, accordingly, faces forward as much as backwards, and, this is why, for all its past and present ambiguities, it offers a home for another kind of Englishness in the 1960s, one defined by anti-militarism and (pagan) pre-imperialist associations. And, this is why exceptionalism in this pastoral context carries with it a particular globalized political and cultural advocacy that has huge implications in the remaking of the popular and the emergence of the counterculture in the mid-to-late 1960s. These forms of progressive exceptionalism create a prism through which the vast presence and influence of American culture is assimilated, with all this culture's own progressive and regressive (militarist and imperialist) retinue. Thus, the links between English pastoral visions, pagan culture, and anti-martial values in the new folk-thinking, is not just incidental to the formation of what defines the English counterculture, but plays a determining role, insofar as it acts as an alternate pole of attraction in its mediation *and* critique of post-war American culture and society.

Consequently, we might say, the origins of the remaking of the popular after the 1950s lies at the intersection of three forces in the wake of Empire: a progressive and anti-martial pastoral exceptionalism; the growing post-colonial pressure building up in response to the reactionary monocultural narrowing of this exceptionalism; and the general impact of American popular culture – as the dominant partner culture in Cold War compliance – on the definition of national culture itself. And, of course, this is a fissiparous combination. What is 'exceptionalism' worth when it is commandeered by racism or xenophobia, or is tied to a global American culture and foreign policy? Thus, if the antique notion of the English as an 'island people' is re-installed post-Empire, it is, therefore, inevitable that its progressive and reactionary meanings will be imme-diately tested against the impact of American culture, for good or ill, as Britain comes under the sway of American hegemony. If England is not Empire, is it now the poor subaltern relation of the US? This was a crucial question. And this is why by the mid-to-late 1960s there is no *special* relationship with American culture to speak of. Firstly, because American commercial culture demands a kind of all-embracing deference to the detriment of local cultural identities and traditions; and secondly, because, after Vietnam and the attacks on the Civil Rights Movement in America, American culture offers another bleak and violent vision of Empire.

So much complacent historical writing continues to talk about the English popular culture of the late 1960s as being in thrall to post-war American commercialization. In many regards up until the early 1960s this is true. Tin Pan Alley, Hollywood and rock 'n' roll sweep all before it, placing English popular music in particular, up until the Beatles that is, in a weakly imitative position. One might talk in customary terms of American popular culture 'capturing' the interests and desires of English musicians and audiences alike. The results were on the whole baleful, and the fount of all attacks on popular music, during this period by con-servatives and radicals alike. Yet, in the wake of the achievement of the Beatles this imitative reflex is undoubtedly weakened, as the Beatles seek to detach themselves from the public vortex of the (American led) 'en-tertainment' industry (certainly when they decide to stop touring after their brutalizing and musically barren tour of the US in 1966). This is the point where the initial deference to American popular music ends, or, rather, becomes radically discriminating. And this takes three crucial and not necessarily complimentary forms.

Firstly there is a conscious embrace of dissident black forms of American popular music, in the spirit of the early English Blues revival (John

Mayall's Bluesbreakers), that did much to confront the racism of English monoculturalism before the wider cultural impact of black musicians in Britain in the mid-to-late seventies; secondly there is a rejection of conventional rock as the only channel of countercultural achievement; and thirdly, certainly by 1966-67, there is an increasing openness to other musics (classical Indian, serial and atonal music, *musique concrète*, as well as the new folk) and other cultural references (Dada, Surrealism, European 'absurdist' theatre). The result is a concerted attempt to mediate the undoubted drive of contemporary American music through a kind of English popular 'exceptionalism,' built as it is, from very non-rock 'n' roll and non-Anglo-American resources, such as the new French and German electronic musics. But, more specifically it is the requirement to produce an English popular music that is *post-Empire* (English and American) that shapes this hybridity.

The Beatles after 1966, with their mocking and sardonic tone, and their increasing resistance in public to their incorporation into a great British success story, are the first band in England to make clear what they are and what they do is no longer assimilable to a narrative of 'British' success and as such to the patronizing grace notes of plucky working class endeavour. Thus, if The Incredible String Band puts the first globalized marker down for a post-Empire music in 1966-67, the Beatles certainly expand its range and dynamism in *Sgt. Pepper's Lonely Hearts Club Band* (1967). *Sgt. Pepper* is the first real codification of an English popular music that seeks to define itself in contradistinction to both Empire and to the 'empire' of rock 'n' roll as a world over-inscripted by the *rites de passage* of teenage life. Indeed, this is the great turning point for an English post-Empire and post-rock sensibility: the heteroclite shifts of the music move decisively in advance of the expectations of their core audience and, the music, as a whole, is mostly 'unplayable' live (it took over 700 hours to record). Indeed, many of the reviews of the album at the time are surprisingly muted or uncomprehending: the narrative of personable, cheeky British rock 'n' roll had been broken. This may be less to do with the use of reverse tapes and strange and eclectic instrumentation and striking orchestration, than a systematic spirit of lyrical incongruity and a kind of stagey, sardonic use of Edwardian song-forms and references, from the title and Peter Blake's cover of the album to the songs 'Being for the Benefit of Mr Kite' and 'When I'm Sixty-Four.' In the context of the album these interludes appear like ghostly stage turns, moments of an English past, that are now – even in 1967 – part of a whimsical tourist industry. To write about benign old age, for instance, at the height of an upsurge of 'youth culture' exuberance almost verges on the churlish. To say, the Beatles, then, are as much preoccupied by popular cultural nostalgia in *Sgt. Pepper*, as they are the demands of a hybridized post-rock, is to miss the 'quotational' or 'conceptual' character of these songs in the overall architecture of the album. The album is a playful exercising and *excising* of English popular motifs. Indeed, compare *Sgt. Pepper's* 'quotational' character to that of Van Dyke Park's American 'conceptual' *Song Cycle* released a year later and obviously influenced by *Sgt. Pepper*, with its ghastly pastiches of Broadway tunes, with jangly pianos, sugary strings and angelic harp arpeggios, and echoey camp vocals, so deep in the mix they sound as if he's singing from inside a fun fair carousel, where no doubt he would have loved to have been had he been able to; here nostalgia does blatantly dry up what made *Sgt. Pepper's* ambition so invigorating.

Thus, if the Incredible String Band and Van Morrison offer a hybridized folk music route into the ruins of Empire and monocultural nationalism, for the Beatles, hybridization is predominantly a matter of humour and bathos, of stretching and ironizing 'Englishness,' at the same time as drawing on its local vernaculars (remember at this time, Paul McCartney was very close to Barry Miles, editor of *International Times* (*IT*), was listening to György Ligeti and Karlheinz Stockhausen, and was also moving in avant-garde poetry and art circles in London and New York, and, therefore, was, if not actually being schooled in a kind of countercultural 'denaturalisation' of Empire-culture, and so was at least was open to its critical influence). In this respect *Sgt. Pepper* is one of the first places in the new music where a post-Empire sensibility draws on a nascent *modernist* indisciplinarity, indebted to neo-Dadaism and Surrealism, and as such, to all the machinery of defamiliarization that European modernism and the avant-garde bring in their wake. Thus, even if this is a largely low-brow assimilation, nevertheless, the Beatles in 1966 and 1967, are part of a continuing shift in critical tone in the popular song-form and rock and countercultural milieu, in which the ironization of authority, and the ridiculing of class hierarchies and presumptions brings an unprecedented modernist disenchantment into popular culture, that also takes in the 'satire boom,' the revival of late 19th century English nonsense poetry (Edward Lear and Lewis Carroll), the anarchism of *Private Eye*, and the radio shows the Goons, and Round the Horne.

Indeed, 1965-75 is England's American Cultural Front (1935-1944) and Germany's Weimar (1919-1933), in which a radical popular culture acts as an ideological clearing zone for all the accumulated imperialist and boosterist dross of nationalist and capitalist self-assertion. And, as with these previous periods of counter-insurgency the incorporation of working class and lower middle class creativity into the reorganization and redefinition of the popular, brings, scepticism, mischief, grotesquerie, exaggeration and sardonic distaste to the fore. This distinguishes the late 1960s decisively from the 1930s in England, where critique and disenchantment was housed largely within a middle class and upper-middle class revolt (T.S. Eliot, Virginia Woolf) against the parlous anti-modernism of ruling English literary taste; the working class contribution to this critique was largely miniscule, confined to a handful of proletarian novelists (Ralph Bates, *The Olive Field* [1936,] Lewis Jones, *Cwmardy*, [1937]),[73] who were CP aligned and themselves highly sceptical of modernism and non-literary culture as sources of progressive transformation. The left's understanding of the popular remained cognitively narrow and predominantly literary. The Beatles, therefore, are one part – if an influential part – of an extensive and belated readjustment of the place of modernist disenchantment and critique into English popular culture, that links subaltern 'techniques of indiscipline' to modernism's own formal indiscipline, opening new lines of connection between music, literature and art. This is why this general mood of sardonic disenchantment follows the bardic uplift of the new folk music, in providing a wholly new and ambitious set of reference points and lines of flight for the popular. And, in turn, this is why the English art school – and its own expansion and finessing of techniques of indiscipline – proves to be so important to the new music and the growing post-Empire sensibility. For the English art school in the mid-1960s, is one of the key places where these new reference points and lines of flight and belated modernist values are given concrete form.

The English art school's impact on popular music in the 1960s is much commented on and celebrated; indeed, its would-be achievements and charms are now part of the standard histories of English postwar history, in a kind of self-flattering narrative of how creative England is and was. [74] The truth is richer, yet less self-congratulatory, than the official histories and 'guardians' of national history would assume. In the early 1960s the

---

73   Ralph Bates, *The Olive Field*, Jonathan Cape, London, 1936; Lewis Jones, *Cwmardy*, Lawrence & Wishart, London 1937

74   See for example, Dominic Sandbrook, *White Heat: A History of Britain in the Swinging Sixties, 1964-1970*, Abacus, London, 2009

English art school was a place filled, on the one hand, with embittered academicians and Realists, and on the other hand, with hard-bitten modernists still fighting interwar battles for Paul Cézanne and Pablo Picasso. The widespread impact of Abstract Expressionism from the mid-1950s to the mid-1960s, then, tends to exacerbate these underlying resentments, re-entrenching the English attachments of the academicians and (Euston Road) realists and the perfumed late Bloomsbury European attachments of the painterly modernists.[75] Postwar American art, 'Americanism,' American culture, were judged by the older generation to be corrupting and presumptuous, or corrupting because they were presumptuous; for younger artists, however, schooled, in a late imperial English 'exceptionalism' and the parsimony of 'proper painterly skills,' or in the genteel mottling of figurative-abstract aestheticism, the formal destablizations of American modernism – particularly Abstract Expressionism – represented a new horizon of achievement. And Englishness whether attached to realist painting or modernism, seemed very tame and epicene in comparison. Yet, one should be careful about Abstract Expressionism sweeping all before it, because it didn't.

If Abstract Expressionism codified 'Abstract Painting' as a fully mature option in the art schools, it still met with a great deal of resistance from Realists and life room stalwarts, intent on re-attaching British art to some stable and civic account of representation and the 'national-popular.' There is no strict left/right fight on these matters, yet something of the 1930s Communist Party's attachment to realism as an artistic cognate of political virtue, shapes the debate, certainly as the Cold War hots up. One conspicuous public manifestation of the debate, before the influence of Abstract Expressionism takes hold in the art schools is the mid-1950s confrontation in *The New Statesman and Nation* and *The Twentieth Century*, between John Berger and Patrick Heron.[76] Berger, Communist Party supporter, takes Realist painting to be the indefatigable home of progressive humanist values, and the new abstraction – in the apocalyptic language of Georg Lukács' writing on the realist novel and modernism in the 1950s – the home of anomie and asocial elitism. Patrick Heron, on the other hand, takes abstract painting and Abstract Expressionism

---

75 For a look at the art student's experience during this period, see Charles Madge and Barbara Weinberger, *Art Students Observed*, Faber & Faber, London, 1973

76 John Berger, 'The Battle,' *The New Statesman and Nation*, 21 January, 1955; Berger, 'The Artist and Modern Society,' *The Twentieth Century*, August, 1955, and Patrick Heron, 'Art is Autonomous,' *The Twentieth Century*, September, 1955

to be the energetic site of a new and invigorating encounter between Enlightenment values and aesthetic experience (the best of the best that bourgeois culture can produce). The premature and partial nature of this dispute is perhaps to be expected. Realist painting by the late 1950s is decidedly dog eared and out of sorts; but perhaps more revealing is Berger's own avant-garde counter-move as he shifts his attention later to photography in his collaborations with the Swiss photographer Jean Mohr: image and text are counterpoised as a double-articulated reflection on representation and the production of historical experience (John Berger and Jean Mohr, *A Fortunate Man*, 1967).[77] Similarly, Heron's expectations for a new public culture of 'sensuous reception' through painting is brought low through the increasing withdrawal of advanced art (in the USA and Europe) from the particulars of painterly aestheticization. Berger and Heron's dispute, therefore, hides a deeper malaise: the strikingly regressive character of the debate on realism, modernism and the avant-garde in the 1950s and early 1960s in England. Berger's defence of murky green and brown figures at work at lathes or building bridges, or Heron's Greenbergian paeans to bright washes of colour, hardly constitute a radical remaking of the culture, or even a 'making new' of recent precedents. Indeed, there is something peculiarly ahistorical about the debate despite both authors' eagerness to call on historical forebears. That is, this is a debate that wilfully misreads, misses or neglects the key shifts and departures in twentieth-century art: Marcel Duchamp's destabilization of traditional skills and the technical and critical introduction of the unassisted readymade; Laszlo Moholy-Nagy's and Alexander Rodchenko's environmental and interdisciplinary forms and post-gallery ambitions; John Heartfield's and Hannah Höch's photographic superimpositions and temporal discontinuities; and André Breton's and Jean-Jacques Boiffard's narrative-literary exchanges between photography and text. Thus, in this respect, we can see what the emerging counterculture releases into the art school in the mid-sixties: a belated recovery of the vast shifts in the form, function and social identity of art in the wake of the crisis of painterly and sculptural tradition at the beginning of the twentieth-century. For the first time there is a systematic introduction of avant-garde – as opposed to the occultation of painterly modernist aestheticisms – into the English art school, a generalized recovery and re-adaptation of the deflationary and ironic techniques and strategies of early twentieth-century art, that the postwar German and French artist took for granted. Hence the impact of the counterculture in the art schools is

---

77   John Berger and Jean Mohr, *A Fortunate Man*, Allen Lane, London, 1967

enormous, for, its belated reconstruction and re-functioning of the early avant-garde provides the requisite tools for a critique of *culture* (capitalist and Stalinist) as opposed, to simply, an aestheticist and representational adjustment to the problems of artistic value and tradition. The opportunities for reinvention derived from this, therefore, cannot be underestimated, given how much of English high culture was still in thrall to formalist and anti-formalist shibboleths borrowed from the 1930s. Art in England recovers a socially engaged and internationalist understanding of the avant-garde, that radically exposes the narrow national mediation of European modernism and realism in English public life; but, crucially, it also provides the opportunity and intellectual means to critically assess the rise and dominance of American art, rather than merely dismissing it uncritically or slavishly adapting to it for fear of being thought provincial. This is why by 1966 the new abstract art and Abstract Expressionism does not crush everything before it in the art schools. Many young artists are persuaded, certainly, on terms borrowed from Heron, Greenberg and others, that this is the future. But for many other artists the new abstract art and Abstract Expressionism, as part of a larger debate about the origins of modernism and the role of post-traditional art 'beyond' painting; and of course, such a position is not provided solely by the early European avant-garde, but by the growing confidence of post-1950s American art itself, which in its own belated version of the early European avant-garde provides new points of re-articulation and departure for non-traditional practices. This is a long way from Berger and Heron's miniaturist spat. It is also a long way from English reticence about linking the production of art to the critique of culture. This is why in 1968 Jeff Nuttall's *Bomb Culture*, is such a focal point for these new horizons and ambitions.

Schooled in the early avant-garde, the new American art, Beat poetics, and the new countercultural musics, Nuttall's inventive conjunction of cultural leftism and hipster new journalism, provides a new set of coordinates for art and politics in England that is comparable (in rhetoric at least) to the fledgling countercultures of New York and San Francisco. Central to his vision is a version of what was rapidly becoming the 'working practice' of so much countercultural activity inside and outside the art schools on both sides of the Atlantic: the confluence of Dada's interrogation of high-culture, nationalism and imperialist adventurism, with a disorderly hybridity. There is even a stand-alone chapter on Dada in the book. Indeed, Nuttall sees the emerging intersection of art, literature and popular music as inciting new kinds of cultural attachment across classes that recalls in spirit, Dada's early years.

> Up to the point of failure of CND it would be
> broadly true to say that pop was the prerogative of
> working class teenagers, protest was the prerogative
> of middle class teenagers, protest was the prerogative
> of middle class students, and art was the prerogative
> of the lunatic fringe. The pop fans despised protest
> as being naïve and art as being posh, the protesting
> students despised pop as bring commercial and art
> as being pretentious, and the artists despised pop for
> being tasteless and protest being drab.[78]

There is a great deal of truth in this perspective, as I stressed in the introduction; and as such, Nuttall is right to suggest that the entry of modernist and avant-garde cultural politics into the landscape of post-Empire English culture reconfigured these prejudices and distinctions. New points of connection between popular culture and high culture were made available to a large number of younger people across classes keen to learn the disaffirmative 'codes' of the counterculture: "there is a great negative work of destruction to be accomplished. We must sweep and clean," as Tristan Tzara declared in 1918, full of disgust for The Great War, and the "world abandoned to the hands of bandits."[79] This does not mean that working class teenagers in the 1960s were reading Tzara in French, or that English art and high culture was completely oblivious to the merits of Dadaist disenchantment and anti-art irony (Robert Motherwell's *The Dada Painters and Poets* [1951] was a much circulated text in the art schools and reference point for the educated general reader).[80] Yet, in the early 1960s there was a palpable unlearning of settled prejudices about elite culture and the would-be antipathy of art and politics that found a new and willing audience.[81] The critical achievements, energy and hu-

---

78 Jeff Nuttall, *Bomb Culture*, MacGibbon & Kee, London, 1968, p114

79 Tristan Tzara, 'Dada Manifesto 1918,' *Dadas on Art*, ed, Lucy Lippard, Prentice-Hall, Inc., Englewood Cliffs, New Jersey, 1971, p19

80 Robert Motherwell's, *The Dada Painters and Poets: An Anthology* [Wittenborn & Schultz, New York, 1951], The Belknap Press of Harvard University Press, Cambridge Mass., 1981. Later, this was supplemented by Willy Verkauf's, *Dada: Monograph of a Movement*, Wittenborn & Schultz, New York, 1957, and Han Richter's *Dada Art and Anti-Art*, McGraw-Hill, New York, 1965.

81 Two English artists who contributed – in their early work – significantly to this belated Dadaist shift, are Nigel Henderson (1917-1985) and Richard Hamilton (1922-2011).

mour of Dada seemed to confirm for young musicians that some of the avant-garde's techniques of refusal were usable more broadly, even if these techniques went under the name of 'humour,' as opposed to negation as such, for those who used them. It is possible to see, therefore, by the mid-1960s how the 'disorderly' ambitions of Dada – even in a weakened form – offered the 'disorderly' ambitions of a new generation of artists and a new popular music a language or mode of address capable of engaging with the British post-Empire landscape, that an outright folk revival or old school rock 'n' roll couldn't provide. That is, above all else, Empire demanded mockery and deflation, a language that rooted out the false gravitas of a national tradition based on high-minded humanism and the patronization of the 'popular' and workers' cultural interests.

Thus, if the clearing out of the retinue of Empire in English culture is attached in art and music to a re-functioning of pre-war techniques of the artistic and literary avant-garde, it is possible to see a little clearer, therefore, why the Beatles, in crucial respects, are a significant manifestation of this new conjunction of forces; they provide a bridge between the growing disaffected energies of a new popular culture and what Nuttall calls, memorably, Dada's "collection of calculated impertinences."[82] By 1964-5, then, the Beatles, are developing their own range of calculated impertinences, opening up a gap between their tentative heterodox interests as musicians and the culture that produced them and their now vast fan base. This shift is reflected, in particular, in John Lennon's increasingly humorous impatience with standard kinds of lyricism, revealed vividly in the two collections of pugnacious short stories and poems he published during this period, *In His Own Write* (1964)[83] and *A Spaniard in the Works* (1965).[84] These two books are worth some close reflection, in the light of Empire, Dada and the 'lyrical incongruities' of *Sgt. Pepper*, for they stake out what was to come for the Beatles and other musicians working through the legacy of Empire.

The texts obviously disclose some of the literary influences that were finding their subterranean way into the group (Joycean paragrammatics and neologisms, English nonsense poetry, Ronald Searle, and Goon-type malapropisms, and Dada sarcasm and syntactic disruption), but they also

---

82   Nuttall, op cit, p88

83   John Lennon, *In His Own Write*, Jonathan Cape, MacMillan & Scribner, London, 1964

84   John Lennon, *A Spaniard in the Works*, Simon & Schuster, New York, 1965

map directly onto a world of Empire that feels as if its gruesomeness is still lapping at Lennon's and the band's feet, as it is for other musicians and artists confronted by the upsurge in racism and anti-immigration rhetoric. Adrian Henri, for instance, incorporates this racial and anti-immigration rhetoric directly into one of his mixed media paintings in 1965, *Liverpool 8 Spring Collage No 5 (for P.G.W and F.B)*. A racist White Britain poster is pasted onto a canvas, partially obliterated by a black painterly and violent Arnulf Rainer-style smear. The poster reads: '9 million coloureds in Britain By 1984 Means The End of Our White Race. Boycott the Perverted Poofs and Degenerate Scum In And Outside Puppet Parliament Who Seek This End.'

Hence, one of the first things noticeable about *In His Own Write* and *A Spaniard in the Works*, is how the writing works over the ideological detritus of the War, Empire, Labour and Tory politics and post-1950s English popular culture, misogyny, racism and anti-semitism as a *mise en scène* for Lennon's anger. "Mammy: 'O.K. Kimu sahib bwana, massa (*she lifts the bundle and eats it*). 'Sho' was naice." (*In His Own Write*)[85]; "a coloured man danced by eating a banana." (*In His Own Write*)[86]; "Otumba kept wogs for poisonous snacks" ("wogs" here being a translation from "frogs") (*In His Own Write*)[87]; "Ai've brot ya a negru Rosebeen from the war y'know." (*In His Own Write*)[88]: "Small wonder on this churly morn I crivy like a black." (*In His Own Write*)[89]; "One place of particularge interest was the Statue of Eric in Picanniny Surplass." (*A Spaniard in the Works*)[90]; "He was like a black shadow or negro on that dumb foggy night." (*A Spaniard in the Works*)[91]; "Well! Mr Wobooba – may I call you Wog? What is the basic problem you are facing." (*A Spaniard in the Works*). [92]

---

85 Lennon, 'Scene three Act One,' *In His Own Write and A Spaniard in the Works*, with a foreword by Jon Savage and an introduction by Paul McCartney, Vintage Books, 2010, p34

86 'Neville Club,' *In His Own Write*, p54

87 'On Safairy With Whide Hunter,' ibid, p56

88 'Halburt Returb,' *ibid*, p65

89 'On this Churly Morn,' ibid, p68

90 'The Singularge Experience of Miss Anne Duffield,' *A Spaniard in the Works*, op cit, p101

91 Ibid, p103

92 'I Believe, Boot…,' ibid p163

But also noticeable is the number of disabled and "crippled" characters in the stories; a cast of dispelled, broken bodies, dwarfs and War casualties. "Eric, I am growth on your very head, help me Eric…From then on you never saw Eric without the big fat scab growth on his head. And that's why Eric Hearble lost his job teaching spastics to dance. 'Were not having a cripple teaching our lads,' said Headmaster." (*In His Own Write*)[93]; "Woenow Attle grazine upone an olde crypped…" (*In His Own Write*)[94]; 'Should I have flowers all round the spokes? Said Anne polishing her foot rest. 'Or should I keep it syble?' she continued looking down on her grain haired Mother. 'Does it really matter?' repaid her Mother wearily wiping her sign. 'He won't be looking at your spokes anyway.'" (*In His Own Write*)[95]; "its not every one what has a real cripple for a father" (*In His Own Write*)[96]; "His very fist was jopped off, (The War) and he got a birthday hook!" (*In His Own Write*)[97]; "The only thing that puzzled [Jesus El Pifeo] was why his sugarboot got so annoyed when he called her his little Spastic in public." (*A Spaniard in the Works,* p88)[98]; "I feel I know why you are here Basil' said Womlbs eyeing he leg. 'It's about Jock the Cripple'" (*A Spaniard in the Works*)[99]; "You don't want me around," he said, "I'm old and crippled too." (*A Spaniard in the Works*).[100]

It would be fair and obvious to say that the wordplay and humour discloses a trauma here, as if the exit from Empire is only in name; a shallow and broken name. Indeed, the emotional register of the writing is caught up in a complex elision between the received racist language and colonialist attitudes and characterization, and Lennon's sadistic scenarios and gallows humour. What it produces is a macabre and miserable England, relieved only by the dadaistic release of the malapropisms, neologisms and substitutions, which are rich and multiple: "Everydobby knows" (*In His Own Write*)[101], "Merry Chrustchove" (*In His Own Write*)[102], "the

---

93 'The Fat Growth on Eric Hearble,' *In His Own Write*, op cit, p18

94 'The Famous Five through Woenow Abbey,' ibid, p27

95 'Nicely Nicely Clive,' ibid, p50

96 'Henry and Harry,' ibid, p60

97 'A Surprise for Little Bobby,' *In His Own Write*, op cit, p64

98 'A Spaniard in the Works,' *A Spaniard in the Works,* op cit, p88

99 'The Singularge Experience of Miss Anne Duffield,' ibid, p102

100 'Our Dad,' ibid p157

101 'At the Denis,' *In His Own Write*, op cit, p16

102 'Randolf's Party,' ibid, p23

Poleaseman speeg" (*In His Own Write*)[103], "To get a goobites sleep" (*In His Own Write*)[104], "Look at that garbet all filby and durby" (*In His Own Write*)[105], "Harassed Wilsod won the General Erection, with a small majorie over the Torchies" (*A Spaniard in the Works*)[106], "my cup kenneth connor" (*A Spaniard in the Works*)[107]. "When they had finished speaching" (*A Spaniard in the Works*)[108], "How many moron of these incredible sleazy backward, bad, deaf monkeys parsing as entertainers, with thier FLOPTOPPED hair…" (*A Spaniard in the Works*)[109], "he fell suddy to the ground weefy and whaley crizeling tuber Lawn." (*A Spaniard in the Works*).[110] Jon Savage in his foreword to the reprinting of both books in 1997, talks of Lennon's "Liverpool Irish-subversion of the ruling-class language."[111] But this is too easy and benign; the works' recalcitrance is formed by the lived grotesqueries and cynicism of everyday working class life, which gives the writing its troubled and uneasy character. In this respect, after 'I am the Walrus' (1967) and *Sgt. Pepper* Lennon doesn't try these acidic 'envoicings' again in prose form; the songs take up the slack; and, by 1970, when he arrives post-Beatles in New York, eager to participate directly politically in the US counterculture, the whimsy and grotesquerie had to be put aside, or least repositioned:

> I wouldn't say I've given up politics in that way. I mean, I never took up politics. Things I do – or for that matter anybody does – are done politically. Any statement you make is a political statement. Any record, even your way of life is a political statement.[112]

But if political Dada finds another voice in Lennon in 1970, Lennon's brief 'literary' ambitions and success lay siege to that new horizon of

---

103 'Sad Michael,' ibid, p29

104 'I Wandered,' ibid, p30

105 'Unhappy Frank,' ibid, p66

106 'The General Erection,' *A Spaniard in the Works*, op cit, p114

107 'Araminta Ditch,' ibid, p129

108 Ibid, p129

109 'Cassandle,' *A Spaniard in the Works* op cit,, p134

110 'Silly Norman,' ibid, p142

111 Jon Savage, 'Foreword,' *In His Own Write and A Spaniard in the Works*, op cit, pix

112 'Elliot Mintz Interviews John Lennon,' *Los Angeles Free Press*, Oct 15-21 1971, quoted in James A. Mitchell, *The Walrus & The Elephants: John Lennon's Years of Revolution*, Seven Stories Press, New York, 2014, p20.

musical, artistic and literary ambition from below that Nuttall rightly hymns. This is why we need to register how unusual it was for Lennon to produce these two books, in the form that he did. Young working class and uneducated lower middle class men and women just did not write and publish books, let alone rock musicians, even famous rock musicians.[113] In the early 1960s literary and critical production was still the preserve of a tiny middle class and upper-middle class minority, centred largely on Oxbridge, even if a few declassed working class novelists continued to find a wide audience (John Braine, *Room at the Top*, 1957) or a small literary audience (James Hanley, *Boy*, 1931, *The Furys, 1935, An End and a Beginning, 1958*).[114]

No better diagnosis of this upper-middle class post-war literary claustrophobia is Elias Canetti's literary memoir, *Party in the Blitz: The English Years* (2005). The divide in empathy between the ordinary English people he meets and befriends, and the elite London literary milieu he mixes with in the 1930s and 1940s, leaves a bitter taste. "It is not easy for me to go on writing about these English things. I often find myself shaking with rage when I think of them."[115] Indeed, the class insecurities of writing outside of the patronage of this small upper-middle class coterie, affected, even defined, the values and expectations of that generation of educated postwar working class and lower-middle class grammar school pupils who did achieve literary success, such as Kingsley Amis and Anthony Burgess. Burgess never really shook off that feeling of being patronized – of being thought worthy rather than exceptional – despite the

---

113 For a striking account of these exclusions during the 1940s and 1950s (albeit within a French colonial context, with powerful echoes of Rancière) see Hélène Cixous, 'Coming to Writing' (1976), in Cixous, *Coming to Writing and Other Essays*, ed Deborah Jenson, with an introductory essay by Susan Rubin Suleiman, Harvard University Press, Cambridge, Mass., 1991

114 John Braine, *Room at the Top*, Eyre & Spottiswoode, London, 1957; James Hanley, *Boy*, Boriswood, London, 1931, The Furys, Chatto & Windus, London, 1935, and And an End and a Beginning, Macdonald & Company, London, 1958. We should also note the achievement of Gerald Kersh (*Night and the City*, Michael Joseph, London 1938), an escapee from the London suburbs, who created a convincing working class and criminal interwar London. *Night and the City* became a bleak noir film starring Richard Widmark in 1950, directed by Jules Dassin.

115 Elias Canetti, *Party in the Blitz: The English Years*, The Harvill Press, London, 2005, p230

achievement of *A Clockwork Orange* (1962)[116] and later *Earthly Powers* (1980).[117] Accordingly, in the early 1960s, to write and try and publish was to feel the full force of class expectations. Hence, young working class men and women just didn't write and publish – period; male skilled manual workers might have a letter published in a daily newspaper or a workers' newspaper, or write an article for a trade union publication, or a specialist technical or hobby magazine, or even publish poem in a tiny poetry magazine, but on the whole, workers did not see writing as part of their daily lives, or expect to write – if they did so – as anything but as amateurs. Workers' writing, then, was never able to achieve a collective level of self-identity, as it did briefly in the Soviet Union and Weimar in the 1920s and 1930s. Thus, writing a playful collection of prose and poems amounted to a frontal attack on the accepted norms of 'working class' literary production. In a provocative sense Lennon's two books were in *excess* of what was required from a working class author: they were not class memoirs or first-person reports on working class experience, neither were they *roman à clefs*, tidying up working class life for a fiction reading middle class audience; they were, rather, extravagant and childlike super-fluities, in which an insistence on a language 'without' stable measure, was open incursion into the realm of the professional modernist poet. There is, then, something of the non-instrumental ambition of Rancière's early 19th century Parisian unschooled worker-poets in the writing; in other words, a test of the authority of that which is allocated to the worker-writer, even if the working class writer in question has access to leading publishers and an audience of millions. *In His Own Write* sold over 200,000 copies in its first year; *A Spaniard in the Works* over 100,000 in

---

116 Anthony Burgess, *A Clockwork Orange*, Heinemann, London, 1962. In this respect, we might also note the reception of D.H. Lawrence (1885-1930) in England's upper-middle class literary metropolitan milieu. Lawrence's proletarian background, was, for his detractors, always taken to be evidence of his weaknesses as a novelist. In 1930, for example, T.S. Eliot in the *Nation and Athenaeum*, attacked Lawrence's 'crudeness of tone,' and later chastised him for not possessing "what we ordinarily call thinking" and a "lack of "intellectual and social training" (*After Strange Gods: A Primer of Modern Heresy*, Faber, London, 1934, p58). See F.R. Leavis, *D.H. Lawrence: Novelist*, Chatto & Windus, London, 1955, for a passionate defence of Lawrence against this Eliotian interwar literary snobbery and condescension. Countercultural radicals were in no sense Leavisites, but something of Leavis's plebeian defence of Lawrence attaches itself to the deflationary drive of the new modernist modes of popular and literary engagement in the 1960s.

117 Anthony Burgess, *Earthly Powers*, Simon & Schuster, New York, 1980

the first three months. These huge figures are instructive, because they reveal the wider compass of the books. They find their way not just into the homes of those who rarely read, but into the young hands of those who begin to see the value of the connection between pop and literary self-definition; rock and its possible wider influence and connection to things that normally would appear 'intellectual' or demanding. And this new threshold of sensibility is perhaps what the counterculture imagined, above all else, was its wider vision for a new culture: a popular culture of reflection and experiment.

Thus, the manifest weakness of Lennon's writing is not the point here; they are obviously works of a young man with limited knowledge, and who is working from what is to hand. But for all the writing's false notes, it does a successful and striking job: it redefines the available voices of working class writerly ambition, in a culture where non-literary and post-literary attitudes prevail, and where working class autodidacticism – unlike today – still carried a certain prestige. In this respect it turns attention to the *social* significance of the song-form in the counterculture, for those, who do not have a daily relationship to writing, that is, the song is not simply an outlet for vocal expression, but quite simply a chance to *publish*. This is not to be underestimated or trivialized in the light of the above; and this is one of the reasons why the song-form becomes so open to poetic reshaping after 1965, and seems increasingly literary in ambition, and why, in turn, a performer such as Van Morrison, can, without a second thought, look back to the Beatles and consider himself a *writer*.

The incursion of Dada's calculated impertinences into literary high culture, then, meets the dissident bardic uplift of the new folk-thinking coming the other way, creating a broad and newly articulated space for popular literary values in the counterculture. This is the achievement of the counterculture in England under post-Empire conditions: the production of an unprecedented realignment of literary self-definition with popular forms in contradistinction to a growing post-literary mass culture. And, as I have insisted, this is inseparable from the popular penetration of neo-dadaism into all areas of the culture, for it is dadaism that provides what the bardic uplift and visions of pastoral Albion cannot provide for the new techniques of indiscipline: a generalized impropriety and humorous disordering of Empire Englishness; and obviously, for those in the art schools exposed to other ways of thinking in art not captured by conventional realism and an aestheticized modernism, this has its own vital attractions. Thus, if the Beatles use art school Dada and

English absurdism to radically transform high culture's condescension towards the popular song, there are others, artists and musicians who – with a far closer relationship to the art schools – adapt it for quite different, even insouciant, ends. One such group of ex-art school musicians was the Bonzo Dog Doo-Dah Band.

The Bonzos, were not 'serious' musicians – that is they had no interest in transforming the popular song-form in any radical sense – however, they were serious Dadaists, and, therefore, had to take seriously what they did as musicians in order to remain serious Dadaists and counterculturalists. In fact, the seriousness and assiduousness of what they did as humourists and satirists was widely influential and haunted what the Beatles and many other musicians did in the late 1960s; in many ways they set the tone for the popular use of art school Dada, as much as the Goons in the 1950s set the tone for radio comedy. Thus, despite their stand-aside eclecticism, pastiche of other songs and genres of popular music, and mannered indifference to the new critical demands of rock, for a while they provided a countercultural chorus for the new techniques of indiscipline, offering a kind of dada 'leadership.' They were also, through the writing and vocal delivery of their lead singer, Vivian Stanshall, surprisingly literary in their sardonic and deflationary attacks on the older popular culture, sixties *mores* and the legacy of Empire, drawing on Stanshall's range of fictive song personas and whip-smart retorts (his influence is certainly detectable in *Sgt. Pepper* and more crucially in *The White Album's* wide range of pastiches and parodies). Indeed, it is largely the acid wit and sprezzatura of Stanshall's writing and vocalization that defines the character and achievements of the band. Formed in 1962 at Central School of Art & Design, the original line-up (Neil Innes, Roger Ruskin Spear, Rodney Slater, Vernon Dudley Bohay-Nowell, "Legs" Larry Smith and Stanshall), lasted until 1970 (although they reformed briefly in 1972), and recorded their first single, a cover version of the 1920s song, 'My Brother Makes the Noises for the Talkies' in 1966. In 1967, they appeared, at Paul McCartney's request, in the Beatles *Magical Mystery Tour*, in which they played 'Death Cab For Cutie,' from their first album *Gorilla* (1967). The best songs and satiric interludes are largely written by Stanshall: 'Big Shot' ("You're eccentric. I like that"), 'I'm Bored' ("I'm bored. With exposés and LSD. I'm bored. With Frank Sinatra's new LP. And so, I'm… bored."), 'Tent,' 'Look at Me I'm Wonderful,' 'Mr. Slater's Parrot,' 'Sport,' 'The Strain' (a *basso profundo*, grunting pastiche of Captain Beefheart [who became a close friend]), 'We Were Wrong,' 'Can Blue Men Sing the Whites?,' '11 Moustachioed Daughters,' and by Stanshall and Innes, 'Kama Sutra,' 'My Pink Half of the Drain Pipe' (perhaps their best; a tale of English suburban envy, pride and boredom sung in glorious mock-Jacques Brel by Stanshall, containing one of his most memorable lines: "Lord Snooty's giant poisoned electric head"), 'Rhinocratic Oaths,' 'The Bride Stripped Bare By "Bachelors"'), although Innes's solo songs tend to be arch in comparison, and betray a too easy desire to write a standard stage-show light comedy rock; ('The Equestrian Statue,' 'Urban Spaceman,' 'You've Done My Brain In'). One of the most vivid interludes, however, is written/produced by Ruskin Spear and Gerry Bron: 'Shirt' off *Tadpoles* (1969); a live vox pop interview conducted by Stanshall on the streets of Willesden Green, in his best urbane 1950s BBC interviewer voice, a wonderful mixture of condescension and perky inquisitiveness:

> Stanshall: Here comes a gentleman. And we're going to
>   talk to him about shirts. Excuse me sir, would you
>   mind talking to us about shirts?
> Man: You what?
> Stanshall: About shirts.
> Man: Shirts?
> Stanshall: Yes.
> Man: I've got plenty at home.

The perfect inanity of it, a deathly miscuing of understanding, echoes the desuetude of many of Stanshall's lyrics and other interludes, in which a lone voice, usually a singer, reflects on their own 'wonderfulness' or exquisiteness ('I Left My Heart in San Francisco,' 'Look at Me I'm Wonderful,' 'Narcissus,' 'The Sound of Music'). Indeed, it is this desuetude that marks out the best pastiches of genres; they hint at the delusions of public acclaim and the self-aggrandisements of 'show business.' But, more generally, the songs, in their reflection on the rituals of suburban dementia and populist sentiment, evoke a 'crippled Englishness' in Lennon's sense.

> The fact that we are able to communicate some-
> thing to people by singing songs about trousers and
> wardrobes was a remarkable thing. People tried to
> categorize us and work out who our audience was,
> but they never could. We were our own audience.
> We went on stage in the hope of entertaining each

other, destroying something and creating something
in its place.[118]

And voice, 'envoicing,' mimicry, dramatically 'throwing one's voice' is
crucial to this process, and to the character of Stanshall's achievement.
Stanshall was from a lower middle class background in Leigh-on-Sea,
but spoke with, and delivered many of the songs in a cut-glass RP accent
that gave the humour an air of imperious incredulousness. The symbolic
authority that comes with such a voice doubles up Stanshall's singing
role: he becomes both a front man and, across the delivery of a wide
range of materials, a kind of cabaret MC with dadaistic overtones of
1920s Weimar and Zurich 1916. Moreover, the adopted authority of
delivery produces a chiasmic effect. The fruity RP diction serves both
to give authority to the humour – to disconnect the jokiness from mere
pastoral buffoonery – and to stage and expose the presumptions of the
authority itself. Stanshall speaks with the confidence of Empire in order
to render the voice of Empire impossible, certainly for maintaining an
echt countercultural profile.

The RP 'upgrading' and modulation of voice was common in the English
theatre in the 1950s and 1960s, in order that actors be 'worthy' of all
roles. One can hear the sneer in John Osborne's voice in his autobiography when he talks of his actress girlfriend Pamela Lane failing to 'upgrade' completely, retaining "traces of a thick burr which RADA had not
completely erased,"[119] just as one hears a similar obsession with upgrade
in Harold Pinter's voice in the early 1960s. A working class boy from
Hackney, his speaking voice has an aristocratic mien and drawl that is
even more polished and fruitier than Prince Philip's (listen to Pinter in
Joseph Losey's *The Servant* (1963) which he scripted, in which he has a
brief role as a restaurant customer, and in the interview he gave to the arts
programme *Tempo*, in 1965). Now, it's possible to imagine such a voice,
schooled in the studios of RADA, offering a working class boy a bit more
confidence in finding a way through the narrow portal of opportunity
into English high culture in the early 1960s. But in the new popular culture this would seem irrelevant, if not a liability: the new demotic song

---

118 Vivian Stanshall interviewed by Keith Altham, *New Musical Express*, 1971, quoted
in Lucian Randall and Chris Welch, *Ginger Geezer: The Life of Vivian Stanshall*,
Fourth Estate, London, 2001, p117
119 John Osborne, *A Better Class of Person: An Autobiography: 1929-1956*, Faber &
Faber, London, 1981, p241

is unambiguously an extension of the new demotic voice. Public school boys, if called on, were not being asked to sing like public school boys. The authority of Stanshall's voice, then, is where the countercultural and dramaturgical meet: like the extraordinary, thespy, self-dramatizing voices of the postwar actors Cecilia Johnson (*Brief Encounter*, 1945), Fenella Fielding and Kenneth Williams (strange, confected voices now long gone from the repertoire of trained diction) Stanshall's voice imposes a character that is seemingly at odds with the demotic requirements of the time. As Dadaists and counterculturalists why hitch so much of what you do to the *class-bound tone* of Empire? (The crisis of the male singing voice is something we will look at in detail in the next chapter). Yet, in this case, paradoxically, it provides the music and the humour with a connection to a range of 'English' musical resources that, like the new English folk, defines the popular in Englishness in tension with American rock 'n' roll; for the Bonzos, the presumptions of American popular music are to be taken down as much as is the condescension of English lower middle class pretence and upper-middle class *hauteur*. Thus, if the Bonzos satire looks down on Empire and its fading suburban relics, the band's pastiche of various song-forms creates a kind of countercultural music hall repertoire, in which the signs and affects of popular Americana are kept at an ironic distance; if Stanshall is the Weimar cabaret MC, he is also the English music hall singer and comedian, with a twinkle in his eye, and risqué pun to hand. 'My Pink Half of the Drainpipe,' for instance, may vocally pastiche Jacques Brel, but it is also an accomplished countercultural version of the English music hall song, with its discernable narrative types: in this instance, the petty-minded and nosy neighbour. Another English theatrical influence was the music-hall neo-Dada cabaret of the Alberts, which featured Bruce Lacey's robotic figures, one of which used to sing 'I'm Forever Blowing Bubbles,' whilst bubbles emerged from its chest. Their now rightly lauded show, 'An Evening of British Rubbish,' at the Comedy Theatre, London in 1962, was much admired by Stanshall. But in the end this space of English dadaist-pastiche of genre is limited, running aground on the band's unwillingness to shift their localised countercultural indiscipline onto a wider and more ambitious stage. This is why finally there is something inescapably conservative about the Bonzos indifference to the critical hybridities of the new music, particularly when they reform in 1972. Dominated by Neil Innes' songs and ideas, the Bonzos in their last album *Let's Make Up and Be Friendly* (1972) have lost Stanshall's aching desuetude, to become a plodding collection of comedy pasticheurs of 1960s girl and boy pop tunes; even Stanshall succumbs, putting in a dreadful Johnny Cash turn in his 'Bad

Blood,' a tale of errant cowboys. The irony, infelicity and deflation now seem more at home in provincial rep. Innes' future membership of The Rutles was assured.

The Bonzos are crucial to the broader reconnection between modernism and popular culture in England in the mid-1960s. Their 'reframing' and deflation of Empire and the presumptions of modernity in postwar American popular culture find strong echoes in the Dada cabaret of the new TV comedy (*Do Not Adjust Your Set* – on which they performed – and later of course, *Monty Python's Flying Circus*). These two TV shows certainly continue an English neo-Dada deflation of Empire and ruling class cultural paternalism, into comedy proper. Yet late Stanshall and the Bonzos, point to one of the problems of English Dada in the 1960s and early 1970s counterculture: the tendency to accept feyness, cosmetic anarchism, and English whimsy as acceptable techniques of indiscipline and calculated impertinence. Indeed, by the early 1970s, the Dada contribution to the new techniques of indiscipline in popular musics and art – particularly performance art – had calcified into a loose repertoire of eccentric behaviourisms and disorderly, anti-medium and anti-syntactic clichés, in which the admix of 'nonsense' and an aesthetics of detritus and dislocated assemblage, become a radical substitution for thinking and the exigencies of *form*: Bruce Lacey, Ivor Cutler, Ruskin Spear's post-Bonzos career ('Roger Ruskin Spear and his Giant Kinetic Wardrobe'), the Peoples Theatre, and vast amounts of street performance (outside high street shops, in public toilets and telephone boxes, outside factory gates, etc), performed by Jeff Nuttall and others, all contribute to the general informality.[120] And this is where we begin to see a sharp fault line in the techniques of indiscipline develop in the counterculture in the late 1960s. The inflation of aesthetic or syntactic disorder as a means of breaking the would-be dulled veils of bourgeois habit and convention and Empire stultification, begin to move out of art and popular music proper to coalesce more generally around highly confabulated figures such as the trickster or shaman, as the neo-Dada attack on cultural hierarchies finds common alliance with the 'hippie' version of English pastoral and the rustic, as the Southern English summer festival circuit grows in influence. The construction of the 'hippie' as a faux-rustic exquisite does much to cement this link, connecting, naturism, the new environmentalism, and

---

120 See, Jeff Nuttall, *Performance Art, Vol 1 Memoirs*, Calder, London, 1979; and Richard Burton's biography of Basil Bunting, *A Strong Song Tows Us*, Infinite Ideas/Prospecta, London and Westport, 2013).

pagan ritual to the anti-statist politics of rural 'self-sufficiency.' This we might say is the 'decadent' period of the English counterculture – a counterculture in political decline – as the aestheticization and mystification of positions associated with the rejection of waged labour, city life and the nuclear family, become excuses for withdrawal from organization, politics and the formal demands of art and music in favour of gestures of anti-worldly defiance.

However, the crisis of neo-Dada is not the crisis of the counterculture itself, just as the aestheticization of Dada fails to weaken, overall, its progressive chiasmic effects in English culture generally: that is, the passage of popular motifs and affects into high culture (art, poetry and theatre), and the passage of techniques of negation into popular forms. The growing aestheticization and mystification of countercultural indiscipline, then, does not diminish the vast changes in cultural expectation put in place across class lines. The inability of popular music and the new art to sustain a progressive dismantling of the dominant culture, does not mean that the ideological work of 'indiscipline' comes to end, as if the impact of the counterculture on class relations suddenly faded away; popular culture's re-functioning of 'techniques of indiscipline' is now embedded in the disaffections of young workers and the educated lower middle class alike. The crisis, rather, is the assumption that gestures of defiance and informality are, *in themselves enough*; or carry any real cultural and cognitive value.

Many musicians, artists and activists in fact began to realize this as a condition of carrying on – that the counterculture in its late period of beatific 'hippiedom' and gestural Dadaism, is now actually a block on new work, and a new politics. Interestingly Hunter. S. Thompson notes this shift, some years earlier in the US, where the self-identification of the 'hippie' with a kind of 'exquisite' rejection of politics, captures a large part of countercultural youth. As he says in 'The 'Hashbury' is the Capital of the Hippies' (1967):

> Students who once were angry activists, were content to lie back in their pads and smile at the world through a fog of marijuana...Even in Berkeley political rallies during 1966 had overtones of music, madness and absurdity. Instead of picket signs and revolutionary slogans, more and more demonstrations

carried flowers, balloons and colourful posters
featuring slogans from Dr. Timothy Leary.[121]

If Thompson fails to register the significance of the neo-Dadaesque framing of the new politics and culture here, nevertheless, he puts his finger
on something that will define the late days of the counterculture in the
USA and England, as the neo-dadaists's withdrawal of politics as usual, is
run down into celebration of 'spontaneity' and the 'primitive': would-be
unmediated expression works hand in hand with the valorization of an
unmediated Nature, in which the critique of industrial culture becomes
little more than a 'back to the land' aboriginalism. This drift into post-po-
litical and anarchist indeterminacy forms the basis of Lennon's increasing
disillusionment with what the counterculture had become, and one of
the reasons he left for New York in 1970. As he was to say famously in
1971: "nothing changed except that we all dressed up a bit, leaving the
same bastards running everything."[122] This is certainly intemperate and
does an injustice to what the Beatles' own investment in the disordering of sensibility achieved. Yet, nevertheless, Lennon does draw attention
to the increasing gap opening up in the counterculture by the earlier
1970s, between 'sensibility,' praxis and politics, and, in turn politics and
form. Thus, one can understand why the content of techniques of indiscipline are by no means settled musically and culturally in this period in
England. Neo-Dada in England is not one thing, indeed, it is possible
to say that its influence bifurcates in the late sixties into a *rigorous informality* (Nuttall, Lacey, rock/theatre in such bands as Principal Edward's
Magic Theatre, or Forkbeard Fantasy or the Peoples Theatre) and a *rigorous reflexiveness*, as the counterculture in popular music, art, poetry, theatre splits around the question of form. Is 'experimentalism' antithetical
to form – and as such at the expense of form – or is it indivisible from
form, new forms? Lennon here, then, could be said, to be coming down
on the side of a rigorous reflexivity, or at least a refusal of aestheticism and
expressivism; 'hippy' informality and spontaneity were not the answer;
sensuous self-display, a distraction; and, of course, his increasing familiarity with Yoko Ono's art as much as his revolutionary politics plays a part
in this. Thus, the issue is not about denying what neo-Dada sensibility
achieved in English culture between 1965-1970, but, rather: what were

---

121 'The 'Hashbury' is the Capital of the Hippies' (1967) in *The Great Shark Hunt:
Strange Tales From a Strange Time*, Picador, London, 1980, p413

122 John Lennon, quoted in Elizabeth Thomson and David Gutman, *The Lennon
Companion*, Da Capo, New York, 2004, p166.

its implications and possible transformative outcomes once the trappings of Empire and conventional rock 'n' roll and the afflatus of high culture had been exposed or ridiculed? There is, therefore, an interesting shift in the tenor and direction of countercultural techniques of indisciplinarity, which has a profound effect on the character of the last years of the counterculture and the remaking of the popular.

A certain kind of *anti-informality* presses its demands on the chiasmic shifts taking place in the exchange between the new popular culture and high culture, forcing the counterculture to accept the critical, as opposed to simply the resistive implications of its indisciplinarity. That is, there is a clear return of the repressed by the late sixties: namely, the recall of the formal discipline of an older modernism, in which semantic and discursive excess prevails over mere indeterminacy or free form spontaneity. The result is a distanciation from the idea of the counterculture as a broad *dissolution* of all hierarchies of value, and the embrace – in various registers – of 'complexity' and 'difficulty.' Yet, it is not neo-Dada as such that is the primary target here, but, rather, the anti-intellectualism that its popularization and identification with English whimsy and eccentricity provided. This is why the semantic, discursive and formal complexity that emerges in poetry (Bunting, Prynne), art (conceptual art) and post-*Sgt. Pepper* popular music (progressive rock), in the late 1960s is not in any sense a rejection of the deflationary spirit of Dada and its ties to the counterculture (a return to high cultural propriety), but, rather, its realignment and re-functioning in the interests of pushing the 'newness' that the English counterculture promised into genuinely unmapped territory. In this respect there is a loop back to what the counterculture had claimed to have left behind in 1965: the old left activism and avant-garde ethos of *learn, learn, learn*. But, in this instance, it is heavily mediated by a critique of the idea that culture and political transformation are somehow isomorphic – as indeed, modernism had long ago claimed, certainly back to the American poet Louis Zukofsky, a CPUSA fellow traveler in the 1930s and 1940s *and* a resolute critic of conventional realism and aesthetic populism. As such, in a variety of work there is a push against satire, pastiche, pathos and performativity – as politically companionable and popular artistic strategies – into a reconfiguration of experiment with a demonstrable intellectuality. The chiasmic passage between popular culture and high culture is put on hold.

In Prynne's poetry, for instance, this takes a frontal assault on both the semantic dullness and conservatism of the Movement poets (Philip Larkin,

D.J. Enright, Elizabeth Jenning, Donald Davie) and Nuttall's romantic histrionics, in the form of a non-lyrical exactitude and abstraction. As Andrew Duncan says of Prynne:

> When compared with…work devoted to hedo-
> nism, gratification, sensation, Prynne's poems
> belong, like those of his followers, with the camp of
> responsibility.[123]

Or as David Trotter puts it, Prynne's poems turn a "Medusa-head on any-one who accosts [the work] with a demand for ready meaning,"[124] Here is Prynne in 1972 in 'Into the Day':

> Gauge at four the pen, demic invasion, the integrity
> of false day. The bud rots with gentle glory, flut-
> tered in chronicle. Vain to ask, you see all there is.
> Memory of curling and soon stalks in the land. It is
> unsullied and, despite this, the assuaged birds soar,
> as they must.[125]

Admittedly there is still a residual lyricism here, but semantic excess is bound to – bound *into* – the poem's 'intractable' granite-like surface. And perhaps it is this lingering lyricism that attracted Nick Drake, and his own chiasmic introduction of the resistive poetic voice into the folk song (which we will look at in the next chapter). Reputedly Drake may have had some contact with Prynne at Caius, or at least some of his cir-cle there or at Fitzwilliam where he was studying. Similarly, conceptual art opens up the ideas and skills that artists bring to the daily problems and methods of art, to autodidactic training in analytical philosophy and philosophical Marxism. Exactitude and abstraction, however, is not sim-ply a way of encouraging 'thought experiments' – intellectual back up for images and objects – but a devastating destruction of humanist categories of 'visualisation,' 'expression' and 'representation' as such, as in the work of Art & Language. Art & Language's writing *into* art, presents a com-parable kind of surface intractability, in this instance, though, through a

---

123 ('Response to Steve Clark's Prynne and the Movement,' http://jacketmagazine.com/24/duncan.html, 2003)

124 David Trotter, *The Making of The Reader: Language and Subjectivity in Modern American, English and Irish Poetry*, MacMillan, London, 1984

125 J.H. Pyrnne, *Poems*, Bloodaxe, Hexham, Northumberland, 2015, p203

resolute refusal of the 'common spectator and reader' in the interests of a new spectator/reader, or spectator *as* reader; art and theory producing an unbending, shared facticity:

> ...we are faced with the – non-deontological (chronic) – ought of mapping if a parameter is not an approximation to a (highly generalizable) pragmatic situation...The projectibility of a mapping has traditionally been the a priori weights attached to a complex (sic) inductive function. There is, however, a mutual dependence between the scalar and vector dimensions of a point of reference and its 'logical' transformations. Instead the values/shopping list of modalities of any fragment of (pre-) language provides an ordinal wave.' Wither anaphor?[126]

Progressive rock, also offers a new reflexiveness, spatiality and abstractedness; new voice-instrument hybridities, drawing on modal jazz, free form jazz, choral music, and the new folk, in order to create a wider range of entry and exit points for an experimental music outside of the 'new music' concert hall. In Henry Cow, for example, post-rock dynamics interfuse, with Weilian and Eislerian song-forms, noise music and free jazz. If much progressive rock does little to refute the familiar accusations of hyperbole, where it does work, however, it works precisely *because* of its excess and hybridity. Thus, if this loose 'camp of responsibility' challenges the countercultural meaning of expanded form, it also, by definition challenges the meaning of techniques of indisciplinarity and excess itself; indisciplinarity converges with a new *re*-disciplinarity, so to speak.

Consequently, we might say, there is a common reflection across the new poetry, conceptual art and progressive rock, on what the techniques of indiscipline might now mean in a context where learning appeared to have stopped, or had become mere countercultural 'dressage,' in Lennon's sense. These moves, accordingly, provide a broader shift: an examination of what the character and effectiveness of the counterculture's opening up of new social relations and forms might now legitimately and realistically be post-Empire. This is the point, then, where (Nuttall's) post-Beat 'free form' counterculture is subject to an internal critique of varying degrees of intensity, in which technique and knowledge, technique and language,

---

126 Art & Language, 'Violins and Cows,' *Art-Language*, Vol 2, No 4, 1974

technique and form, are disassembled and *reassembled*. That Marxism, analytic philosophy, late modernist poetics, and a radical politics of culture play their part in this shift is perhaps not fortuitous, certainly in Prynne and conceptual art. For, if, as I have emphasized, neo-dadaism in England, above all, provides a working framework for dislodging the living entanglements of Empire-culture and breaking the identitary and ethnographic signs of class, neo-dadaism also enables a rise in theoretical ambition and temperature. Neo-dadaism, then, doesn't just facilitate the rise of a deflationary humour in its attack on the presumptuousness of high culture and conservative popular cultures; it also releases a new desire for formal learning amongst artists and musicians – hence the semantic and discursive and intellectual excesses of Prynne, conceptual art and progressive rock, as opposed to, the simple, even benign, acceptance of the would-be correlation between anti-formality and liberation. Learn, learn, learn becomes operative of what it is to make poems, musical works, and works of art that demand an active and strenuous correlation between the radicality of form and cultural politics. And in this way, to these ends, with these strange heteronomous materials, this new work is unprecedented in English culture, let alone the counterculture. Between 1970 and 1974, at the tail end of the counterculture, Prynnian poetics, conceptual art and progressive rock, define an indisciplinarity/re-disciplinarity therefore, that is largely at odds with the radical informality of the counterculture and rock 'n' roll spirit, or at least, draws on its muted presence (present merely in the folds and clefts of the counterculture). Attentiveness is opposed to unexamined pleasure; learning is opposed to spontaneity – as an absolute value that is.

In fact, we might talk of this in terms of an epistemological and ideological shift: the move from Dada and the critique of Empire and post-war high cultural deference, to Adorno and Debord and the critique of mass culture and the society of the spectacle. As a result, the ground on which the remaking of the popular, popularity, and the assumed exchange between high culture and popular culture – definitional of the counterculture as I have stressed – shifts. The pole of attraction is not about finding some mutual space of negotiation between the avant-garde and the popular (Lennon's ideal), but the reassertion of avant-garde indisciplinarity itself: namely, the notion that the unlocking of meaning is irreducible to the idea that things of value are always and necessarily companionable if they are to find an audience. Companionableness, on the contrary – as exemplified by the Movement poets and Pop art at the time – can hide a deceptive authoritarianism, particularly when it's attached to conservative notions of English exceptionalism and its conservative correlate 'common sense.'

Hence, if the Beatles and other musicians and artists in the sixties in England, quote the avant-garde – gesture towards it – the new poetry, conceptual art and progressive rock, actually – at last – *enact it,* that is extend and rearticulate its historical achievements, in new forms, without any of the deferential baggage of earlier generations of English artists and musicians. In short, they create a range of works that define their *own* terms of reference in defiance of establishing an external framework that allows the audience to situate the work before they actually encounter it. This points then to the growing tensions in the English counterculture between attention to form – as a politics – and the radical remaking of the popular. This is why Van Der Graaf Generator's *H to He Who am the Only One* and *Pawn Hearts* (1971) are in key respects far more innovative than *Sgt. Pepper;* they make no concessions to pastiche and 'rock 'n' roll' rhetoric; yet are obviously situated in the space of an expanded electronic, 'rock' music. In these terms, we should be clear: Prynnian poetics, conceptual art and progressive rock, provide a kind of rectification, even clear-out of some of the clichés of companionableness that had come to define the counterculture's 'hippy' and Pop-sensualist appeal. But, at the same time, we should recognize this is very much a *minoritarian* moment within the counterculture as a whole; the counterculture assimilates some of the radical temper of these moves – largely through music – but on the whole, this is a way of poetry and art saying goodbye to the optimistic political claims of popular culture, in an Adornian gesture of dismay. Art & Language, for example, soon attack the counterculture for its posturing and radical *sentimentality.* [127] Basil Bunting dismisses poetry that is caught up in its own demands for performativity (he had little time for Ginsberg's writing, for instance, despite being a friend). But if the new poetry and conceptual art exit the counterculture, the minoritarian status of progressive rock is a different matter altogether, certainly in relation to the most engaging progressive rock of the period. That is, progressive rock is not simply the telos of avant-garde 'formality' in action in the counterculture; the great and final flowering of the counterculture's musical ambitions. This is because contrary to those who identify progressive rock with a new seriousness and musicianship in popular music,[128]

127 *Newcastle Writings,* Robert Self/Northern Arts, London and Newcastle, 1977

128 Bill Martin, *Listening to the Future: The Time of Progressive Rock, 1968-1978,* Open Court, 1998

what defines the best of progressive rock, is not the extension of rock into jazz and noise music and new classical forms per se – as if popular musicians were now 'proper' musicians – but its reworking of the song-form as a radical refocusing of popular sentiment and literary and musical ambition.

In this respect the best of the music departs from the anti-pathos of the counterculture's late minoritarian avant-garde shift, in that it retains the counterculture's links to various companionable techniques and strategies: pathos, satire, and performativity. This is why, where progressive rock defines its formal independence it does so largely through its *melding* of the literary, dramaturgical and the musical. Thus, if the minoritarian shift in poetry and art, and some of the new music, uses formal self-definition to move beyond the neo-dadaistic strategies of the counterculture, the progressive rock that retains its relationship to the song-form also retains its political relationship to the remaking of the popular, as a recognition of what the popular and the voice in music enables. As such there is an undeclared Brechtian assessment here (although Henry Cow, come closest to addressing the question of the popular in these terms): what defines the real radical achievement of the counterculture is its opening up of popular music to the hybridities of the European *gesamtkunstwerk* and its bridging of traditions; the song-form, therefore, is indispensable to this move, *as* are political pathos, didacticism, bardic uplift, François Villon, Tristan Tzara, popular sentiment and theatrical performance, all the things that new folk-thinking and the new rock carry in their wake. That the English avant-garde in poetry and art of the early 1970s discards much of this repertoire (particularly in poetry) does not diminish its achievements.

Prynne's poetics and the English development of conceptual art have contributed extensively to the critical horizons of much of the advanced poetry and art at the end of the twentieth century and the beginning of the twenty first century. This is not in dispute (even if Bunting's judgement on Ginsberg is misguided). However, the song-form resists these calls for formal independence, precisely because of its deep attachments to music as a collective experience *beyond* the concert hall. And as we have noted in this book so far, what defines the extraordinary successes of popular music of the 1960s and early 1970s in England is its connection between new forms of collective experience, the song-form and insurgent and experimental techniques of indiscipline, that the working class and lower middle class felt some notional control over and attachment to. The English progressive rock committed to the song-form (fully or intermittently) therefore, rightly, did not want to give up the 'political relation' to voice and song, by moving completely into free jazz, noise or minimalism. Robert Wyatt's eventual split with Soft Machine is predicated upon this as a political question; the other band members finding his singing an irritation and distraction. Indeed, we might say, in expanding and re-working the song-form within a post-rock setting there is in much progressive rock a resistance to the overdetermined liberationist telos (and theology) that linked spontaneity with freedom, and that was driving the counterculture and its critique in its end years.

But ironically, English progressive rock's incorporation of the song-form is not a clawing back of working class autonomy and the demands of self-representation, in response to the new intellectual atmosphere of popular music. Working class musicians may have listened and drawn on much of the new progressive rock (as Johnny Rotten and Mark E. Smith did),[129] but few of them actually played it, particularly given the absence of guitars. As such, with the rise of progressive rock we see another dynamic at play in the relations between class, form and the techniques of indisciplinarity: the incorporation of trained musicians, invariably from public schools and academies. A snapshot of this change is revealed in the public school education of four of the period's leading keyboardists: Richard Wright of Pink Floyd (Haberdashers' Aske's Boys' School), Tony Banks of Genesis (Charterhouse), Hugh Banton of Van Der Graaf Generator (Silcoates School), and David Bedford (Lancing College), occasional pianist and arranger for Kevin Ayers. One way of looking at this, of course, is evidence of the growing professionalization of popular music and the increasing middle class encroachment into its domains (that punk was so rightly enraged about in 1976); another, is seeing it as part of the egalitarianism and 'communization effects' that were driving the collective character of the new music. The truth lies within the terms of both positions. That is, it is certainly the case that the entry of schooled musicians into popular music was redefining the horizons of musicianship and professionalism – as rock music became 'respectable' – but middle class musicians were as much driven by the liberating effects of the counterculture at its height as anyone else, and as such contributed to some of the counterculture's striking achievements. The mistake,

---

129 Reputedly Mark E. Smith sent a copy of every single, EP and album he released with the Fall to Peter Hammill. See 'Invisible Jukebox,' Peter Hammill, interviewed by Mike Barnes, *Wire* Magazine, No 138, August 1995

however, is to assume that progressive rock was therefore fundamentally antithetical to the great wave of popular cultural insurgency; that it
somehow betrayed the experiential vitality of the new rock culture. On
the contrary, in the period of counterculture's flight into rock recidivism
and the fetishization of spontaneity in the early 1970s, English progressive rock – through its own re-disciplinary reworking of techniques of
indisciplinarity – it was able to sustain, briefly, a dialogue with the great
deflationary force and energy of the counterculture; indeed, in the period
of the counterculture's demise, it redefined its most salient achievements
in contradistinction to progressive rock elsewhere. Yet, the fact that these
redefinitions were not accompanied by a further broadening and deepening of countercultural insurgency is of course, one of the reasons for the
demise of the counterculture and progressive rock. By 1975, progressive
rock, despite all its hopes, was a critical constituency with a contracting social base, as was most music attached to the counterculture. The
extra-musical conditions that had sustained the counterculture felt ex-
hausted, subject to forces that were beginning to dissolve the radical links
between cultural form and politics. I will discuss the character of these
changes and the fate and achievements of progressive rock at length in
Chapter 4, as part of my general musical assessment of the counterculture. In the next Chapter, though, I want to examine in more detail the
character of the male singing voice and song-form during this period, as
evidence of a crisis of performance under Empire and post-1950s rock
'n' roll. In this we will take a further look at the new folk-thinking and
bardic uplift, the deflation of the signs and regalia of Empire and the
legacy of American rock 'n' roll, as a preparation for our final reflections
on English progressive rock and the remaking of the popular.

CHAPTER 3
FEMINIZATION AND THRENODY

WHEN CHET BAKER SANG AT THE SALLE PLEYEL IN PARIS, ON SEPTEMBER 22 1955, he was given the 'bird.' His tenor voice, hesitant, thin, plaintive, was not what the majority of the audience, there to listen to his beautifully limpid yet pearl hard trumpet playing, expected or wanted to hear. Baker had been singing on stage for a couple of years already, and recorded *Chet Baker Sings* in 1954 in Hollywood, yet this had not been a wholly satisfactory development. Just as audiences – in particular East coast be-bop audiences – found it difficult to adjust to his winsome and wispy singing, his backing musicians on *Chet Baker Sings*, found the ghostly mannerisms, off-key sibilance, and repeated takes that drifted into vaguery, deeply frustrating.[130] Indeed, criticism of his voice amongst musicians, jazz aficionados, and critics was widespread and stinging. His singing was

---

130 See James Gavin, *Deep in a Dream: The Long Night of Chet Baker*, Alfred Knopf, New York, 2002, p86

considered emotionless, distant, fey, effeminate, morbid, affected, and aimless; whereas his trumpet playing captivated, his singing appeared to suck the very air out of a room. On the French tour *The Melody Maker* was unambiguous: 'CHET'S VOCALS NOT WANTED.'[131] The outcome was immediate; severely shaken by the criticism he didn't sing again on the tour of France. Yet, by the late 1950s, with the success of *Chet Baker Sings*, whatever professional and critical scepticism remained about his singing skills was offset by a growing popular acceptance of his voice as possessing a languid authenticity. His voice and trumpet playing were now considered synonymous with an unadorned truthfulness and sangfroid, particularly for audiences who had little interest in whether Baker met or didn't meet the requirements of conventional male jazz vocalization, and therefore were much more interested in his vulnerable persona, such as (non-jazz interested) young women and gay men. They felt a greater attachment to what Baker's voice suggested and promised – its access to an emotional landscape of lost love and inarticulate desire – than anything so stringent as his lack of demonstrative song delivery. In fact, the very sense of withdrawal, of bruised reticence, was the key, to Baker's eventual success, giving his slow and slightly disconnected treatment of conventional repertoire of lovelorn modern standards, an alluringly novel quality. Through this withdrawal and bruised reticence, Baker seemed to have access to feelings and sensitivities that male singers with a greater vocal range and assertiveness failed to touch on as convincingly. In this, his aura of defeat and resilience gave an unprecedented confessional quality to standards that, in other hands sounded merely sentimental or frivolous; with Baker the effervescence and brittleness of Tin Pan Alley's confident encounter with the world drifted away.

As such, Baker's voice both caught, and began to define, a loosening of how the male jazz singer and popular singer might perform intimacy, as opposed to simply stating it. In ways that echoed the great black female singers of the 1930s such as Billy Holiday – the palpable sense of having just being dragged out from the shadows of a tumultuous love life to recount the tale in the spotlight – Baker gave to the male singer an interiority that defied the clichés of masculine control. This was electrifying, because the singer didn't just offer the signs of experience, but evidence of a life lived without the usual masculine defences. The trick then, was that Baker appeared to be both the actual author of the words of the songs and the privileged interpreter of their hidden and irreconcilable

---

131 Ibid, p120

truths; and this is why, the hushed intimacy of the delivery felt so solicitous to the non-jazz aficionado; it sounded as if Baker had discovered
and released an emotional language for the male singer that allowed a
new and candid conversation between men and women, men and men,
women and women. One might call this a *non-dominative* register. No
wonder, therefore, that his singing seemed so out of place within the
standard male jazz and blues repertoire, and emerging rock 'n' roll. Frank
Sinatra and the Nelson Riddle Orchestra, Louis Jordan's jump-jive, Elvis
Presley, Jerry Lee Lewis, Little Richard and Screamin' Jay Hawkins, are
all concerned with conquest and display, with hubris and bravado, and
as such with triggering sexual expectation; Baker conjures the opposite: a
forlorn reflection on loss and hoped for reconciliation. This is why he was
attacked so vociferously by jazz cognoscenti: he had feminized his music
in order to win, it was claimed, some spurious popularity from a female
audience, who in the end invariably despised the 'hard' values of jazz and
therefore the 'real' emotional disclosure of musical performance, the bitter and sweaty graft of male improvisation. There was a hint of an accusa-
tion of jazz betrayal to these criticisms. At one level these musician-critics
were right; all the cool discretion and de-masculinization was, of course,
a carefully managed pose, a way for Baker to settle into something that
he actually felt comfortable with, an extension of his feelings of loss and
hurt in his life, as opposed to anything as grand as the restructuring of
the male jazz voice. Indeed, Baker loathed the accusations of homoerot-
icism and feminization that came with the brickbats and praise and was
quick to denigrate 'faggot' musicianship. There was certainly little or no
shared intimacy in his personal life with women. But on another level
his musician-critics were profoundly wrong. The absence of conventional technique was not a cynical ploy – Gerry Mulligan having dismissed
the emotional resonance of Baker's voice as the result of sheer incompe-
tence – but, rather, the mastery and channeling of limited technique into
something more ambitious and redefining: the recognition that would-be
poor technique can register feelings and affects that outreach pure, slick
or classically trained technique. Something of this derives from Baker's
self-trained non-professional background – the resistance to professional
doxa – but other aspects derive from the sense that the singing had to
connect with the reality of his own experience, even if it meant inflating
the air of vulnerability a little.

It is no surprise therefore that Baker's perceived flawed and vulnerable
masculinity finds its own bohemian place in the anti-heroic masculinities
of the new popular culture, as was the case for instance with the films of

Marlon Brando and James Dean. Baker, Brando and Dean, all provide moments of non-dominative respite from the stultifying martial masculinities of the Cold War. All secure the promise of a male sexuality not defined by submission to suburban marriage and patriarchal authority; all play their small part in the growing Beat sensibility. However, it is Baker's voice and demeanour that does more of the work of ideological de-acclimatization. Unlike Brando and Dean's calculated surliness and introverted preening, Baker's voice produces an overt withdrawal of masculine desire from the physical display and assertion of the male body. It is perfectly understandable then, that such a voice and such a demeanour would also appear to derive from another, less lovelorn home: 1950s LA drug culture. It is hardly revelatory to say that the reticence and withdrawal also have some emotional entanglement with the drug addiction that accompanied his career from the mid-1950s. Baker's solicitousness and otherworldliness is no doubt shaped by the daily memory of other states of wretchedness than those of love's lamentations. Yet, whatever the true emotional origins of the voice, it nevertheless establishes a space inside and outside the masculine policing of jazz, for other desires and projections not beholden to the excruciating conformities of the day. And therefore, whatever reservations Baker might have had about the voice's feminine solicitousness, his singing shifted the emotional focus of the song-form irrevocably. But it would take a very different kind of culture, a post-jazz, post-rock 'n' roll, and post-Cold War culture for this shift to appear more than simply 'exotic' or adventitious.

If the bardic uplift of the new folk-thinking opened a space in the 1960s for male singers who wanted to 'sing the song' in the voice of the poet, Baker's emotional withdrawal as a vocalist allowed an additional set of moves for the singer against the narrow registers of priapic rock 'n' roll, pop effervescence and traditional folk. Indeed, to 'sing against singing,' to create a voice indifferent to the rock 'n' roll body and jazz exaltation, was to embrace an indisciplinarity that bordered on self-negation. Yet, in conjunction with the plaintive interiority and bardic ambitions of the new folk music, Baker's reflective and non-dominative envoicing seemed particularly compelling for a popular music intent on clearing away the rhetoric of Empire and Cold War militarism. Thus, a number of English male singers followed Baker into a non-dominative aesthetic, in which interiority and exsanguinuation are prized as a respite from declamatory noise and busyness. This is not to say, that Baker stands behind these voices, as if he is the template for countercultural demasculinization, or that the singers are consistent in these moves. But, rather, that his

flattening of articulation and timbre opened up another way of singing of loss and desire that is unmistakable. This establishes a range of
voices and song-forms that are marked by melancholia and lamentation,
or, a gentle threnodic visitation of the past. Kevin Ayers, Robert Wyatt,
Syd Barrett, Nike Drake, and Richard Sinclair for example, use non-de-
clamatory phrasing and flat, 'feminized' voicing, to create a landscape of
withdrawal, drift and disconnection. In Drake this borders on the clin-
ically depressive, creating a consciously darkened pastoralism, in Wyatt,
Barrett, Ayers and Sinclair it captures a playful indolence, that touches
on the nursery rhyme and the play school, in keeping with the neo-Dada
and countercultural affirmation of nonsense and childlike disavowal of
authority generally. The overall, tone, though, is not comedic: its spirit of
deflation is defined by quietude, reflection and regret.

Why the emergence of these kind of male voices in popular music in
England after 1965? What kind of musical and ideological adjustments
are being made? How are these voices continuous with, and interior to,
the opening up of the new techniques of indiscipline? It is actually difficult to say exactly why this cluster of threnodic voices appear at this
particular point in England, with such surety, and not elsewhere, but it is
clear that they all are indebted, at some level, to the space that the turn to
modernist *poiesis* opens for interiorized reflection in the new folk-thinking in England, and in turn, therefore how this subjective shift enables
musicians to define what they do as counterculturalists as part of the general resistance to the hard, even severe, masculinities of Empire and the
Cold War alike – that American rock 'n' roll did not so much relieve as
deflect. The new folk-thinking and the new voices of lamentation, then,
are not the same, yet, they do share an unparalleled introduction of reflective uncertainty into popular music that marks out a sharp break with
a certain tone and expectations of an abrasive, front-loaded rock 'n' roll.
In this sense Baker's non-dominative break with expressive body-voice
couplet in jazz at the height of hystericized forms of masculinity in politics and popular culture, is undoubtedly culturally significant in terms of
what male singers might comfortably do or not do, even if Baker's direct
influence on the English singers was slight, with the exception perhaps
of Wyatt. Thus demasculinization in these years is not something that is
produced *alone* by the rejection of the rhetoric of Empire and the Cold
War, for there was no 'critique of masculinity' in left politics or popular
culture in the 1950s and early 1960s;[132] anti-masculinity, as a marginal

132 Outlier, gay and bisexual writing, was, however, beginning to emerge, drawn in part

position in the 1950s in the critique of the arms race and warmongering, was invariably attached to or associated with pacifism; and the bad memory of pacifism during WWII in the fight against fascism, was still raw and suspect, and therefore carried little or no moral authority. Even Bertrand Russell, for instance, a conscientious objector in World War I and a leading member of CND, was always, in the wake of the defeat of fascism, keen to talk about not being a "theoretical pacifist."[133] Consequently, demasculinization had to be produced culturally in response to the general crisis of martial Cold War values; and as such had to find a space and set of alternative values that could test the prevailing framework of masculinity without falling into the bad faith of anti-masculinity and misanthropy.

The extension of a non-dominative aesthetic in these male voices of lamentation, then, defines this tension. It marks out an aspect – if an important aspect – of what will be the testing ground of identity, expression and techniques of indiscipline in the counterculture overall: the refusal of a 'straight' or armorial masculinity based on a rejection of familial and patriarchal order, sexual (heterosexual) propriety, and disciplinary reason. We need to make a distinction in the counterculture, then, between the 'feminization' of appearances in general and a non-dominative masculinization, in the specific. The counterculture inherited some of the 'feminized' subcultural moves of the Mods and Teds that preceded it: the emphasis on self-display and sartorial self-consciousness. This is where the counterculture opened up some initial point of contact with post-ethnographic working class identity and energy; techniques of indisciplinarity crossed from musicianship to style, and back, and that appealed greatly to a new generation of male working class and lower middle class musicians, intent on leaving the cultish and commercially exploitable and reified aspects of working class life behind. In the counterculture one could be working class without advertising it as a narrow form of belonging. But nevertheless, if the 'feminization' of appearances had their own attractions, a non-dominative masculinity was a minority

---

from the pioneering work of Edward Carpenter (*Homegenic Love and Its Place in a Free Society*, Redundancy Press, London, 1894 and *Some Friends of Walt Whitman: A Study in Sex-Psychology*, J.K. Francis, London, 1924, republished Folcroft Press, Folcroft PA, 1969). See, in particular (although published at the end of the counterculture), Colin MacInnes, *Loving Them Both: A Study of Bisexuality and Bisexuals*, Marti Brian & O'Keefe, London 1973

133 Bertrand Russell, *Unarmed Victory*, Penguin, Harmondsworth, 1963, p11

position and sensibility, certainly in music performance, and therefore, was a form of indisciplinarity that limited working class musicians' identification with this subject position, and crucially limited the appeal of this music to most listeners. Let us not forget this threnodic, non-dominative male vocalization was not shaped by the women's movement or feminism, and therefore, whatever mimicry of introspection-as-femininity it announced, it was not backed by the wider values and challenges of women's liberation; the impact of women's liberation to the contribution of women in popular music occurred largely after the counterculture (although Dagmar Krause, the singer in Henry Cow, and Sandy Denny, were two female musician who prepared the ground for this shift). Hence although, the counterculture was not exactly alien to the women's movement's contribution to the critique of masculinity, certainly by 1973 the emergence of the demasculinized singer and a non-dominative aesthetic was less a concrete ideological response to the women's movement, than a rejection of the postwar interpellation of young men as loyal images of their fathers, men who mostly had fought in the war. (Reflection on this crisis of fathers – derived from a popular Freudianism and an anti-Cold war sentiment – is wonderfully played out in Nick Ray's 1956 masterpiece, *Bigger Than Life*, starring James Mason as an overbearing American high school teacher).

In the end, the marginality of these voices within the counterculture of the time, then, was determined by those values, that in most instances, were seen unproblematically as that which defined what was most distinctive about the counterculture: the confrontational and declamatory character of the rock revolution. Thus, let us also not forget: it was the *big* voices of this period – even on the avant-rock periphery – that defined the counterculture: Mick Jagger, Robert Plant, Roger Daltrey, Paul Rodgers, Jim Morrison, Alex Harvey, Janis Joplin, Captain Beefheart. Indeed, it was these big voices that shaped the drama of rock's confrontation with the old popular culture and high culture; no vocalization in popular music, before, had sounded so threatening, indomitable, intimidating, sexually forbidding and foreboding. This is reflected in the relative poor sales of most the new folk (particularly *Astral Weeks*), and the new threnodic singing in England; if this work contributed to the radical transformation of the popular, it did so in a subsidiary role, or, through the creation of a certain general tone, that once the amplified and distorted guitars and clatter of drums had died down, everyone could pay due respect to and feel comforted by, if not, in the end, embrace: the acoustic and the contemplative. And it is this essential ambiguity over these non-dominative techniques of indiscipline – in a counterculture that appeared to incorporate all distinctive voices of resistance – that so, confused those musicians and listeners who were unsure precisely what direction rock culture should be traveling. Were these non-dominative values tied to the deflation of rock *culture*, key or expendable? Was the counterculture an extension of new folk-thinking and post-rock forms, and new forms of listening and attentiveness, or of the general intensi-fication of rock 'n' roll as a sonic and fully industrialized assault on the senses, in which a band like the MC5 were the vanguard? One could appreciate the reach of the mythic resonances of the Incredible String Band's 'new world' music in creating a counterculture without musical boundaries, but, how might this music also move bodies and attack the invidious 'good manners' and 'civility' of the old popular culture and high culture? In what ways was its genteel sense of community and tradi-tion 'revoiced' able to compete with the volatility and power of bodies in motion, that Led Zeppelin and the Who and others could channel and bring to the public arena?

In this the new folk-thinking was confronted by its own moment of cri-sis, as was traditional folk in 1959-60, when pop swept all before it. By 1972 the big rock bands began to determine not just that which was popular, but the minoritarian and majoritarian values of the counter-culture; the new folk-thinking's extension of rock, the new threnodic song-forms were felt to be secondary to the necessarily urban content and confrontational character of the new rock, even if a band like Led Zeppelin drew directly on the new folk-thinking itself, in particular The Incredible String Band and Sandy Denny, who they were close to and collaborated with. Indeed, Led Zeppelin is the one globally successful English rock band that assimilates these values productively.

This tension between majoritarian and minoritarian countercultural values arises, in many ways, through the mediation of Englishness 'ex-ceptionalism,' under conditions where the 'rock business' and the coun-terculture were becoming increasingly interconnected and defined by international markets. The bands that were very successful, on the whole conformed to an increasing American-led and 'non-parochial' concep-tion of rock brinkmanship and masculinized transgression; the new folk-thinking and the new threnodic song-forms as they mutated into progressive rock, felt too heterogeneous, *too* English, too 'feminized' by comparison. Nick Drake suffered from this more than most. He could never work out why his albums hardly sold at all, despite the vitality of the new folk-thinking, the achievement of *Astral Weeks*, and his belief in the centrality of what he was doing to the core shift in popular values in the counterculture. Yet, as we have noted, the new folk-thinking may have determined the musical horizons and direction of the counterculture, but not its commercial identity. Below, then, I want to continue to examine the minoritarian significance of the new non-dominative aesthetic as it intersects with a heterogeneous 'Englishness' shaped by both the new folk-thinking and neo-Dada. For it is how these minoritarian values are mediated by this heterogeneous notion of 'Englishness' that contributes to the development of the song-form in these new songs of lamentation, and in turn, their further reworking in progressive rock. The development of the song-form in the work of these singers, consequently, offers some insight into the direction progressive rock takes in the English counterculture.

Much has been written about the 'Canterbury scene' as the crucible of these new song-forms and voices of reflection; the Canterbury description though is a misnomer, none of the music had any relationship to the place *geographically*, and as such it holds up a distorting mirror to the music's origins. Yet, this does not mean that the music does not emerge from a distinctive place, it is just that this place encompasses an area far wider than Canterbury itself: namely, the South East down to the coast (Herne Bay, Whitstable). It is this larger swathe of Southern England that rightly could be said to form the social topos of these songs; a provincial and largely pastoral area, but in easy reach of London. Hence it is important to note, again, that some of the most significant contributions to the English counterculture emerge from the borders and edges of metropolitan England; indeed, the collective achievement of the counterculture is the outcome largely of musicians arriving from the provinces with their own distinct experiences and affiliations. In this instance, however, these edges and borders – as with Vivian Stanshall in Leigh-on-Sea further down the coast – bring a particular class dimension to these contributions from the cultural margins.

This South East area of England in the mid-1960s was characterized by the absence of heavy industry, semi-rural habitation outside the coastal towns, an extensive, if seasonal, tourist industry – serviced by a growing lower middle class (traders, hoteliers etc.) – a long-settled commuter middle-class traveling back and forth to London, and a large and itinerant number of unskilled rural and urban workers. But, with the exception of the population of the coastal towns, still attached to what remains of the fishing industry and to a tourist industry overwhelmingly geared to the needs of working class visitors from London, the South East hinterland is conspicuously middle class. This is that sector of the English middle class, that from the 1860s certainly up to the 1980s, linked English 'middle-classness' with rural landownership, 'gentlemanly' farming (*pace*, Sackville-West), entry to public school education and the 'professions,' public service and committee work (charities, hospitals, the magistracy), and of course Tory or liberal-centre politics. These values and attitudes are not peculiar to the conservative commuter belt in the South East, but in the South East, they do benefit from the umbilical cord of economic attachment to London, and, conversely, the easy escape from its stresses and pollution (large sections of the Midlands and North in the early 1960s were still affected by coal-based smog, as was London). The South East's contribution to the restorative virtues of the English pastoral myth, existed, therefore, for good material reasons. It was on the whole pleasant to live there.

These details do not pretend to be anything other than a snapshot of demographics in the South East in the mid-1960s. We have seen how much of the English pastoral is also underwritten by depopulation of the countryside and rural poverty. Yet, it does point to one of the distinguishing characteristics of these class relations in this period in the South East: a middle class corridor of genteel semi-rural prosperity (drawing on London), living cheek by jowl with a coastal working class, largely engaged in non-industrial production for low wages. The result is an area in which class detenté is conspicuous and artisanal consciousness widespread, given the weak presence of trade unions in the area and absence of large industrial conglomerations and the semi-rural character of public life. As such, the sons and daughters of the professional middle class and lower middle class (the latter the greater beneficiary of the 1944 Education act), find themselves part of middle class upbringing free from the immediate conflicts and signs of industrial labour and culture. The radicalization of this generation of Southern provincial lower middle class musicians, accordingly, is accompanied and shaped by many of the privileges – in particular musical training, classical and jazz, and access to a certain metropolitan *savoir fair* – that working class musicians in the North and Midlands had little or no access to, certainly those who went to secondary modern schools. Consequently, we should not underestimate how this access to leisure and culture – as a distinctive training in listening and looking – for the London and South East middle class and the grammar school educated lower middle class alike in the 1960s, provided a certain élever les sentiments in their countercultural rejection of their parents' deference to the old high culture and popular culture. As Robert Wyatt intones in 'Hulloder' from *The Soft Machine: Volume Two* (1969): "as I'm free, white and 21, I don't need more power than I've got, except for sometimes when I'm broke." Of course, there is deliberate irony here, but nevertheless, it reveals, a conspicuous sense of confidence (if not entitlement in Wyatt's case), that derives from the Southern English experience, given its historically defining and hegemonic capture of 'Englishness' since the 1860s. As a young man Wyatt was a regular visitor to Robert Graves in Mallorca!

These conditions are an expression of the deep social and cultural roots of the minoritarian topos that both helps kick-start and eventually redefine the counterculture in its progressive rock period. That is, the inherited skills of acculturation (and even bohemian values) of this Southern milieu, allows this generation of lower middle class and middle class musicians the space to play with the tone and expectations of the new industrial popular culture and its definitions of 'Englishness.' In other words, training produces capacity, widening the range of post-rock and cultural references. In 1969 Black Sabbath's Tony Iommi up in the West Midlands, working in a steel mill, was not citing Thomas Pynchon or Alfred Jarry. Access to this acculturation thus produces a wider palette of techniques of indiscipline than many other bands at the time, drawing on post-bebop jazz, non-standard jazz-rock time signatures, the new folk, the hymnal, choral music and *musique concrète.* And of course, like Van Der Graaf Generator key to this is the transformation of the song-form and voice as they detach themselves post-*Sgt. Pepper*, from the remnants of traditional 'rock culture.'

But if both Viv Stanshall and the Beatles in 1968 and 1969 use song pastiche to disentangle themselves from the clutches of this culture and Empire, Kevin Ayers and Robert Wyatt in the first two of many incarnations of Soft Machine, resist – like the new folk-thinking and Van Der Graaf Generator – the overtures of pastiche as a route out of the rock 'n' roll cul de sac (although Ayers, seemingly indifferent to his own achievements with Soft Machine, is drawn in part back into its orbit in *Joy of a Toy* [1969] and after). Thus, both singers, within a broadly post-bebop jazz framework (Mike Ratledge on organ and piano, Hugh Hopper on bass and his brother Brian Hopper on soprano and tenor saxophones), produce a post-rock that has a formal integrity in keeping with *Astral Weeks* and *H to He Whom am the Only One*; the 'totality' of sound being definitional of the links between songs and accompaniment. In *Soft Machine* (with Ayers singing), and *Soft Machine Two* (with Wyatt singing) voice and instrumentation find new spatial and dynamic relations beyond a standard verse chorus verse structure. Indeed, *Soft Machine Two*, with Wyatt on lead vocals (after Ayers has left) – particularly in the integrated song-sections – is comparable in scope to the spatial achievement of Morrison and Van Der Graaf Generator, even if it lacks an overall thematic resonance. And crucial to this is Wyatt's loose, playful and 'feminized' voice that offers contrast with and release from Ratledge's beautifully darting and aggressive organ playing and Hopper's percussive melodic bass. As Marcus O'Dair notes: "Robert's voice is as reedy as a soprano saxophone but tremendously affecting despite – or because of – these idiosyncracies. Knots and grain exposed, it is imbued with the same vulnerable, ingenuous quality he has as a human being."[134] Indeed, Wyatt's high, sweet voice produces a threnodic dissonance, providing the music with, if not atmospheric coherence, then at least a striking tone of levity and lightness that the organ, bass and saxophone push against. Combining autobiographical reflection, recitation of the alphabet, softly spoken asides, non-threatening sexual invitation, Spanish, and neo-Dada incantation, Wyatt's lyrics are delivered in a kindergarten sing-song and insouciant soprano, that leak at points into 'la-la-ing,' squeaks, whispers and mutterings. However, for all their sardonic wit, Wyatt's swooping, lilting voice carries with it a serious intention: to exact a new voice-song relationship from a post-rock music that has learned from what jazz can do to the timbre, structure and density of a song. In this the extended spatiality of song and music (not simply accompaniment we might say) on *Soft Machine Two* is as innovative in its way as *Astral Weeks*. But if *Astral Weeks*, marks a distinct meeting between jazz and the new folk-thinking, *Soft Machine Two* – despite very little of the album being in $\frac{4}{4}$ – is shaped by the energy of the rock ensemble, particularly through Wyatt's drumming. Yet, even so, it is also not jazz rock. Not because it relies on the song-form, but because it has precisely this relationship to a threnodic sensibility that marks out what will become the compelling achievement of this progressive rock: the re-assemblage of voice, song and heterodox instrumentation.

We see a continuation of this sensibility in the next Soft Machine album, *Third* (1970), and Wyatt's solo album for CBS, the free-form *The End*

---

134 Marcus O'Dair, *Different Every Time: The Authorized Biography of Robert Wyatt*, Introduction by Jonathan Coe, Serpent's Tail, London, 2014, p55

of an Ear (1970). There is actually little of Wyatt's voice on the latter re-cord, but where it does appear, as on the version of Gil Evans' 'Las Vegas Tango Part One (Repeat),' it follows the lapidary Pataphysical sound-me-anderings of the non-word vocals of parts of *Soft Machine Two*. Indeed, unnervingly today the electronic treatment of Wyatt's voice sounds like the babbling of the cartoon Minions – and maybe that's no bad thing. On *Third* Wyatt is still writing lyrics. But now the song-form and Wyatt's voice are subjugated to the overall drive of jazz rock instrumentation with the arrival of the saxophonist Elton Dean; and Wyatt's vocal contribution is restricted to a single track 'Moon in June.' In fact, *Third*, is the cut-off point between progressive rock and jazz rock, that Soft Machine in its next incarnation, with the virtuoso guitarist Allan Holdsworth and Ratledge (*Bundles*, 1975), does much to establish. Jazz rock as I insist in Chapter 4 is not progressive rock. Yet in 'Moon in June' Wyatt and Soft Machine will point to what will in many ways define the reassembling of the song-form, within what I have been calling this minoritarian shift to non-dominative aesthetic, drawing on some of the vocal mannerisms of *Soft Machine Two*: the instrumental stretching of the song-form, in which lapidary vocals appear as an interruption or return intermittently, as part of an extended instrumental section or soundscape.

'Moon in June' begins directly with Wyatt's voice, and then follows with his voice in unison with Ratledge's piano line, followed by Hopper's skip-ping bass, then Wyatt's voice, then percussive organ, voice, piano and organ, voice, organ, voice, (10 minutes), then an extended passage of fast, fuzzy, snarling organ later accompanied by Wyatt's sopranic scat sing-ing, followed by a slow and low pastoral drift of organ and drums, that transforms into a repetitive piano figure, then into a screechy smudge of violin, piano figure, and electronic tweets, and Wyatt's occasional nursery rhyme style accompaniment, followed to the end by Dean's low moaning soprano saxophone (9 minutes). Wyatt's vocalization, then, within this stretched structure, comes in and out of focus, providing not so much a weaving of voice and instruments into a continuous non-standard song-form in the manner of Morrison on *Astral Weeks*, than a sequence of fragments, some verse-like, some not. If the effect is lapidary it is because the singing at points seems to drift away from the melodic and percus-sive drive of the music, allowing the music to follow its own dynamic. Although Wyatt's voice closely follows Ratledge's organ at points, the elongated and broken character of the song-form and the threnodic and child-like quality of his voice, gives a disconnected, forgetful character to this singing. And this is why Wyatt's apparent de-masculinized delivery is so distinctive in its contribution to this non-dominative aesthetic. It appears to give the prevailing neo-Dada aesthetic contribution to the post-rock song-form a new deflationary direction that is quite different from the use of pastiche in the Beatles and the Bonzos, and as a result provides a new quality of subjectivization to the male rock voice generally: a voice happy to disappear, drift, and 'gurgle' in and out of view. This is less humorous, therefore, than evidence of the unwillingness on the part of the singer to force the music into alignment with voice and song – a kind of indisciplinarity of the voice – in which the voice takes a welcome secondary role. At points this gives Wyatt lapidary style a ghost-like or reticent quality, as if the words don't really belong there or are merely incidental; and this fleeting quality is perhaps, more than any other set of attributes what distinguishes the singing of the other threnodic and lamentary singers of the period, particularly the work of Kevin Ayers.

After Ayers left Soft Machine in 1968 he recorded *Joy of a Toy*, a collection of songs that didn't make it onto *Soft Machine One*, or were written independently. The collection though is a retreat from his contribution to *Soft Machine One*, falling back into pop pastiche and Tin Pan Alley and show-tune inflections ('Joy of a Toy Continued,' 'The Clarietta Rag,' 'Girl on a Swing'). This may have something to do with a bid by Harvest his record company to turn him into an English Tim Hardin, a singer too easily won to a saccharine version of the counterculture. But it doesn't work, as it doesn't for Syd Barrett after he leaves Pink Floyd – although for different reasons. *Joy of a Toy*, simply gets the post-*Sgt.Pepper* and *Astral Weeks* countercultural conjuncture wrong. If the countercultural song-form is to sustain itself and move on then it has to accept the need for work on those heterodox forms of instrumentation (from modal jazz and the new folk-thinking) and moments of formal negation, that The Incredible String Band, the Beatles, Van Morrison, Van Der Graaf Generator and the Soft Machine, all provided, in their respective ways. The return to a child-like sensibility (of sing-alongs and circus themes), as opposed to the invocation of a child-like *détournement* of technique (as in Wyatt) was therefore a mistake. And it reveals, as a consequence, how music, as much as art, demands that the potentialities of a given conjuncture are recognized and developed before they are pushed aside in the interests of new or other commercial possibilities.

However, in his next album, *Whatevershebringswesing* (1971), one of the great titles of the period, things change, as if a realization of the weaknesses of *Joy of a Toy*, and the achievement of *Soft Machine Two* had brought him up short. But, realistically, this perhaps has less to do with his powers of critical reflection alone, than the fact that David Bedford, the classical musician, finally joins his band The Whole World as pianist and as arranger (he also played piano on *Joy of a Toy*). The move of classically trained musicians into playing with, or acting as arrangers for, rock bands is not so unusual at the time. Bedford is no different to many other trained classical or modern atonal musicians in this respect. However, Bedford has a musical pedigree that was unprecedented for the majority of young classical or new music composers in Britain: he trained with the great Luigi Nono in Milan in the late 1950s. A Marxist and an Italian Communist Party (PCI) member, until his death in 1990, Nono is the major figure of post-*musique concrète* and post-Schoenbergian atonality. But unlike the formalist interpretation of this legacy, with its abstract complexity and teleological assumptions about the need for a music that refuses all concessions to heteronomy (pathos, affect, representation), Nono draws on the multiple legacies of the modern and premodern past to produce a music of historically inflected shards and fragments; atonality is the emotionally wrought and politically grounded framework for sound as representation and gateway to historical trauma. Key to this move is the extended spatiality of sound, in which the shards and fragments of violent sound break through extended sheets of drifting noise or silence. Importantly, these effects are produced by a process of assemblage and dis-assemblage of taped electronic sounds and voice and live orchestral instruments and voices, creating an environmental soundscape as opposed to instrument-centred musicianship; composition and improvisation, fugitive or intractable soundscape and instrumental and 'voice-blurts' combine. The overall, impression, as in *Como Una Ola De Fuerza Y Luz* (*Like a Wave and Strength of Light*) from 1972, a requiem to the murder of one of Nono's comrades in Chile, Luciano Cruz, is of listening to sound as trace; the extended sheets of background sound acting as the empathic landscape to this act of historical reimagining. Bedford doesn't impose a Nono aesthetic on Ayers in *Whatevershebringswesing*, as if Ayers' music could conceivably accommodate it. However, he does bring an extended spatiality to some of Ayers' songs, which recalls the environmental sound of Nono, as much as they reflect the extended song-forms of Wyatt and Ratledge. And this is not only revealing in itself; but it enables Ayers' music to recover in some respect that which is compelling about the stretching of song-form during this period. In other words, Bedford's contribution – in part at least – serves to refocus the best qualities of Ayers' own (minor) contribution to a lamentary, non-dominative aesthetic. Thus in 'There is Loving/Among Us/There is

Loving,' the soft baritone voice is a fleeting, circumspect presence, sand-wiched between a long intro, beginning with trilling and flaring flutes, followed by an Eisler-like orchestration of organ and trumpet, followed by soft wah-wah guitar and trombone, and atonal violin scratching, and then after the short vocal, an extended, stately drift of tuba, trombone and reprise of the gentle wah-wah guitar and trombone. The quality of this song though is marginal to the overall tone of the album. With the exception of 'Song From the Bottom of a Well,' with its repetitive in-dustrial slabs of distorted and spiky guitar, and Ayers' macabre growl ('This is a song from the bottom of a well I didn't move here, I just fell"), Ayers again reverts to jaunty pastiche (rag-time, country and western, and intermission music). The overall effect is confusing to say the least, if less disappointing than that of *Joy of a Toy*. Similarly *Shooting at the Moon*, released in 1970, with Bedford on piano and organ prefers rock eclecticism to taking on the legacy of Soft Machine – despite the fact, that Ayers is also helped on the album by Lol Coxhill ('Underwater'). But perhaps, Bedford's contribution was never meant to be other than dec-orative or contingent; and perhaps Ayers never saw himself as anything other than a pop singer, drawn to English whimsy before anything so destabilizing as the avant-garde in rock. Ayers's next album *Bananamour* (1973) would suggest this. It is certainly his best (utilizing the talents of Bedford, Wyatt, Ratledge and Steve Hillage); it has a continuity and coherence that the others lack; and possesses an inviting languidness. But the threnodic qualities of Ayers' voice are largely subordinate to an ac-commodation to the comforts of soft rock ('Shouting in a Bucket Blues'), with the exception of the hazy, guitar repetitions and electronic drones of 'Decadence'; the album's success is precisely the result of its conservatism.

It is therefore hard to position Ayers as a key minoritarian figure in the English remaking of the song-form at the end of the 1960s and the begin-ning of the 1970s: everything interesting about the moment in his songs either comes in and out focus or gets drained out altogether. Yet, one cannot understand the move to threnody within the Southern English countercultural milieu without the impact of Ayers' own lapidary con-tribution. Like Wyatt he establishes a place for the male voice that is at home in lamentation and disenchantment; and this reveals a fracturing of rock culture that lies under the surface of the English counterculture's and the new rock's assault on 'straight' culture. If it is fair to call this a de-masculinization of the voice, it is also fair to say that in its capacity for 'interiorization' it breaches or deflects the affirmationist character of the times. Their voices withdraw consent, as did Baker's. But withdraw consent from what actually? From namely: those expectations of masculine expressiveness and assertion that define the majoritarian values of the counterculture. That Ayers' repertoire is highly eclectic does not change this; his voice, like Wyatt's, is haunted, in these terms, by a loss of relation. These are voices, then, that flow the other way into the counterculture: from the privileges of middle class acculturation into the heterogeneous upsurge of techniques of indisciplinarity.

This negotiation of middle class acculturation is also discernible in Hatfield and the North, who combine exacting post-rock musicianship, an English deflationary pastoralism, with Richard Sinclair's 'feminized' and louche vocals. Sinclair had been in the Wyatt/Ayers Wilde Flowers, played bass and sang with Caravan (leaving in 1971 after *In the Land of Grey and Pink* (1971)) and played bass in Wyatt's Matching Mole. Another singular vocal contribution to this Southern English milieu, Sinclair's sweet, and solicitous tones are part of the same high tonal register as Wyatt (Wyatt in fact singing on 'Calyx' on *Hatfield and the North* [1973]): broken sopranic, even falsetto, scattish, singing and humming over extended instrumental sections (Dave Stewart's drifting washes and fuzz-box distorted stabs from his electronic piano and organ), with the occasional lyric-based song. The effect on a track such as 'Son of 'There's No Place Like Homerton,' ' is choirboy-like, on 'Aigrette' jazzy in a supper-club kind of way, in which his falsetto mimics the melody line, and on 'Fol de Rol,' imitative of medieval plainsong. But whatever identity the voice takes, it has a shifting, temporary presence. In this the punctual vocalization and extended instrumentalization offer another version of the extended song-form familiar from Soft Machine and Ayers and indeed Caravan, who on *In the Land of Grey and Pink* lay down a template for the band. Thus, as on *Third*, the overall structure of the music – the continuous passage and mutation from one track to another – tends to favour ensemble playing – although 'Fitter Stoke Has a Bath,' brings together standard versification and extended instrumentalisation. Sinclair and Hatfield and the North are one minoritarian version of what happens when these de-masculinized, post-rock voices meet progressive rock; or rather continue to define what it could be.

The lack of relationality in these voices is not a *subjective* condition of the singers' 'sensitivity,' even if the re-definition of the subjective in popular music is what is at stake here. On the contrary, the loss of relation is the objective condition of the middle class, bohemian musician finding a voice. Wyatt, Ayers's and Sinclair's countercultural loucheness then is grounded experientially in the alienated social conditions of its production; it is not a form of artistic ventriloquism. And, consequently, what we hear as lamentation and withdrawal, or choirboy 'flightiness' in the case of Sinclair, is the outcome of the singers' dissonant mediation of this English middle class acculturation. This is why these non-relational qualities take on the characteristics of class belonging and class alienation; they resist the conventional forms of English middle class acculturation, yet at the same are at odds with the dominant forms of masculinity that continue to drive the counterculture and working class indisciplinarity. However, this does not make these qualities of reticence, withdrawal or faux naivety, alien to working class singers and working class creativity; such qualities are of course not class, race or gender specific. But that, in this instance, these dissonant forms of male middle class acculturation are able to take the lead on a non-dominative (countercultural) aesthetic space that others can enter and transform according to their own image and needs. The emergence of the male threnodic, minoritarian voice, then, is an important instance of how singers and musicians negotiate a place for themselves in the counterculture, confronted with the intimate relations between class, gender, race and technique. And of course, one singer who negotiated this relation, with a certain difficulty after he leaves Pink Floyd and the disciplinarity-indisciplinarity it provided, is Syd Barrett. In 1967-68 Barrett was at the centre of Pink Floyd's reconfiguration of the masculinities and spatial form of rock, but by 1969 after leaving, much like Ayers in *Joy of a Toy*, he underestimates what the song-form is now or could be. This is disappointing, for it is Barrett along with Drake – who we will discuss below – are two figures that adapt the non-dominative turn into the confessional and self-disclosure in ways that relink the popular song-form to a poetic affirmation outside of the new folk-thinking. But if Barrett is happy to retain some of his neo-Dada loucheness from his Pink Floyd days without further poetic reflection, and confuses 'girlfriend problems' with emotional disclosure, Drake, resists, all such sardonic and sentimental entreaties. The difference in quality and affect as a result is stark, but instructive.

After leaving Pink Floyd, Barrett records *The Madcap Laughs* (1970) for Harvest with help from his ex-Floyd mates David Gilmour and Roger Waters (they produce most of the tracks). Recorded mostly in 1969, there are thirteen songs, a number of which chart his romantic obsessions ('Well, oh baby, my hair's on end about you,' 'Terrapin'), and some which are quirky playroom ditties (the soft rock 'Octopus'). Speaking-singing in a flat semi-catatonic, love-whiny way, or bouncing along, to Ayers-type seaside and music hall jollities, or just drifting along in guitar-voice dirge mode, the collection is conspicuously weak and disjointed; there is an inadequate transformation of materials and clear evidence of self-indulgence on the part of his producers. The social detail and narrative vividness of the early Pink Floyd songs ('See Emily Play,' 1967) is long gone, leaving Barrett, with the limp pathos of his pop days hanging over the session. In 1969-70 the counterculture didn't stop, indeed it pushed on ruthlessly. Barrett clearly thought that all it still took was 'well, oh baby' songs loved-up on Surrealism to recapture the energy of 1967. The non-dominative voicing of some of the songs, then, are not allowed to breathe, to reconnect with what was happening elsewhere; at times he bashes on like a countercultural George Formby;[135] he just wasn't listening. Some of this is down to his impending illness, some of it down to hubris, but more crucially it is a visible indication of all the spontaneitism that was beginning to sweep through the late English counterculture and that progressive rock and Nick Drake were determined to resist (and that, it had to be said, Pink Floyd wanted no part of). In 1970 there was no place for jolly countercultural Lotharios, artful tricksters, or Anthony Newley-type, West End boho rocksters, even if Richard Neville still thought there was.

Drake's achievement is now widely acknowledged, certainly since the 1990s. Of all the threnodic singers of the late English counterculture, he is perhaps the one that has mostly 'escaped' the defining context of the new folk-thinking, indisciplinarity, and the vicissitudes of the minoritarian male voice; his work is now part of a tradition of romantic singer-song writers whose tragic 'interiority' is celebrated for its would be hard-won emotional insights. However, whatever popular therapeutic status his music now commands on the market, he plays a crucial part in this non-dominative shift, in as much as his own withdrawal from certain expectations of expressive masculinity, link aspects of the Southern English singers to the wider preoccupations of the modernist *poiesis* of the new folk-thinking. Drake was not a neo-dadaist, or neo-Dada vocalist; he was a *poet of the text*, struck down, much like the Incredible String Band and Van Morrison, and all the other singers who had come under the sway of the counterculture's bardic uplift, by the opportunities for *singing poetry*, or at least, retrieving a poeticized vision of the song-form

---

135 Although, this is to do a political injustice to Formby. In 1946 on tour in South Africa he insisted – unprecedented for visiting entertainers – on performing to black audiences.

from the relentless denigration of language and subjectivity in the senti-mental heartlands of the old popular culture.

Wyatt and Ayers (and Barrett) of course, would claim a similar connec-tion to language. But in Drake, there is a greater attachment to the post-Dylan song-form as a literary-popular form that pulls the music back into alignment with the new folk, as opposed to the new folk-thinking's heterodox contribution to progressive rock. This makes the songs, despite their tonal innovations and arresting orchestral arrangements (Robert Kirby and Harry Robinson) and jazz infusions (Danny Thompson, bass, Ray Warleigh, alto sax and flute, Chris McGregor, piano), largely con-ventional in their structure, and their vocalization and instrumentation. Drake's primary concern is the song as a core, tight, even hard, experi-ential focus, in the way a poet controls syntax and semantic content, in order to create a continuity of pitch and atmosphere; and as such, it is the formal integrity of each song as part of the whole of each album that is prioritized. There are no stylistic wanderings, no rock indulgences, no pastiche-follies.

There is therefore a remarkable consistency of delivery and emotional range across the three albums, *Five Leaves Left* (1970), *Bryter Later* (1970), and *Pink Moon* (1971) even if *Pink Moon* (Drake accompanying himself on guitar) is the most bare and unadorned of the three. Each album has a melancholic fluency in which Drake's plaintive and evenly mod-ulated voice, impatiently, relentlessly, creates a confessional, if oblique landscape of fateful encounters and failed encounters, of lost moments of connection and beauty: "And think about people in their season and time," ('Saturday Sun,' *Five Leaves Left*); "Forgotten while you're here" ('Fruit Tree,' *Five Leaves Left*); "And what happen in the morning when the world it gets/So crowded that you can't look out of the window in the morning" ('Hazey Jane 11,' *Bryter Later*). The effect is immediately elegiac, in a way that the other threnodic singers of the moment are not, as if the songs have already said goodbye to the counterculture and have established an emotional connection elsewhere. This is perhaps why the albums did not sell, as opposed to any particular aesthetic resistance to their pastoral quietude: their diffident, reflective qualities didn't seem to issue from anything resembling what people imagined the hybrid ener-gies of the counterculture to be and what they believed the new music stood for; the gentle resignation in Drake's voice defies all the usual ex-pressions of uplift, and the disordering of sensibility.

Thus, if Drake rejects all the affectations of rock 'n' roll, his identification with the new folk, is itself, deflated and understated; he also resists aligning his self-image and pastoral imaginary with the utopian horizons of the new folk music, with its powerful evocations for a 'new spirit' of mind and body, creative labour and community. His own contribution to new folk-thinking, therefore, may be unimaginable without Dylan, The Incredible String Band, and Van Morrison's *Astral Weeks*, but it also forges its own reflective path away from the public and declamatory qualities of these other musics, in which his elegiac vision, dissolves all local colour in an indeterminate – even mythic – reimagining of the recent past. It is easy to say that these expressions of withdrawal and acts of social deflection derive from his class background and education – Marlborough, and Cambridge undergraduate (Fitzwilliam, 1967-69) – and that therefore this explains the asocial tendencies of the music. But in a sense, that's to say nothing beyond the obvious and to diminish his achievement; the middle class has no monopoly on melancholy and withdrawal, as I stressed below in the case of Wyatt and Ayers. Yet, there is no doubt that a certain class disconnection does haunt and define the quality of these songs, in which the expression of non-relation derives less from a managed anger at class alienation, than a particular reading and acceptance – even adolescent reading and acceptance – of modernist *poiesis*, as a way of coping with the loss of relation and alienation. In other words, what drives the mythic 'I' of the songs, and their general and *accomplished* feelings of irresolution, is a particular learned relationship to modernist self-identity. In these three albums Drake is not a singer-songwriter, lover-troubadour, or a tribune, but a modernist poet who sings songs that can't be sung truthfully without the necessary mordancy, self-disgust and self-elimination of the task. In this sense, despite the severe emotional registers of the songs, the unadornedness of the songs in *Pink Moon* have a tough external carapace that is clearly indebted to the modernist anti-informality of the last years of the English counterculture. There is a demonstrable indifference to formal elaboration, but without any of the purist affectations of the traditional folk revival. As the producer of the album John Wood recalled: "Nick was determined to make a record that was very stark."[136]

One should not, therefore, underestimate what he learned or absorbed from the poetry circles he moved in at Cambridge about anti-pathos. Whether he met Prynne or not at the Caius Breakfast Club, is, in a way,

---

136 Patrick Humphries, *Nick Drake*, Bloomsbury, London, 1997, p173

beside the point. He was certainly part of a dialogue on poetry that took in many of the things that had swept away the legacy of the Movement poets. And this points to at least one modernist axiom, made familiar by William Empson amongst others, that was certainly taken seriously in these circles: one must learn a style *from* despair (as opposed to simply inviting despair fascistically into the poem as in Philip Larkin). As Drake's Cambridge near-contemporary Veronica Forrest-Thomson said, who died in 1975 (Drake died in 1974): "Poems teach one that much: to expect no answer" (that is formally).[137] And Drake, accepted that, or accepted it as far possible as someone who was writing popular songs. Thus, his work asks an important question of the new folk song: How do you sing like a modernist of things interior? This is a substantive issue for a songwriter moving far away from anything resembling rock culture, and not one that Wyatt or Ayers come anywhere near, or to be honest are interested in 1970-71 (until that is, Wyatt's completed and exalting move into the song-form, in *Rock Bottom* [1974], after his life changing accident). That Drake's songs, asks this question, puts his threnodic qualities then largely outside of the charmed circle of the Southern English neo-dadaists and 'voice-changers.' His songs are withdrawn, circumspect, lamentary, but not louche or playful. This does not make them any better accomplished as songs. But it does reveal very different aspects of a non-dominative aesthetic in play across this generation: that is, withdrawal carries with it a kind of modernist *responsibility* to the integral presentation of form. Indeed, there is an earnest and provincial character to the resoluteness of Drake's songs and singing, a refusal to take his eye off where the songs have come from (a place of privilege), and where he hopes they are going (a place of common acceptance and celebration). This is where the question of technique, class, race and gender come into play. Drake's songs are a major contribution to the minoritarian shift in the English counterculture. Their poetic song-form ambitions are comparable to those of the Incredible String Band and Van Morrison. But, as I have mentioned, they don't seem able to achieve any kind of stable symbolic place in the counterculture's disorderly logics, in the way that The Incredible String Band, Morrison, Wyatt and Ayers and even Barrett do. It is as if the songs melancholic consistency and relentless threnody are involved in purgative displacement of the singer from the demotic horizons of the counterculture.

---

137 Veronica Forrest-Thomson, 'J'étais plunge dans une de ces reveries profondes,' *Meantime* No 1, 1977, p63.

Drake's techniques of indisciplinarity, then, find their class expression through an extended repertoire of self-negation, even self-loathing. Thus, what the counterculture gives and allows Drake – a profound sense of escape from the duties of privilege and male expectations – cannot be freely internalized for fear of un-acceptance and unworthiness. The result is a traumatic repetition of this failure to assimilate in the form of lost, impossible or imagined love. Again, such a response is not about the singer's heightened 'sensitivity,' but rather about, the contradictions of social experience. If Drake was inside the counterculture, produced by it, he was also not comfortably of it, insofar, as the counterculture threw a sharp light on the cultural presumptions that defined him. The songs strip away a lot; but in the end they cannot provide Drake with a defence against the aporias of his class background. The counterculture was not set up to give opportunities to singers like himself; he might create a place for himself, but found it difficult all the same to fall under its egal-itarian demands. Interestingly, during his time in London having moved from his parents' home in Tanworth-in-Arden in Warwickshire, he hung out with the aristocratic Chelsea-hippie set, I would imagine not because he had anything in common with them, but he felt more comfortable and could disappear more easily. Hence to note that techniques of indis-ciplinarity in the counterculture are class inflected is to begin to note how and in what form the voices of the counterculture find their enunciative range and establish their relations with the outside world. Drake's mod-ernist poet's voice of withdrawal and non-relationality is clearly a political decision. A way of establishing what he felt comfortable with in a coun-terculture that had mostly other things on its mind; these are techniques of indiscipline not from below, then, but nevertheless from somewhere where the pain of social adjustment to a world not of his making could find some leverage. And that is no small thing. That he looks away from the counterculture in order to find a place within it is neither to his dis-advantage nor advantage as a singer and songwriter. It is simply what he needed to do in order to make and sing the songs that he wanted to sing without shame.

The rise of the threnodic male singer and the de-masculinized shift in tone is one of the great, localized achievements of the counterculture in England. It re-assimilates the *poiesis* of the new folk-thinking as part of a general confrontation with the accumulating idiocies of a mainstream Americanized rock 'n' roll, which even by 1971 is beginning to sound like an advertisement for hippie capitalism. Whatever the unevenness of these singers and songs, therefore, they defy the affirmative reading of popular music in the counterculture that would see it as no more than a new soundtrack to hedonism and a new kind of dance music, or, at a stretch, 'rebellion.' The recourse to singing 'songs of experience' at a melancholic distance from what rock 'n' roll expected of musicians and audiences, is consequently, a move that draws value from other parts of the counterculture that by 1971-72 the new market for popular music was keen to close down, or sideline into specialist niches, such as the new song-forms' relationship to modernist *poiesis*.

As such, there is a clear ideological struggle around the minoritarian and majoritarian during these years as the marketing of the 'big voice,' 'the big sound,' 'the big experience,' 'the big spectacle,' become ways of excising what is inconvenient. But, we should also be circumspect musicologically here. The minoritarian shift to a non-dominative aesthetic, demasculinized song-form is not a confirmation of the absolute decline of rock or evidence of these singers hardening antipathy to American popular music. In fact, if we exclude the major achievements of the minoritarian moves of the English new song-forms and progressive rock – it is American rock/blues, that represents some of the abiding and distinctive music from this period of the counterculture: The Band (*The Band*, 1970), Curtis Mayfield (*Roots*, 1971), Tim Buckley (*Greetings From LA*, 1972), Big Star (*#1 Record*, 1972), and, in a very different register, Captain Beefheart (*Trout Mask Replica*, 1969, and *Lick My Decals Off, Baby*, 1970). In their various ways these albums either held the line for the innovative reworking of the American blues-rock legacy (Robbie Robertson's 'Up on Cripple Creek,' Alex Chiltern's 'The Ballad of El Goodo') or, as in the case of Beefheart, completely re-function it, in a dissonant and fractured syncopation of voice, drums and guitars. Yet, even if we take Beefheart's music as being exceptional (which we will discuss further in the next chapter) and in dis-alignment with conventional rock, all this music is nevertheless borne from the self-mythologizing forge of the American 'rock song,' as American rock becomes central to the popular syntax of the new boosterish American 'scene.' American rock music, as it takes on the hegemonic 'leadership' of rock's subaltern and rebel associations, increasingly encloses rock music into repetitive images of 'flight' and 'deliverance' (with Bruce Springsteen picking up the baton in 1974). This is a big canvas to play out the fantasies of rock 'n' roll transcendence. Hence these English songs and voices of lamentation are not so much about a rejection of rock or American popular culture per se, but a way of keeping open the possibility of *other* voices, *other* stories (and myths), that the American scene, as it loosens itself from the counterculture and attaches itself to the music industry proper, was beginning to erase, particularly through the use of the 'big' voice, whether this voice was conventionally inscribed into the legacy of blues-rock or not. That the minoritarian male voices of the English counterculture between 1968-73 take the form of feminized withdrawal and non-relationality is not fortuitous in this respect.

Rock culture's resistive position within the counterculture is caught up in the unstable sexual dynamics of popular culture, mass culture and high culture; and the new threnodic song-form plays its part in defining this. Implicit in both conventional bourgeois humanist and leftist critiques of mass culture in the 1960s is that mass culture is passive and feminine; it produces supine, undiscriminating, pliable consumers, particularly in the domain of popular music, where 'affect' readily dominates 'listening,' the 'somatic' overwhelms the 'cognitive,' and 'feeling' trumps 'thinking.' The significance of rock to the *counter-hegemonic* success of the counterculture is that it breaks with these reified perceptions; by 1967-68 with the impact of *Sgt. Pepper* (and the Beatles disconnection from their teenage female audience)[138], the associations of popular music with passivity and empty 'affect' is beginning to fracture. Complexity, disorder, even difficulty, now displace these feminine associations as popular music absorbs the 'masculine' – modernist – strategies of refusal and non-compliance. Yet, inversely, for many musicians and audiences this absorption of the difficult and the heterodox is identified with a de-masculinizing

---

138 It is difficult to make a hard and fast generalization here, but the emergence of pop in the UK and the US in the early 1960s, does not achieve its hegemony without strong opposition from the old folk guard, on the grounds that it, allowed a pacification of the listener (largely directed at young women) to enter popular music, in a situation where the 'song of protest' had a strong and defining presence in the civil rights movement and the anti-nuclear campaign, and encouraged the contribution of women as performers. This is what the 'audience wars' in the UK, during Dylan's tour in 1966, and the vituperative booing during Dylan's performance at the Newport Folk Festival in 1965 were principally about; Dylan's 'electrification' appeared to conspire with rock's libidinal drive to split the popular from the political. See the extraordinary comments of two working class girls, interviewed after Dylan's concert at Newcastle City Hall in 1966. After one girl attacks his set as a "half-concert," the other girl calls the new 'electric' Dylan "a fake neurotic" (*No Direction Home: Bob Dylan*, director Martin Scorsese, 2005). For a discussion of Dylan's US-UK 'audience wars,' see Greil Marcus, *Invisible Republic: Bob Dylan's Basement Tapes*, Picador, London, 1998

and feminizing move against 'straight' and official culture, hence the significance of new folk-thinking in the countercultural revolt against the old popular culture; new folk-thinking helps release the new music from the narrow instrumentalities (masculinities) of traditional folk and the old popular music. But in a further *détournement*, these shifts are themselves mediated by the sexualized division between popular culture and high culture: if modernist difficulty is construed as being masculine, popular culture invariably traduces high culture for being effete, opaque, ambiguous – in short 'feminine' – in a reversal of high culture's critique of popular culture's would-be femininity; and, as we have seen, rock's majoritarian masculine logic in the counterculture continually enforces this popular critique of high culture as a nominal condition of the countercultural revolution in values. This is why the avant-garde is always an ambiguous presence in the musical counterculture; its place in the re-making of the popular threatens at various points the very integrity of the masculine, libertarian economy of rock.

Thus, rock music is constantly shifting its countercultural identity across the unstable opposition between the feminine and masculine depending on how it mediates its attachments to class, gender and race in relation to the wider division between high culture (feminized or masculinized 'difficulty') and popular culture (feminized or masculinized 'affect'). And this is why the counterculture's techniques of indisciplinarity are not just defined by gender and class in the abstract here, but by the *cultural mediation* of femininity and masculinity, in which women singers and musicians utilize the codes of masculinity to attack a corrupted femininity or masculinity, and male singers and musicians utilize the codes of femininity to attack a corrupted and inert masculinity. But, of course, these inversions and shifts are not symmetrical across the feminine-masculine. The feminine remains the secondary term; but it is a secondary term that doesn't know its place. If the masculine seeks to subsume the feminine under the sign of order – in musical terms dissolve or resolve it in tonal music back into the tonic, and in post-tonal music into the atonic – the feminine as the heterodox is always the residual excess which stretches or breaks the logic of masculine musical resolution, and that the masculine itself desires and coverts. Indeed, the modern history of both opera and non-vocal music reveals a history of male composers appropriating the signs of would-be feminine excess (in chromatic female vocal performance and characterization, in terms of the climaxes, strong cadences and structure of musical composition), in order to undermine the teleology of masculine tonal/atonal resolution. That many male composers, in the end, submit themselves to closure in these (virile) terms – ending a section or a piece on a masculine cadence (emphatic beat) – does not alter the disruptive place and desire for the imagined freedoms of the feminine on their part. In the world of the classical canon from 1600-1900 (and in traditional narrative from which it borrows its gender-politics), there *are* no 'feminine' endings, so to speak, or rather, no feminine endings that are considered *satisfying*: "in most tonal music in the eighteenth and nineteenth centuries, nothing less [than the masculine cadence] will suffice for purposes of concluding pieces than complete resolutions onto the triad," as Susan McClary, puts it.[139]

In this respect, these male threnodic singers' attachment to a non-dominative aesthetic, appropriates the secondary-excessive signs of the 'feminine' as a commitment to formal and syntactic openness; song structure and vocalization/lyrics drift, voices 'disappear' or fade, flatten or sweeten, dissolving the declarative 'I' at points into a post-gendered 'we,' or at least producing a blurring of the feminine and masculine. This does not mean the songs avoid conventional 'masculine' cadences or resolutions (Drake), but rather, that the feminine as an excess of 'emphatic closure,' becomes a way of refiguring the relationship between song-form and the male voice that is unprecedented at the time among male singers. This commitment to openness and irresolution is, consequently, a better way of looking at 'feminization' than seeing these young singers as simply appropriating or ventriloquising a feminine 'interiority,' in order to its draw on its excessive power. There is *masculine deflation here, not feminine inflation*; a de-masculinization of affect, rather than a kind of Nietzschean celebration of the successful male artist as possessing the 'complete female' within his powers of expression.

These singers certainly adopt lamentation and threnody as feminine forms, but they do so without relying on the emotive clichés of the female lament, invariably codified by male composers and musicians before the twentieth century as a sign of female hysteria and instability. To do so would be to ridicule both themselves and the destablizing excess of the feminine.

Prior to the twentieth century the male adaptation of the lamentary was a way of mocking both hystericized women and hystericized men

139 Susan McClary, *Feminine Endings: Music, Gender & Sexuality*, University of Minnesota Press, Minneapolis, 1991, p62.

in order to recall both men and women to (musical) order (to the sta-
bilizing rationality of the tonic). Thus, for example, when strong male
characters in operas, such as the overbearing and charismatic Orfeo in
Claudio Monterverdi and Alessandro Striggio's *L'Orfeo* (1607) appropriate the lament for their own rhetorical ends, they are seen as surrender-
ing to the untruth of high emotion and musical irrationality. (In Orfeo
acting the male hysteric in order to win our affectations, he undermines
his own moral standing, by appearing self-consciously to manipulate the
audience).[140] The threnodic singers do not appropriate the feminine as
high emotion in this respect; indeed, the very opposite is the case: mute-
ness, murmuring, withdrawal, loucheness, lapidariness are the dominant
qualities. This is because, what is stake here, is an (English) voice, that is
seen to distinguish itself from the hystericized (male) delivery of the 'big'
majoritarian (American) rock voice; an English voice inflected by history
and pathos. In these terms this threnodic turn in the English counterculture has a deeper resonance with the minoritarian. These voices, as part
of the broader pastoral and post-Empire sensibility, are resistive of the
Dionysian energies of majoritarian rock as spectacle and ecstatic community. They refuse to participate in the bigger countercultural libidinal
frenzy and commercial pagan circus. They want a different kind of space,
different emotional attachments. This does not make these singers the enemy of rock 'n' roll, or dissident purists. But it does make them question
the reified identification of the countercultural with the popular cultural
critique of the avant-garde and the identification of new folk-thinking
and the new musics as subordinate (feminine) forms. The minoritarian
in these terms mobilizes a different set of energies that are irreducible to
the binarisms of 'masculine' and 'feminine.'

Thus, if we need to give due space to the achievements of the new
folk-thinking and the new extended and threnodic song-forms, we don't
need thereby to cast rock and the Dionysian completely outside of the
counterculture. There is no 1960s counterculture without the 'libidinal
frenzy' that rock brings to the destruction of the proprieties of both high
culture and the old popular culture. The new folk-thinking alone could
not have achieved the shift in sensibility, wider cultural attachments, and
transformation in class relations that rock and its audiences were able
to provide. This is because rock broke open the repressed link between
working class and lower middle class desire, indisciplinary technique and
collective experience. Yet, what it gives, it also takes away, in its drive

---

140 Susan McClary, op cit,

to endlessly reproduce the ecstatic powers of this communal experience. Rock's secularization of religious submission continually invests in this ecstatic moment over and above the demands of indisciplinary technique. Indeed, in most rock, indisciplinary technique gets in the way of this experience, and the pleasures of repetition. And not far behind this – certainly in the 1960s – is the cognate idea that rock is the place where reason dissolves and desire begins. What is innovative about progressive rock, however, is that it refuses to submit indisciplinary technique *to* the libidinal expectation of repetition, and to the mythos of popular music as an escape from reason. Yet, progressive rock is not a version of post-1950s theoretical/atonal music: it is shaped *by* the libidinal drive of popular music, certainly those forms of rock that retain the song-form as a focus for an expanded musicality. Thus, we might say that English progressive rock – as it emerges out of the threnodic, lamentary de-masculinized song-forms of the Southern English countercultural moment – brings indisciplinary technique into a *new alignment* with the libidinal drive of rock. In its adaptation of the extended song-form, particularly the song cycle, heterogeneous instrumentation and new voice-sound spacings, it seeks to reconnect and rethink 'affect' with indisciplinarity (experiment). The result is a re-totalizing move within the remaking of the popular (across the 'feminine' and 'masculine') as progressive rock repositions voice, song, soundscape and instrumentation as a form of *gesamtkunstwerk*. It, consequently, brings the minoritarian into a wholly new register. It is this wider framework that I now want to discuss in the next chapter.

CHAPTER 4
EXTENSITY AND THE SONG-FORM

As I STRESSED IN THE INTRODUCTION AND CHAPTER 2, PROGRESSIVE rock is not the teleological summation of those elements that preceded it. It is not what happens programmatically to rock once traditional rock is bypassed. Yet, nevertheless its dynamism and character are indivisible from the heterodox new folk-thinking, 'post-rock,' 'post-jazz,' forms which determine the countercultural development of popular music in the late 1960s. Progressive rock, then, participates in that general deflation of, and detachment from, the cultural signs and practices of Empire, conservative majoritarian accounts of popular culture, and a narrow, indeed, proprietorial understanding of high culture or the avant-garde. In this respect, it generates a range of structural forms, vocal and instrumentalist strategies and techniques that reconfigure the relationship between non-vocal music, the song-form and the theatrical presentation of music (opera, cabaret, choral music, musical theatre). Consequently, the best of the music does not just, borrow from post-bebop jazz and free jazz, new folk-thinking and post-1950s atonal music – as in some grand *synthesizing* act – but, rather, produces a new set of indisciplinary relations between the song-form and instrumentation, that generally, can be defined as antipathetic to traditional rock, folk and jazz. As a result, English progressive rock creates a discernable shift in priorities for popular music; it defines a 'post-generic' space of experimentation that detaches musicians and audience from certain expectations about what counts as pleasurable and affecting in rock. But, it is precisely its relationship to the song-form that secures this. When progressive rock abandons the song-form in the interests of hybrid *musicianship* (Ian Carr's Nucleus, Gary Boyle's Isotope, Chick Corea's Return to Forever, John McLaughlin's Mahavishnu Orchestra, and late Soft Machine), it returns to the 'comforts' of genre and musicology and the formal distractions of instrumental virtuosity. This is why the most significant progressive rock of the period accomplishes two significant things in relation to the restructuring of the song-form: it reassembles voices and instrumentation as the basis for a hybrid expansion of rock into the realm of the total-art-work, or *gesamtkunstwerk*, and, coextensively, it reclaims and repositions definitions of the popular on the basis of the literary and political as a way of 're-landscaping' the structure and dynamic of the song, or in some instances song cycle.

Thus, if progressive rock draws on new folk-thinking, post-bebop jazz, free form jazz, post-1950s atonality in order to generate a new and unprecedented spatiality in rock, this is always at the behest *of* the song, and voice, even, when the voice is a marginal or intermittent presence. This is where Nono's striking environmental extension and framing of voice-fragments clearly has a relationship with the heterodox vocalization of progressive rock, beyond its echo in Kevin Ayers' work, as much as the attenuation and drift of Van Morrison's singing on *Astral Weeks*. In other words, progressive rock is a music of expanded vocal interiority and spatiality as opposed to being simply a form of heterodox post-rock instrumentation – with or without voices. And this is why there is good reason to argue that the hybridity of the best of progressive rock is not a synthesizing move. On the contrary, progressive rock dismantles and re-assembles the musics and traditions it uses as a means of prioritizing certain voices, affects, voice-instrument relations, rather than other kinds, in order to secure a space of experimentation that is not just a hospitable 'meeting of genres and traditions,' as if progressive rock was selecting what is 'best of the rest.' Its character, accordingly, is formed as much as by what it includes and excludes under the name of 'experiment' as what it excludes and includes under the name of the 'popular.' This is why the status and identity of musical virtuosity is crucial to understanding progressive rock's embrace *and* critique of trained musicianship, particularly in relation to jazz.

Progressive rock certainly draws on jazz musicianship for its spatial attenuation of the song-form; it also prefers, on the whole, keyboards and brass instruments, as opposed to guitars, although one of the first progressive rock bands King Crimson, tends to be guitar-centred through the innovative work of Robert Fripp, paving the way for the band's eventual transmogrification into jazz rock proper. But, as a rule of thumb progressive rock has no interest in the improvisational performativity of jazz, that is, in jazz's fundamental commitment to the exchange of musical chops and the competiveness between soloists and backing band. This is not because progressive rock abjures improvisation altogether, but where it works, it places little value on individual instrumental virtuosity over and above that of group musicianship and the 'conceptual' demands of the music; there is a rejection of the 'working space' of improvisation – so prized in jazz, even in free jazz with its valorization of 'shared, collective listening' – as a demonstration of muscular innovation. When virtuosity takes over at the expense of song-form, as in the guitar work of Holdsworth, Steve Howe, Zappa, and McLaughlin, for instance, it pushes the music into the realm of the academy or the coterie salon – the fate of jazz itself in the late 1960s as it moves out of the clubs for support into the university and the 'arts centre.' Jazz rock in these forms (particularly in the US) becomes a rococo swirl of dizzying speeds and non-standard time signatures, for fear that, like late-bebop, if it slows down and decomplexifies, it will lose its gravitas and authenticity.

Jazz rock, then, is what happens to progressive rock when the relationship between popular techniques of indisciplinarity and the collective are weakened by musicianship, or rather, more precisely, jazz rock is what happens to progressive rock when progressive rock bypasses the literary-musical hybridities of the *gesamtkunstwerk* to be driven *solely* by the musicological demands of cognition; jazz rock can mobilize new forms of musical cognition on the heterodox edges of countercultural indisciplinarity – certainly – but it cannot provide a *representational and subjective focus* for the popular transformation of values. This is not because pure non-vocal music is elitist and vocal music is demotic; many song-forms historically have had small audiences. But, rather, because of the way the sonic excess of progressive rock as a form is channeled – that is, the way virtuosity becomes identifiable with a delimited notion of cognition in a quasi-Adornian separation of popular musical form from non-musical use values. Thus, if the counterculture had consisted of jazz rock and non-vocal rock forms alone, there would have been no counterculture and collective transformation of values from below to speak of; the cognitive and social impact of music's innovations would have been slight, contained within the increasing specialist demands of jazz and high culture as a narrow 'corrective' to mass culture. This is why virtuosity and the exigencies of soloing, key to jazz rock's split from progressive rock in the early 1970s, is inflected with the fractures of class.

Much of the breakneck virtuosity, particularly on guitar in the move of jazz rock out of, or the blurring, of song-based progressive rock is the work of white non-academy trained working class and lower-middle class male musicians striving for jazz 'academy' status, in an echo of the driven and self-lacerating ambition of an earlier generation of black male jazz musicians intent on smashing through the racist vocabulary of 'black primitivism.' What is at stake ideologically is obviously quite different, nevertheless, paradoxically these largely self-taught musicians shaped by the new horizons of the counterculture have their sights set on something more than the imprimatur of the counterculture in a resolute separation of post-rock technique from mere pop and rock 'n' roll. Allan Holdsworth's extended guitar solo on 'Hazard Profile' (*Bundles*), with its fiery modal clusters, is genuinely extraordinary and marks a high point for technical accomplishment in popular music (from a self-taught working class musician), but it is not *of* the counterculture; in some sense symbolically it has exited it in a flurry of pleonastic self-display.[141] Detractors

---

141 One might compare Holdsworth's solo on 'Hazard Profile' to Mick Ronson's solo on David Bowie's 'Moonage Dream' (1972). I've hardly mentioned David Bowie in this book. This is partly because his own achievements skirt the radical formal encounters of the counterculture in the late 1960s and early 1970s; he seems, like Nick Drake, to be looking elsewhere for his orientation. Yet, his primary focus was always the song-form, and, in his collaborations with Mick Ronson, and in his debt to modernist montage/cut-up techniques, he saw the song as a place for 'world building' through voice and word. As such the songs set out to reclaim a new moral economy for the popular, a world beyond its dead zones, no more so than in the early songs, and in particular 'Moonage Daydream,' distinguished by the wonderful Ronson guitar solo at the end. Despite appearances to the contrary there aren't many outstanding guitar solos during the English counterculture. This, however, is one of the best, perhaps even the best. This is because, unlike Holdsworth's modal solo

of progressive rock and jazz rock of this kind invariably talk about such ambition in terms of pretension. This would be a mistake – as if pretension, were morally suspect. However, indisciplinarity as it shifts emphatically into ambitious, technically complex non-vocal forms, reveals how close pleonasm in music is to the conventional overachievement of the petty-bourgeois amateur, the artist who 'tries too hard,' and in trying too hard overelaborates and misses the point. It would be trite to say the splitting of jazz rock from the core vocal forms of (the best) progressive rock, are down to 'untrained' musicians trying too hard and missing the point, in order to enter an academy of counter-musicianship of their own self-devising; there is much in progressive rock that, suffers from the same problems. The band Yes, for example, are driven by the sweep of Jon Anderson's songs, yet, as an ensemble their playing is weakened by a self-conscious virtuosity, in a synthetic assimilation of various styles. Admittedly, the Royal Academy-trained pianist Rick Wakeman – always keen to show off his technical ability – is a serial offender here, but the other non-School trained band members (Steve Howe and Chris Squire) do their bit as well. The result is a progressive rock with a lot of sonic detail and energy (and some spatial invention, certainly in *Tales From Topographic Oceans*, 1973), but little coherence of form, allowing the music to be structured around frenetic bursts of instrumental flamboyance and exercise-type interludes, creating in the end an arbitrary conjunction of elements and figures (*Fragile*, 1971, *Close To The Edge*, 1972): a baroque and filigree complexity that stands in cognitive dissonance to the organicist pre-industrial sentiment of the songs (largely indebted to Herman Hesse) and the band's sub-Tolkien visuals (Roger Dean's album covers and stage design), what Edward Macan has called Yes's "cosmic optimism."[142] In this respect, the band's technical indisciplinarity and lyrical range is largely accommodating to tradition: that is, there is an *affirmative transposition* of 19th century classical form (particularly the sonata) and motifs, post-bebop intricacy and rock dynamism, into a 'progressive' framework. This is not the kind of progressive rock I am interested in or consider to be central to the most significant shifts in, and critical demands of, the counterculture, as is also reflected in the music of

---

on 'Hazard Profile' Ronson's solo looks 'outwards,' giving us, as the song closes, a defining vision of popular music's power of disclosure and utopian longing. Dipping and weaving, its echoing, sustained and controlled, distorted notes lift the song into the future – where it still lives.

142 Edward Macan, *Rocking the Classics: English Progressive Rock and the Counterculture*, op cit, p78.

Emerson, Lake & Palmer (ELP), Jethro Tull, Genesis, and Gentle Giant, who, similarly, all suffer from this eclectic spirit of accommodation. In the following, my focus will be on those (few) progressive rock bands, who, in their own adaptation of the *gesamtkunstwerk*, and the legacy of 'new folk-thinking' and bardic uplift retain, a disaffirmative and modernist-literary relationship to the song-form and popular musicianship; a music, in other words, struggling to find a post-generic dynamism, as opposed to either the extension of genre or their combination.

This is why in this chapter I am at pains to make a fundamental distinction between progressive rock and jazz rock, not simply on the grounds of jazz rock's sonic and modal, non-vocal complexity, but more significantly on the basis that jazz rock and some progressive rock's musicology, narrows the *symbolic, semantic and importantly scenic content* of the contribution of popular music to the countercultural. The sonic excess of jazz rock, in particular, reduces this scenic and semantic content to a tightly orchestrated subversion of conventional rock technique. Indisciplinary technique becomes squandered in an assertive display of academic musicianship. In this sense, synthesis and hybridity are localized at the level of musical values, constraining the semantic and scenic richness of the *gesamtkunstwerk's* openness to the literary, theatrical and filmic. And, if the enduring significance of counterculture's achievement, lies anywhere, it lies here in this unprecedented shift in the re-functioning of popular music as a platform for non-musical values and knowledge. Now, of course, all musics, non-vocal and vocal, produce non-music values; all music makes a claim on the social; musical values and social experience are indivisible and coextensive, that is, produce a sense in which music is:

> simultaneously doing other things – thinking and remembering, feeling, moving/being, and co-operating, co-ordinating, and sometimes colluding with others.[143]

Music-as-discourse and music-as-action converge. However, during the counterculture the production of non-musical values was the outcome of a radically counter-hegemonic process, in which working class and lower middle musicians shaped the creative and collective character of these political 'extra-musical' values. Methodologically and politically, then,

---

143 Tia DeNora, *After Adorno: Rethinking Music Sociology*, Cambridge University Press, Cambridge, 2003, p155

it is important not to let progressive rock be separated from the wider capacities and ambitions of popular music during the counterculture in order to sanctify it for musicology alone. Thus, if this means keeping a focus on the song-form as a core principle, it also means keeping a focus on the multitudinous uses of the song from, cabaret, musical theatre, opera, choral music, to the 'mass song' (Eisler, Weill, Guthrie). For, in these terms, we are in better position to explain the continuities between progressive rock and the heterodox vocal music that preceded it, and, consequently, the continuing impact of 'new folk-thinking' on the broad achievements of the period. And, we are, therefore, in a better position to explain why progressive rock at its best is largely an English phenomenon, given English rock music and folk music's origins.

Van Der Graaf Generator was formed in 1967 at Manchester University, and released their first album, *Aerosol Grey Machine* in 1969. In the following year, they released, *The Least We Can Do Is Wave to Each Other*, the album that begins to define their mature, jarring, discontinuous, sci-fi-operatic, organ and saxophone-based sound (Hugh Banton and David Jackson), with Peter Hammill on vocals and guitar, Nic Potter on bass and Guy Evans on drums. Indeed, *The Least We Can Do Is Wave to Each Other*, is, along with King Crimson's *In the Court of the Crimson King*, of the previous year, one of the defining moments of what will come to be known as progressive rock (the band was formed in London in January 1969 and by July was performing with the Rolling Stones at the massive Hyde Park concert in memory of Brian Jones). Like *In the Court of the Crimson King*, it follows the 'poetic shift' in the new folk-thinking in using the song lyric to create a distinct imaginative world or register (in the case of King Crimson's an allegorical medieval world of illusion and tyranny): Hammill's words and Banton's organ combining, to shape, a gothic, lamentary landscape of ruins and apocalyptic spectres. But unlike *In the Court of the Crimson King*, there is no recourse to countercultural pastoral motifs and folk instrumentation in contrast to the overall driving, operatic and atonal-rock structure; in this respect *H to He Whom Are the Only One* and *Pawn Hearts* are unprecedented in their integral post-rock drama and dynamism. In *In the Court of the Crimson King*, flute (Ian McDonald) and acoustic guitar (Greg Lake) ('I Talk To The Wind,' the middle section of 'Epitaph' 'Moonchild'), however, establishes a dominant tone of lyrical pastoralism, that sits between the bookends of Robert Fripp's fierce and fast post-bebop and stretched atonal guitar lines on the rightly celebrated '21st Century Schizoid Man,' and the mellotron driven grandeur of 'The Court of the Crimson King.' Yet, if this pastoralism (and Pete Sinfield's wan allegorical lyrics) had prevailed overall, the album would not have had the influence it had or sit so squarely at the beginning of progressive rock. The pastoralism is tone-setting, as opposed to a new folk rethinking of voice and instrumentation. It is Fripp's guitar work on '21st Schizoid Man' and the innovative 'symphonic' use of the mellotron, then, that gives the album its critical character, and defines its radical break from the dominant blues-rock idiom of the time. As Fripp says in an interview he conducted for the reissue of *In the Court of the Crimson King* in 2009: "The empowering impulse of Underground Rock, which became Progressive Rock, was the belief that we can change the world; even the act of listening had power."[144]

Yet, if *He to He Whom Are the Only One* and *Pawn Hearts* and *In the Court of the Crimson King*, have quite different relationships to late sixties rock, and therefore assimilate the new folk-thinking, post-bebop and free form jazz, and post-1950s atonality, in quite different ways, they nevertheless share a literary-poetic form, that had largely disappeared from popular music: the song cycle. The song cycle is what critics and audiences in the sixties would tend to call the vocal 'concept' album: a collection of songs – historically poems not written by the composer, set to music – that through their internal relations, or established theme, would form a collective whole, creating a scenic structure for characterization and incident. "Often they were based around a poetic topic: the seasons or months of a year; a collection of flowers or colours; the experience of wandering; a sequence of emotional states."[145] In some instances the song cycle tells a story, in some instances it sets a mood, or creates a space for disparate incidents and ideas. An example of the former would be Serge Gainsbourg's baffling and arch *Histoire de Melody Nelson* (1971) (orchestrated soft, guitar-based, rock, with spoken and sung parts) which tells the story of a rich, middle aged man (Monsieur Gainsbourg!) riding around Paris in his Rolls Royce, who, having knocked an English girl off her bike (Melody Nelson), creepily falls in love with her; and, an example of the latter, is Van Dyke Parks, *Song Cycle*, which we have already mentioned in passing, which contains a series of vignettes of 1960's Californian life. If these are not terribly good advertisements for the use of the modern song cycle (it is as if Gainsbourg and Parks were confusing the song cycle with the song-sequence of the West End or Broadway musical), both King Crimson and Van Der Graaf Generator – but especially Van Der Graaf

---

144 Robert Fripp, Booklet, Reissue of *In the Court of the Crimson King*, Panegyric, 2009.

145 Laura Tunbridge, *The Song Cycle*, Cambridge University Press, Cambridge, 2010

Generator – adopt the song cycle in ways that refocus its connective and critical possibilities. Indeed, the song cycle, in Van Der Graaf Generator provides a bridge to a wider musical framework, in the way that the domestic or salon form of the early song cycle (Franz Schubert, Robert Schumann) in the 1830s and 1840s moves into the public form of the orchestral song cycle at the end of the 19th century (Gustav Mahler). In Van Der Graaf Generator's *Pawn Hearts*, the domestic scale of the song cycle (vocal and piano accompaniment) becomes expressly a modernist resource for a hybrid music-theatre, incorporating, Ornette Coleman type atonality, elements of German *Lieder* and choral music, as well as operatic and sonic 'environmentalism' (Ligeti and Nono). The modernist bardic uplift of the 'new folk-thinking' is given a new sonic platform to work with. This is also evident in the striking first album of Comus, *First Utterance* (1971). Formed in 1969 at Ravensbourne Art College in Bromley, Kent (David Bowie's old alma mater), by Roger Wootton and Glen Goring, Comus are perhaps the only English progressive rock band that extend the heterodox voice-instrumentation possibilities of the 'new folk-thinking' into an innovative post-rock idiom. Employing, viola, violin, choralic voices, flute, acoustic guitar, bassoon, bongos, but *no drums*, the band produces a driving, searing, gothic 'dark folk'-song cycle, in which the threatening scraping of the strings ('Diana') gives way to drifting pastoral acoustic guitar interludes ('Song to Come') and to gentle Japanese inflexions on acoustic guitar ('The Prisoner'), reminiscent of the Hon Kumoi Shiouzhi pentatonic scale. In this respect, the respite of the pastoral is never far away from nature raw in 'tooth and claw' (the grinding, droning and sawing of violin and viola). As Rob Young, puts it: "Comus were nabobs of negativity, prophets disrupting the feast with unwelcome harangues."[146] Wootton's vocals swooped "from a saturnine soprano to a guttural, lecherous goading, shadowed by [Bobbie] Watson's angelic counterpoints and milk-souring disharmonies. Their repertoire was snarled tales of innocence corrupted, brutal ravishment, clinical derangement and murderous gore."[147] After the release of *First Utterance*, Lindsay Cooper joins the band on bassoon for their next, and disappointingly far weaker album, *To Keep From Crying* (1974); she later joins Henry Cow.

And this is precisely what I mean by the *gesamtkunstwerk* space of early English progressive rock. The move out from the traditional song cycle

---

146 Rob Young, *Electric Eden*, op cit, p512

147 Ibid, p509

into a hybrid and scenic musical theatre provides a space for the presentation of voice and instrumentation that enables the singer and band to link and extend the form of songs within a thematic/literary structure across the duration of an album. This does not mean, however, that, *In the Court of the Crimson King* and *H to He Whom am the Only One* and *Pawn Hearts*, take the classical form of the song cycle, in which the hero or heroine undergoes a journey of self-discovery, as in Schubert's *Winterreise* (1828). In this classical form (voice and piano), the cycle is made up of a number of self-sufficient, yet tonally and thematically related lyric poems, in which the journey of self-discovery – represented formally through voice and piano 'wandering' through a number of keys – is resolved at the end by returning to the opening key and home (but in possession of new knowledge or wisdom, particularly on matters of love), in an echo of the sonata. In this sense the cyclical musical form is attached to the chastened development of the poems' 'song voice': the sentimental and restitutive education of the 'lyric-I.' Little of this early Romanticism attaches itself to early English progressive rock's use of the song cycle (unlike in Gainsbourg's neo-Romantic song cycle, which may have something to do with the residual attachment in French popular culture to the chanson as a romantic form). On the contrary, in Hammill's songs, and even in Sinfield's lyrics, there is no narrative of wandering self-development, no attachment on the part of the writer to a spiritual or redemptive journey, no cyclical movement as such, given the fragmentary nature of the 'lyric-I'; connection and integration of elements take a non-developmental and montaged form (in contrast to *Close to the Edge*, which follows the classical song cycle form: at the end the piece the seeker looks down from a mountain on all that he has overcome!). In *Pawn Hearts*, for instance, Hammill's 'lyric-I' passes through various states of disorientation and loss ("I am the lost one, I am the one who crossed through space, or stayed where I was, or didn't exist in the first place"), distinct from any narrative of transformation; indeed, in the final track, the expressly operatic and sci-fi 'Pioneers Over C,' Hammill's 'lyric-I' ends its tribulations 'lost in space.' ("I have no frame"). Similarly, *In The Court of the Crimson King*, Sinfield's 'lyric-I' (or 'troubadour-I' more precisely) is clearly on some journey or remembered journey, ("I've been here and I've been there," 'I Talk to the Wind,' "As I crawl a cracked and broken path," 'Epitaph,' "I walk a road, horizons change," 'The Court of the Crimson King'), yet at the end of the song cycle, the 'lyric-I' remains fixed in the same state of confusion and uncertainty.

This lyric non-developmentalism is, of course, to be expected. These may-be popular songs but they work over, and work through, the de-temporalizations and fragmentary spaces of modernism, particularly Hammill's far more ambitious writing, which is far richer, allusive and demanding than, Sinfield's mytho-pastoralism and constructed 'innocence' and pre-lapsarian tone. This difference, is also reflected in the integrated atonality or post-tonality in Van Der Graaf Generator's reworking of rock structure and instrumentation; in *In the Court of the Crimson King* and *In the Wake of Poseiden* (1970), in contrast, these demands seem largely down to the efforts of Fripp and his desire to restructure the language and repertoire of rock guitar, in an attempt to stretch the prevailing tonalities in a non-standard, dissonant, whole-tone, direction (one of the formal problems of *In the Court of the Crimson King*, is that the influence of Fripp's innovative guitar work is with the exception of '21st Century Schizoid Man,' marginal). This obviously is one of the reasons Fripp eventually reorganizes the band as largely a post-vocal, post-rock 'research unit' in the mid-1970s ('Frippotronics'), in the wake of *Starless and Bible Black* (1974) and *Red* (1974). Nevertheless, both bands use of the song cycle in the late sixties and early seventies produce a distinct scenic frame for the extended song-form, creating a fictive and theatrical whole that exceeds even the usual themed song collections of the time (such as Bowie's *The Rise and Fall of Ziggy Stardust And The Spiders From Mars*, 1972, and *Diamond Dogs*, 1974). *H to He Who Am the Only One* and *Pawn Hearts*, in this sense are the post-rock equivalent of the orchestrated song cycle, extending the simple and intimate interaction of voice and piano, into the greater dynamic and frame of the song cycle as a public and collective experience. Yet it is not Schubert and Mahler or Ligeti (*Atmosphères*, 1961) that stand directly behind *He to He Who Am the Only One* and *Pawn Hearts* – and other ambitious progressive rock of the time – but, of course, *Sgt. Pepper*, with its own particular reading of the European *gesamtkunstwerk*.

Again, so much in these years travel through *Sgt. Pepper*, particularly in the work of those musicians who at some level recognized its novel, integrated approach to different song-forms. *Sgt. Pepper* is not strictly a song cycle, yet in its opening and closing symmetries and interrelated themes, it seems as if, it owes its scale and dynamism to a programmatic aesthetic external to that of pop and rock, and this was incredibly liberating. David Jackson, spoke for many rock musicians of his generation, when he said: "there was this incredible buzz of sheer disbelief [when *Sgt. Pepper* came out]…Suddenly with this astonishing music anything seemed possible."[148] Similarly, the Beatles heterodox use of song-forms also had an immediate impact in avant-garde, new music and post-bebop circles, particularly in the US. Carla Bley also spoke on behalf of many of her generation who were growing disenchanted with free-form jazz, when she said she was astonished on hearing *Sgt. Pepper* in 1967. As Amy C. Beal recalls:

> She began cultivating a musical alliance with what she considered to be her true culture: European and European American music. In particular, she had lost her tolerance for long solos full of emphatic self-expression. With this significant change in attitude, she felt as if she experienced the beginning of a new musical life. Coinciding with these reevaluations, her friend Michael Snow introduced her to the Beatles' newest record, *Sergeant Pepper's Lonely Hearts Club Band*, which had been released on the first day of June 1967, on the eve of the so-called Summer of Love. Snow told Bley that many visual artists were already listening to this record instead of the avant-garde jazz they tended to favor in the past. In particular, Bley remembers Snow playing her the album's last song, "A Day in the Life," and being astounded by what she heard. The sonic adventurousness of the album and the audacity of its larger musical architecture impressed her. The "concept album," a record beyond a set of short, unrelated songs, suggested an intriguing possibility for Bley.[149]

And this possibility was the systematic reintroduction of the song-form into a post-free jazz and new music framework, in opposition to both a Colemanesque free-form 'expressivism' and non-vocal, post-tonal scientism (Pierre Boulez, Milton Babbitt). This does not turn Bley into a progressive rock musician nor does it have any discernible influence on US rock counterculture of the late 1960s. But it does show how wide reflection on the song cycle was during this period as a means, in both popular music and the avant-garde, of shifting frozen allegiances and

---

148 Mick Dillingham. 'Van Der Graaf Generator: The David Jackson Interview, Part One,' *Ptolemaic Terrascope* 2, May 1991, p6

149 Amy C. Beal, *Carla Bley*, University of Illinois Press, Champaign, Illinois, 2011, p34.

reified teleologies. That Bley collaborates with Jack Bruce soon after, drawing on the song cycles of Eisler and Weill as part of a song-focused, yet instrumentally and tonally mobile aesthetic (*Escalator Over the Hill*, 1971), is revealing, then, of how significant *Sgt. Pepper* was in shifting both popular music and avant-garde practices away from various forms of *miniaturism* and narrow disciplinary expectations. Bruce clearly stood in Bley's eyes for something that *Sgt. Pepper* also stood for, or, rather represented something of the Beatles world she could channel. "Bley took *Sergeant Pepper's* [forms] as an open invitation to venture into something more grandiose – program music, and the high expressivity typical of romanticism."[150] *Escalator Over the Hill*, composed with lyricist Paul Haines, a two-hour, non-linear song sequence and jazz interludes, ends on a twenty-seven minutes Ligeti-type buzzing oscillation. Utilizing multiple singers and musicians (including Bruce, ex-Manfred Mann singer Paul Jones, Linda Ronstadt, Charlie Haden, Don Cherry, Gato Barbieri, John McClaughin, and Don Preston), the piece is her own 'holding of forms in tension and cohabitation,' or *gesamtkunstwerk*; and for all its New York jazz scene affectations, noodling and langours, is about as close as the exchange between popular music and the avant-garde gets in the US in the early 1970s to English progressive rock's own post-*Sgt. Pepper* anti-miniaturism.

We might say, therefore, that one of *Sgt. Pepper's* functions, historically, was to both re-establish and rethink notions of the programmatic; re-establish it in popular music in defiance of the particularisms of traditional rock and traditional folk music; and rethink its relations to the post-tonal avant-garde's programmatic indifference to music history and formal heterogeneity. A lot rides on the song-form in progressive rock then. It becomes a space for the rethinking of the popular, the production of new (post-formalist) programmatic content in the avant-garde and a renewed reflection on the extra-musical content and collective or 'communization effects' of popular music as such, in line with the critical horizons of the counterculture as a whole. In this sense the return to the song cycle is not a conservative move, but a return to its dynamic functions as it moves out of its domestic realm at the end of the 19th century: its capacity for voice-instrumentation innovation.

> The once modest song cycle became a potent vehicle
> for lofty ideals: for exploring new methods of text

---

150 Beal, *Carla Bley*, op cit, p40

setting and modes of musical representation, new
vocal and instrumental techniques, new harmonic
territories. In this sense, the song cycle interacted
more actively with changing conceptions of musical
modernity than did any other genre.[151]

Consequently, the use of the song cycle in progressive rock enables a
new complexity and affective space for the song-form. The post-rock
musicianship and literary-scenic ambitions reframes and rearticulates the
spatial extension of 'new folk-thinking' and bardic uplift, within an unprecedented theatrical space.

In this respect, progressive rock continues the post-ethnographic dynamic within late sixties popular music that we noted earlier: with a shift in
class relations in cultural production from below, there is a loosening of
the conservative class and cultural identities of working class and lower-middle class musicians that dramatically reposition the symbolic attachments and affects of 'untrained' musicians to the popular. This transformation is of course very uneven, but even in the largely lower-middle
class and middle class world of progressive rock its effects are still discernible. Progressive rock enables some white working class musicians and
many white lower-middle and middle class musicians, to re-align their
extensive or minimal musical training (self-education) with de-hierar-
chized conception of value and images and practices of a dissident collec-
tivity, defying what is both proper to serious musical ambition (a respect
for the authority of high culture) and the easy companionableness of the
popular. In a mass culture, then, intent on clawing back some of its lost
profit margins in the early 1970s, invariably through the re-pacification
of working class musical production and taste (Status Quo, Slade, Sweet),
this is not be underestimated; progressive rock is that realm of symbolic
and cognitive superfluity and excess that early pop's post-ethnographic critique of working class identity imagined for itself, and helped put
in place. But if the conservative new-*conservatoire* inspired progressive
rock (Yes, ELP, et al) along with some of the more ornamental jazz rock,
sees this new expanded place for experiment as opportunity for assertive
virtuosity and the de-stabilization of cultural hierarchy, it also reaches
– particularly in the commercially successful progressive rock – for an
affirmative and synthetic musicianship and communitarian 'spiritualism'
that de-rationalizes and deflects the aporias and contradictions of music's

---

151 Laura Tunbridge, *Song Cycle*, op cit, p4

relationship to social experience, technique and politics. In other words, this kind of progressive rock falls into the trap of treating late countercultural anti-informality as a musicological *solution* to cultural division, as if fast guitar solos, symphonic grandeur, and "cosmic optimism," or transcendental humanism (leavened by anti-technological rhetoric) could, as an 'integrated or organic whole,' provide a workable and mobile enough framework of engagement with the remaking of the popular and the avant-garde.

What characterizes the progressive rock I have so far foregrounded, then, is the very obverse of this: a sceptical relationship to virtuoso musicianship as a solution to form; a resistance to organic metaphors generally; and a greater emphasis on the relational functions of the tonal and atonal, as opposed to seeing atonality ultimately as needing harmonic correction. Thus, without wanting to capture this kind of progressive rock for a stable tradition of achievement in popular music post-1965 – as if all we are doing here is canon building – this is what the continuation of modernist-literary techniques of indisciplinarity in popular music might look like after Dylan and the Beatles: a *poeisis of disaffirmation*, that continues to take words *and* music seriously.

One can see, therefore, what links Van Der Graaf Generator, King's Crimson's '21st Century Schizoid Man' and Comus' 'Diana' to the integrative hybrid moves of the 'new folk-thinking,' without, thereby weakening what separates this new music from the folk moment as such. Even if the adaptation of the song cycle as a framework for voice/new instrumentation experimentation distinguishes this version of progressive rock from the new folk, there is, nevertheless, a comparable emphasis on indisciplinarity as conflictual and negating. Progressive rock in this form, consequently, uses the scenic and the literary possibilities of the song cycle in ways that are the direct inverse of any "cosmic optimism." Van Der Graaf Generator's, *Pawn Hearts*, for example, is structured as a series of discontinuous and dramatic violent shifts in tone and timbre, in which Hammill's voice appears constantly in a state of stress and destitution, very different from Jon Anderson or Greg Lake in ELP singing 'above the fray' so to speak. This is perhaps why Van Der Graaf Generator had a large following in Italy more than anywhere else, connected as their performances in the country were at some level to the non-sectarian and critical left public culture supported by the PCI during the 1970s, whereas Yes and ELP were incredibly successful on the North American rock arena circuit, drawing on the dying embers of the American 'hippie' counterculture, as it began to mutate into New Ageism. As the American counterculture felt the cold draft of decline, Tolkienesque visions of "cosmic optimism," were a much more commercially palatable vision of English pastoral 'eccentricity' than the drama of selves "who didn't exist in the first place."

Yet, one of the surprises – even striking aporias – of Van Der Graaf Generator/King Crimson/Comus' form of modernist progressive rock is its rejection or indifference to overt political song-forms derived from 'new folk-thinking' and post-Dylanesque bardic uplift. The mythic, apocalyptic, and the allegorical, outweigh any interest in the diurnal detail provided by the everyday ballad or movementist 'mass song.' Indeed, modernist-literary progressive rock may draw on a European legacy of the 19th century song cycle and *Lied*, opera, *musique concrète* and modern atonal music, for its post-rock bearings, but it had little use for the political modernism of Brecht, Weill and Eisler, where as we have seen, this music had some leverage in jazz in the early 1970s (where Weill and Eisler's music ultimately had its origins in the 1920s; Weill, for instance famously collaborated with Ira Gershwin – *Lady in the Dark,* 1941). This omission has much to do with the broader political bearings of progressive rock and the counterculture generally. The critique of waged labour and the nuclear family, of traditional masculinities and industrial city living, made it difficult for those singers and writers engaged in extending the countercultural scope of the song-form to find any working relationship with a partisan political *aesthetic*, no matter how heterodox. What we have called the demise of that spirit of learn, learn, learn, and the breakdown between the lyric 'I' and the 'people,' is heightened in progressive rock, in its modernist architecture of social crisis. The narration and symbolization of collective experience (the alienated 'I' of narrative non-development) is grounded first and foremost in the critique of abstraction (of modernity), as opposed to reflection on history and collective struggle. This shift of course has deep cultural and political roots, and as such whatever appears to be lost as part of this process, is outweighed by its apparent gains: there are other struggles over the sign than those contained by images of labour; the representation of class struggle for the working class musician is always a reminder of their own subordination as musicians to the wage-form and their extra-musical status as cheap labour, and, as such, this feels like a defeat, as much as an act of solidarity, certainly when the musician is compelled to repeat it. This is something that Adorno was particular sensitive to in his own ambiguous relationship to the cognitive possibilities of the song-form. This is why pop and rock during the counterculture years were so liberatory for professionally active working class and lower-middle class musicians; it briefly relieved working class musicians of the speech of *being* workers, of being captured by the image of their own labours, a privilege of course always possessed by the non-working class musician and artist. Even in the early 1950s one sees how key this is to workers' struggle. In parallel with the reflections we have already noted in Bob Darke's 'resignation memoir,' *The Communist Technique in Britain*, there are two remarkable scenes from Paul Dickson's documentary drama *David* (1951) shown at the Festival of Britain (1951), that highlights this expectation.

Set in a Welsh mining village it follows the daily life of an aging school caretaker, ex-miner and part-time poet Dafydd Rhys, based on the ex-miner and amateur poet D.R. Griffiths. One flashback scene shows the twelve years old Rhys/Griffiths sitting down in the pit to eat his lunch and being handed a book by an older comrade, seated next to other comrades who are also reading; and a contemporary scene of late-night drunkenness in which a miner-trombonist – 'Evans the Trombone' – is shown leading a group of revelers across the village church graveyard. The structures of autodidacticism are quite different in the communist/non-conformist Welsh mining valleys than in the industrial communities North and South of England, even in the 1950s. Raymond Williams notes this about his time at Cambridge before WWII: he wasn't there as a lone scholar, but as a representative of the (Welsh) working class. "I had a very strong sense…of having my own people behind me in the enterprise."[152] Yet the film makes clear – even under the weight of its own romanticism – that individual autodidacticism is not enough. If progressive rock, then, is not the teleological outcome of popular music under the sway of the counterculture, nevertheless, it represents that continuing transfer of the ideal of 'autonomy' in the counterculture to relatively unschooled musicians.

Yet, if this kind of literary progressive rock finds its modernist bearings outside of the legacy of the political aesthetics of the 1930s – in a way broadly Adornian – in its final days English progressive rock and the English counterculture, in the work of Henry Cow, belatedly recasts the 'mass song' within an avant-garde setting as if as the corpus of work on the song-form in progressive rock had now finally a chance to reassess the

---

152 Raymond Williams, *Politics and Letters: Interviews with* New Left Review, NLB, London, 1979, p37

wider modernist bearings of the song-form from the recent past. That this doesn't last long, and doesn't fulfill its potential, doesn't detract from the heuristic possibilities of the reconnection. In a retroactive recovery of the avant-garde culture of learn, learn, learn, Henry Cow, reconnect the post-1965 popular song-form to its movementist pre-war origins. In this they step back beyond the new folk and Dylan to the legacy of Brecht, Weill and Eisler. If, I have made clear why this break with the past was necessary in order for the counterculture to effect the inclusion of workers and the lower-middle class as musicians and listeners in the countercultural remaking of the popular, nevertheless, it is still extraordinary to note how the 'song of struggle' and the 'song of experience from below' were removed from most forms of Western popular music after the late 1950s demise of the traditional folk revival. It is therefore too simplistic to talk about the Cold War and high cultural condescension/exclusion as reasons for this. Rather, more crucially from the early 1960s there was a growing sense that formally, the images and rituals and practices of class belonging could not alone secure the cultural emancipation of workers. The affective attachment of workers to techniques, practices and images outside of the world of waged-labour, thus, contained an undisclosed utopianism external to the struggles of labour itself. This is why the inclusion of working class and the lower-middle musicians in creative alliance in the remaking of the popular in the counterculture in the 1960s, is a *productive* transformation from below, a release of the collective energies of anti-pathos in the revolutionary spirit of the modernist culture of the time. In periods of class flux and working class self-assertion – of the reordering of hierarchies – struggle as creative repossession overrides struggle as representation, or certainly repositions it, as in the US in the mid-to-late 1930s and revolutionary China in the 1940s. And this is why *Sgt.Pepper* is so important politically. It was a manifesto for working class *creativity*. In this sense, then, the philosophical avatars of May 68 were right: these years of transformation from below made the old collective images and allegiances, if not redundant, then at least delimiting.

Yet, nevertheless pathos and history are not that easily dismissed or dissolved, particularly so when revolutionary or emancipatory struggle ebbs away into amnesia or cynicism. Pathos comes to be seen as a way of reflecting on the recent past and its achievements and failures, of reconnecting feeling to representation. One can see, therefore, why the 'mass song' in Henry Cow pops up in 1974-5: these songs are not just a reengagement with 'songs of struggle' but a lament on the gathering crisis of the counterculture. That is, the politics of these songs speak as much to the crisis of the place of modernist or avant-garde progressive rock and the legacy of 1930s political modernism in the counterculture as to the counterculture itself.[153] Thus, if these songs (such as the gorgeous and stirring, 'Beautiful as the Moon, Terrible as an Army With Banners,' and 'Living in the Heart of the Beast' from *In Praise of Learning* [1975] written by Chris Cutler and Fred Frith, and Tim Hodgkinson respectively) reestablish the partisan role of pathos as historical consciousness as part of the armoury of the modernist song-form, this return does not escape pathos itself. That is, we would be misunderstanding the band's recovery of this lost modern tradition – a tradition absent, on the whole, from the great musical transformations of the English counterculture – if we see it as a call to arms in desperate days. This is because the tradition that they repossess here is a tradition whose would-be populist political credentials was subject to critique at its inception, certainly by Adorno, and which has been internalized in the very avant-garde practice of the band.

There are a number of things going on here therefore: obviously, the re-establishment of a popular movementist aesthetic, and the rethinking – again – of the song-form in an avant-garde, progressive rock/countercultural context (after Weill; after Guthrie), but also, the building up of some critical distance between the use of the 'mass song' form and the idea of a mass politics through music. There is, consequently, given, the formal ambition of 'Beautiful as the Moon…,' and 'Living in the Heart of the Beast' a detectable antagonism to the idea of the populist song-form as a 'class' antidote to the avant-garde, formalism, theoretical music, atonality, etc., in the wake of Cornelius Cardew's post-Stockhausen apostasy in the early 1970s. Cardew's awful, risible recourse to standard popular tunes ('Croppy Boy,' from *Four Pieces on Ireland and Other Pieces*, 1974)) as a possible route for the trained avant-garde musician back into the affections of a popular working class audience, is remarkable for its delusion in a period when working class musicians *did* have a working class audience for their (popular) songs. In a way Cardew's early 1970s ('rightist'/'ultraleftist') Maoism repeats the ethnographic trap of MacColl and Henderson; they all want a working class audience without workers' negation of their own proletarian identity. We might say, then, at the end-days of the English counter-culture, that one of the achievements of Henry Cow is to re-foreground some of the key fractures in music and

---

153 For a discussion of the tensions of this legacy and the politics of progressive rock, see Chris Cutler, *File Under Popular: Theoretical and Critical Writings on Music*, November Books, London, 1985

politics within modernism between song-form and non-vocal music, between music as action and music as cognition. In this sense, their music offers further scope for reflection on the remaking of the popular and the fate of modernist-literary progressive rock.

Formed at Cambridge University in 1968, Henry Cow are the only progressive rock band in the early 1970s in England to draw on the Brecht-Weill and Brecht-Eisler legacy, shifting the modernist-literary focus of late progressive rock in the English counterculture away from the critique of modernity as such, to an explicit critique of capitalism. In this, if there is a residual post-Beatles countercultural Dadaism attached to their musical allegiances, they none the less strip out all the mythopoeic, apocalyptic and cosmic machinery of modernist-lyrical progressive rock. This is initially the outcome of their post-rock free-form formation, but also crucially the direct result of the band (Fred Frith, Tim Hodgkinson, John Greaves, Lindsay Cooper, Chris Cutler), joining up in 1974 with the post-rock band Slapp Happy, whose members Dagmar Krauze, Anthony Moore and Peter Blegvad (who left after *In Praise of Learning*), brought with them an intimacy with 1920s German political aesthetics and the 'mass song' song cycle. The ensuing assimilation and collaboration radically changes the post-rock and free form dynamic of the group, from an instrumentalist ensemble, close in spirit to the growing influence of jazz rock in progressive rock, to that of an avant-garde musical theatre. And absolutely definitional of this is Krauze's voice, with its Germanic intonation, and air of 1920s Berlin cabaret, particularly on Slapp Happy and Henry Cow's earlier collaboration *Desperate Straights* ('Some Questions About Hats,' 'Bad Alchemy,' 1975). With Krauze fronting the band, the music shifts its cognitive focus and timbre; song and voice re-channels the band's avant-garde socialist cultural politics through a melancholic, yet soaring and operatic exaltation. But if this move is undoubtedly rooted in the aesthetics of the 1920s, there is nothing antiquarian about the songs, no revivalist tone nor evidence of historical deference – although in 1988 in *Tank Battles*, she records, in a kind of classical homage, an extensive selection of Eisler's songs, including the gorgeous, mournful 'Song of a German Mother.' As such, their metric innovation, particularly in 'Beautiful as the Moon…' has little in common formally with Weill or Eisler. Indeed, Weill's, quasi-marching rhythms and Eisler's *Lied* style, seem almost mundane in comparison. There is therefore, no sense that this is a regressive, pseudo-populist move, a Cardewian sop to some fantasy of the 'mass song' as a 'mass politics.' Indeed, Henry Cow's

musical and lyrical sense of the political in the song-form remains defiantly modernist.

> We exchange words, coins, movements – para-
>   lysed in loops
> of care that we hoped could knot a world still.
> Mere words, toothless, ruined now, bulldozed into
>   brimming pits
> – who has used them how? Grammar book that
>   lies wasted:
> conflux of voices rising to meet, and fall,
> empty, divided, other…
>
> Clutching at sleeves the wordless man exposes
>   his failure:
> smiling, he hurls a wine glass, describing his sad-
>   ness twisted
> into mere form: shattered in a glass, he's changed…
> Now dare he seize the life before him and discom-
>   pound it in
> sulphurous confusion and give it to the air?
> He's rushing to find where there's a word of
>   liquid syntax
> - signs let slip in a flash: "clothes of chaos are my rage!"
> he shrieks in tatters, hunting the eye of his own storm.
>
> ('Beautiful as the Moon…')

The song-form, therefore, was still a source of extended possibilities, still
a site where 'politics' might be done, even if the political effects of such
experimentation were unpredictable and unstable. Another significant
factor in this shift is the impact of Captain Beefheart's radical, guitar-ori-
ented, atonal, reworking of the blues-rock song-form in *Trout Mask
Replica* and *Lick My Decals Off, Baby*. These two albums were an enormous influence on Fred Frith, the band's guitarist. As Frith was to say in
an article he wrote on Beefheart for the *New Musical Express* in 1974, the
year that Henry Cow supported Beefheart and the Magic Band on tour
in Britain:

> It is always alarming to hear people playing together
> and yet not in any recognizable rhythmic pattern.

> This is not free music; it is completely controlled all
> the time, which is one of the reasons it's so remark-
> able – forces that usually emerge in improvisation
> are harnessed and made constant, repeatable.[154]

Henry Cow's performances were not 'controlled all the time' – free-form de-structuring remained key to the overall character of the music – how-ever, the band certainly saw in the tightly controlled metric changes of Beefheart's songs one way of reinvigorating and renewing the declara-tive directness of the 1920s mass song. The jerky shifts of metre, yet sweeping continuity of 'Beautiful as the Moon…' is clearly marked by what Beefheart, Bill Harkleroad, Jeff Cotton, Mark Boston, John French and Victor Hayden achieve on *Trout Mask Replica*. Indeed, the spiky, twisting, atonal lines of Harkleroad's scintillating guitar on *Trout Mask Replica*, provide a striking precedent for Frith's guitar style, which switch-es between angular spurts and splurts and the use of rhythm as a lead line. Thus, Henry Cow's songs do not revisit the Brecht/Weill and Eisler's 'mass song' to the letter: they open up their legacy to a post-rock recon-struction, in much the same way Beefheart disorders the components of the standard American blues/rock song.

> We don't make political statements in a passive
> way…[we are doing] what most so-called revolu-
> tionary artists aren't doing, which is expanding the
> form we're working in, which I think is the most
> important…[155]

The result is a Henry Cow song-form that sits within the now standard attenuated form of progressive rock instrumentation; the songs are parts of an extended, instrumental whole. But the songs also have a formal in-tegrity in themselves; they are not simply stitched into the instrumenta-tion as details, but are crucial to the scenic structure of the music overall. In this they owe far more to Van Der Graaf Generator's drama-setting links between voice and instrumentation. Yet, these are songs without the 'lyric-I,' songs in which the drama of self and other is subordinate to

---

154 Fred Frith, 'Antennae Jimmy Semens: "Dali's Car."' *New Musical Express*, 1974, re-printed in *The Lives and Times of Captain Beefheart*, compiled by David Britton, Babylon Books, Manchester, 1977, p57

155 Fred Frith, quoted in John Wickes, *Innovations in British Jazz, Vol 1., 1960-1980*, Soundworld, Chelmsford, 1999, p175

the pathos of struggle and class-consciousness. Nevertheless, the songs avoid demotic observation and detail. In contrast to Guthrie, and early Dylan, and keeping with the modernist literary metaphysics of progressive rock, the pathos of struggle remains largely abstract. In this sense the songs are not so much popular 'mass songs' at all, as songs that draw on the partisan voice and lamentation of Brecht and Weill and Brecht and Eisler's songs, in order to create a political tenor or theatrical affect. That is, the band borrows the tenor of these songs for their rich historical and semantic tone, that fact, that these are first and foremost communist songs of *struggle in defeat*. This, indeed, is the character of their signifying power; this is why Eisler's use of the *Lied* form is so compelling, it fills the romantic origins of the form with a terrible sense of loss and attrition (most of the songs – the 'Hollywood song-book' as they are known – were written in exile in the US in the early 1940s).

The Brecht, Weill and Eisler legacy, therefore, becomes a way of giving the pathos of struggle, as the political and countercultural struggle wanes in the early 1970s, a historical connectedness and solidarity. So, in the light of my remarks above, these are songs of crisis in a form that deliberately pushes the would-be radical attachments of the English counterculture into an expressly internationalist direction. As I have stressed throughout this book the idea that the popular music of the English counterculture was largely in thrall to American popular music is a myth. In fact, most ambitious music of the period – led by the example of the Beatles – resisted the clutches of commercial Anglo-American popular music in favour of European and global music, defining the 'Englishness' of the music as a space where this might happen; a space where heterodox modes of native English music (folk, choral, modern classical), might facilitate this exchange. And this is why the belated impact of modernism in English popular culture between 1965-1975 is so powerful, because it successfully destroys – from below – the professional and managerial English cultural provincialism of the interwar years, that sanctioned the middle class's control of a nativist high culture as a manifestation of 'good sense,' and its judgement on working class investment in popular culture as a manifestation of failed (feminine) or ersatz taste. Popular music under countercultural working class and lower middle class indisciplinarity, becomes, in contestation of this, a space for all kinds of productive hybridities. Yet, as I have also stressed, this breakdown of cultural borders was not framed by any explicit revolutionary avant-gardism; the neo-dadaism and Surrealism that transformed English popular culture and high culture in these years and the meaning of indisciplinarity, was mostly stripped of its European and revolutionary cultural context and political complexities. With a few exceptions the counterculture's mediation of modernism and the avant-garde in England, was shorn of its European radical and (anti-Stalinist) communist determinates.

So, what we find in Henry Cow is something of an anomaly: a moment when progressive rock and the countercultural find a way into post-rock forms through an explicit politicized and European avant-garde context, in which Brecht and Weill and Eisler are the focus of formal and political interest, as opposed to Duchamp, Tzara and Breton. And this is perhaps why the band represents one of the more exacting manifestations of that late flowering of anti-informality in the counterculture in England. The pathos of the songs combined with the anti-pathos of the free-form and post-rock musical architectonics produce a *gesamtkunstwerk* mobility of means and ends reminiscent of Brecht's theatre, in which pathos and anti-pathos are never far apart. This does not mean, that Henry Cow manage as a progressive rock band to neatly join up the musicological and political dots, and therefore point us towards a satisfying resolution to our analysis of song-form and the counterculture. Henry Cow do not get the song-form/instrumentation, pathos/anti-pathos mix 'right' so to speak. They don't give us a determinate materialist musicology as opposed to an indeterminate "cosmic optimism." However, they do allow the song-form to recover some of that older movementist energy, albeit reshaped in post-ethnographic and bardic ways that opens other possibilities and connections. In this *Trout Mask Replica* and *Lick My Decals Off, Baby*, are closer to this shift and to the preoccupations of late progressive rock in England than we might initially think. Thus, there is a way of looking at Captain Beefheart's early songs as a kind of avant-garde movementism. Captain Beefheart's neo-Beat and fractured songs of ecological crisis, social entropy, the empty rituals of commodity culture, animal welfare, form an extended Robert Creeley-like modernist song cycle across *Trout Mask Replica* and *Lick My Decals Off, Baby*, in which Beefheart's voice takes on a growling, bardic propheticism.

> Space-age couple
> Why do you hustle 'n bustle?
> Why don't you drop your cool tom-foolery 'N shed
>   your nasty jewelry?
> Cultivate the grounds
> They're the only ones around.

Space-age couple Why don't you flex your magic
   muscle?
Hold a drinking glass up t' your eye after you've
Scooped up a little of the sky
'N it ain't blue no more.
What's on the leaves ain't dew no more.

('Space-age Couple')

What is perhaps extraordinary in this light is that reputedly Beefheart's favourite record – *favourite*, not one of his favourite – was A.L. Lloyd's and Ewan MacColl's *Blow Boys Blow* (1960) a collection of English sea shanties sung by Lloyd and MacColl. Zappa lent it to him, and he never gave it back. The idea for the cappella song 'Orange Claw Hammer' off *Trout Mask Replica* may "well have sprung from this root, as although the song is narrative, the tune is in simple, repetitive cadences reminiscent of a sea shanty."[156]

The idea of Beefheart, then, as a Creeleyite, Howlin' Wolf obsessed, lover of English traditional songs, puts an interesting swerve not only on the shared concerns of English and American musicians during the late 1960s, but on the place and post-ethnographic treatment of the traditional song-form in the counterculture. Beefheart's songs offer a similar attempt at the modernist refiguration of the traditional song-form to the English 'new folk-thinking' and progressive rock, even if Beefheart is much closer to his sources than the English singer-songwriters. He brings bardic uplift and modernist disorderliness to bear on the blues song and folk song. Indeed, in *Trout Mask Replica* and *Lick My Decals Off, Baby*, with their famously 'scored' atonalities, and brisk changes in metre, there is a clear affinity with the anti-informality of late English progressive rock, a resistance to traditional rock-blues companionableness, as if Beefheart's sense of what he wanted was far closer to the modernist-literary ambitions of the English counterculture than anything contemporary American rock culture could provide (including Zappa), even though he had no interest in the extended, attenuated song-form – most of Beefheart's songs are two or three minutes long.

This affinity with the minoritarian moves of the English counterculture is reflected in the sustained reception his work received in Britain in the

---

156 Mark Barnes, *Captain Beefheart: The Biography*, Omnibus Press, London, 2011, p97

early 1970s: *Lick My Decals Off, Baby* managed to reach No 20 in the album charts in 1971, unprecedented for anything of comparable difficulty. Revealingly none of his albums released in the US ever broke into the charts. Consequently, we might say that Beefheart and the Magic Band, if not strictly Anglophiles, were critical allies of an English-driven re-functioning of the traditional song-form. And as such their work made a great deal of sense in a situation where the song-form was being stretched and beguilingly expanded; and when Beefheart's later work didn't live up to the expectations of the early work, his supporters in Britain were concerned and disappointed that the innovations had not been sustained. Thus, knowing that he carried on the spirit of MacColl's rendition of traditional English songs through the early years makes his own programmatic and avant-garde encounter with the traditional song, not just poignant, obviously, but musicologically compelling. It as if all the key breakthroughs in the popular music of the counterculture were dealing with the same problem: *how to critique the traditional song, without leaving it behind and moving onto non-vocal music.* Because, if the revival of traditional song-forms were no longer possible confronted as they were with the exigencies of rock music and the avant-garde, the refusal of the song-form was catastrophic in terms of politics, movementist or otherwise. And this is why Henry's Cow's reconnection to Brecht, Weill and Eisler in the early 1970s in an avant-garde countercultural context, in a way that is critically engaged as opposed to nostalgic, opens up again all the old, longstanding wounds about the respective character of the popular and the avant-garde that Adorno did so much to frame in the modern period.

This is not the point to give a lengthy discursus on Adorno's theory of music; this is not the kind of book where it is warranted. However, Adorno's analysis of the song-form and popular culture hang over the achievements of the counterculture, insofar as the achievements of the counterculture defy Adorno's sociology and musicology. It therefore makes sense to bring – briefly at least – some further theoretical reflections to bear on the counterculture's extension of the song-form. Because if it is songs that have defined the popular in music in the modern period, it is the re-functioning of the song-form in the counterculture that defines the remaking of the popular (and its audience), something that Adorno had little concern for.

In his much discussed and critiqued 'On the Social Situation of Music' (1932), Adorno makes clear what he thinks of popular song and any ambitions it might have for claims to seriousness.[157] The popular song – or light music as he calls it – is "anal" and "narcissistic"[158] insofar as it subordinates itself to the most restrictive and banal harmonic-formal relations in order to win the easy affections of its audience. It "inclines to smile at itself in order to pass by without being challenged."[159] The hit popular song, in particular, is the most alienated of all music in society:

> it no longer expresses anything of social misery and contradiction, but forms rather in itself one single contradiction to this society. This it does by falsifying the cognition of reality through the satisfaction of desires which it grants to man. He is forced away from reality and divorced from both music and social history.[160]

Popular songs become fetish objects, then, forbidding analysis at the expense of feeling aligning themselves, without qualms, to existing consciousness. Adorno calls this objectivist or "use" music: music that attempts to make the listener believe they are part of a living community, and consequently, invites a fantasy of belonging, no matter how spectral, over and above any real and authentic community. Adorno, therefore, makes little concession to the adaptation of the popular song on the left. Even if in this instance this is "elevated"[161] use-music, it likewise subordinates musical cognition to easy affect and fantasies of community. However, this argument is not un-nuanced; he is not blind to the achievement of Brecht and Weill's and Brecht and Eisler's songs, acknowledging their work as a break with the fetishization he maps out. He recognizes that through their use of montage – of musical and literary re-contextualization – their music introduces a modernist disaffirmation into the space of the song, "unmasking" "common compositional means" – which he calls intriguingly a version of "Surrealism."[162] Indeed, in Brecht and

---

157 Theodor W. Adorno, 'On the Social Situation of Music' (1932), in *Essays on Music*, ed., Richard Leppert, trans Susan H. Gillespie, University of California Press, Berkeley and Los Angeles, 2002

158 Ibid, p432 & p431

159 Ibid, p427

160 Adorno, op cit, p425

161 Ibid, p408

162 Ibid, p409

Weill's *Threepenny Opera* and *Mahogany*, these techniques are "admirable."[163] They

> sketch innovations of the opera theater in the sudden illumination of moments which simultaneously turn dialectically against the possibility of the opera per se. It is beyond question that Weill's music is today the only music of genuine social-polemic impact.[164]

Similarly, he recognizes that the communal achievement and "agitator value"[165] of Eisler's choruses is "beyond question"[166] Eisler, the favoured pupil of Schoenberg, is the "most consequent"[167] of all the proletarian-aligned composers of the present. Hence, given the self-imposed character of the music and political demands of the times, only "utopian-idealistic thinking could demand in its place a music internally suited to the function of the proletariat, but incomprehensible to the proletariat."[168] Yet, if he concedes some ideological ground to Weill and Eisler's re-functioning of the song-form – to its scenic extension we might say – he nevertheless rejects the broader formal and subjective possibilities of the popular song as a whole. As "soon as music retreats from the front of direct action, where it grows reflective and establishes itself as artistic form, it is obvious that the structures produced cannot hold their own against progressive bourgeois production."[169] In Adorno's language the modern song-form places fetters upon the musical productive forces. And Adorno is right, of course. The song-form cannot carry the weight of musical expressive-subjectivity and progression, irrespective of the introduction of modernist inflexions. However, he is 'right' for the wrong reasons, based, as his reasons are on false premises. Thus, there are a number of partial musical assessments and sociological reifications that are at work here that need clarification.

Firstly: Adorno has too narrow an understanding of "use" and consciousness consequent upon his ontological commitment to the immanent-aesthetic development of modern music derived from Schoenberg.

---

163 Ibid

164 Ibid

165 Ibid, p411

166 Ibid, p410

167 Ibid, p411

168 Ibid

169 Adorno, op cit, p411

That is, Adorno's defence of Schoenberg's subject-expressive mode of composition – of "extreme variation and through-construction"[170] – channels musical cognition into a very narrow band of attention and listener-competence. Thus, given Adorno's empirically undifferentiated account of fetishization of music under mass culture and the culture industry, this cognition carries with it an unbearable ideological burden as a negative model of praxis. The attentiveness of the listener, demanded by Schoenberg's immanent-aesthetic model, takes on teleological finality in which all other claims to music-praxis and "use" seem compromised and submissive by comparison. The relationship between critical cognition in music and community is abstracted from the actual multiple, conflicted and unstable uses of music in people's lives. Gaining pleasure and solace from a popular song, does not necessarily turn the listener into a mass cultural dupe or model capitalist citizen; it can transform a moment of reflection into action, as Weill and Eisler knew. Similarly, listening to music that has removed those "combinations that don't go to their familiar destinations," to quote Milton Babbitt,[171] or that have removed the usual crutches of the diatonic (Adorno), do not automatically open up listening to sustainable critique and the expectation of a 'new commonality' (Babbitt); they can just as easily lead to melancholy and resignation and to aesthetic indifference. As Tia DeNora argues:

> In short, Adorno's socio-musical landscape is sparsely populated…we are not offered a sufficient view of people *doing* things, that is, of actors caught up in the contingencies and practical exigencies of the local spheres of action. All action in Adorno is *post facto*; it is primarily seen once it has congealed in musical form, composition. It may be an exaggeration but with a grain of truth to say that the only process to which Adorno actually attends is the process as exemplified in musical form.[172]

In this sense Adorno's weakness does not lie in pointing out the subjective-expressive limits of popular music – which are real enough; there would have been no sixties counterculture without musicians taking on

---

170 Ibid, p401

171 Milton Babbitt, *Words About Music*, eds., Stephen Dembski and Joseph N. Strauss, University of Wisconsin, Madison, 1987, p167

172 Tia DeNora, *After Adorno*, op cit, p25

this principle actively at some level – but rather in assuming that critical use values can only be sustained by the development of an immanent method, in which the resistance to the mobilization of emotion and affect necessarily prevents regression and false community. This is why his assessment of the popular song and Weill and Eisler in 'On the Social Situation of Music' go to the very heart of my defence of the expanded countercultural song-form here. For what underwrites Adorno's assessment of objectivism and use-music is an undisclosed Caecilian prejudice against the sonorous voice, as a destabilizing influence on 'true' community. But whereas the Caecilians called for a return to the purity of the Gregorian chant in order to rid the Catholic worshiper/listener of distracting affects, Adorno sees the voice freed, or in excess of, the immanent-aesthetic demands of non-vocal music as complicit with an egregious weakening of the listener's autonomy. We need to read Eisler, therefore, sharply against Adorno's assessment of the song-form, if we are to establish a more dynamic account of the popular and a post-Schoenbergian immanent-aesthetic or concept of the avant-garde. For in Eisler there is a clearer view of the multiple use values of the popular and the demands of an immanent-aesthetic, and, accordingly, a more direct understanding of the production and reception of music in its social contexts. We might say, consequently, that whereas Adorno pushes Brecht out of his understanding of music and use-value after Schoenberg, Eisler brings Brecht and the legacy of Schoenberg into fruitful tension, as a productive, modernist site of the popular.

In his interviews with Hans Bunge from the late 1950s and early 1960s Eisler recognizes a similar cultural problem to that of Adorno: the popular easily renders listeners susceptible to authoritarian forms of cultural regression. Music, cognition and social experience are intertwined, and therefore listening is not 'innocent.'[173] But this does not thereby mean that musical form is simply a 'reflection' of the social. On the contrary, music is *constitutive* of the social, that is, its musicological and formal choices are indivisible from claims on modes of extra-musical sociality – music's collective and social function in the world; and therefore, as discourse and action, it is a site of conflicted forces and identifications.

---

173 Hanns Eisler, *Brecht, Music and Culture* [1975], Hanns Eisler in Conversation with Hans Bunge, ed, and trans. by Sabine Berendse and Paul Clements, Bloomsbury, London, 2014. See also the early writings: *Hanns Eisler: A Rebel in Music: Selected Writings*, ed and intro, Manfred Grabs, trans. by Marjorie Meyer, Kahn & Averill, London, 1999

Adorno and Eisler are in relative agreement on this. But where they differ is how and under what terms, and to what ends, this sociality enters music. On 'what side' is music to resolve this antinomy between the popular and the immanent-aesthetic method? In the end, there is only one answer for Adorno as we have noted: there are strict limits to what music's sociality can legitimately accomplish, before the immanent-aesthetic demands of attentive-listening are jeopardized.[174] For Eisler, though, this split is a false, even idealist, problem. In an additional dialectical move, he rejects the Adornian notion that the popular and the immanent-aesthetic are simply torn halves of a whole. Rather, the immanent–aesthetic is *itself* split open by social contradiction, that is, by the everyday demands and expectations of people's uses of music.

> This metaphysical, blind belief in 'the development of music' produces results, which are entirely detached from the social circumstances of the people! If only Adorno would understand once and for all that music is made by people for people – and that even if it develops, it is not abstract, but can be connected in some way to social conditions…[175]

And this is why Eisler does not privilege non-vocal music over and above the song-form or the song-form over and above non-vocal music. As he was to declare on the 10th Anniversary of Schoenberg's death: "We don't want to proceed dogmatically. We don't want to withhold anything valuable from the new youth."[176] Yet, he recognizes, contra Adorno, that the song-form, given its historical place in the production of emancipatory and critical thought and popular experience defines a kind of elevated relationship to the political and extra-musical, that non-vocal music (certainly post-Schoenbergian atonality) cannot achieve, certainly in conditions where close listening is so rare and attenuated. "I know how important…song cycles are in the history of music and what significant role they can play."[177] "Music without words is not a natural phenomenon

---

174 Theodor Adorno, *Quasi una Fantasia: Essays on Modern Music* [1963], translated by Rodney Livingstone, Verso, London and New York, 1992

175 Hanns Eisler, *Brecht, Music and Culture,* op cit, pp14-15

176 Eisler quoted in Günter Mayer, 'Arnold Schöenberg im Urteil Hanns Eisler's,' *Beiträge zur Musikwissenschaft,* No 16, 1976, p209

177 Eisler, *Brecht, Music and Culture,* op cit, p32

but a historical one…"[178] 'Autonomous' or 'pure' music – concert music – only really begins after 1750. And, as he says, reflecting on the popular and Schoenberg:

> I gradually develop such an aversion to the whole system [mass culture] when by chance I hear three bars by, for example Schoenberg, I suddenly think they are the greatest expressions of humanity. Why? Because with Schoenberg there will at least be an expression of grief or lamentation, not all this liveliness, this false enthusiasm, this pathetic zest for life expressed in a waltz, or a jolly polka – nor, indeed, the foolishness of my young colleagues who, with the best intentions try to write something for the working class movement. It is simply unbearable. So, here is a serious challenge for our people: to try to write in popular genres that don't have this terrible, hackneyed banality, this conformity to the past of which Brecht was acutely aware.[179]

Recorded in 1958 this interview could almost be a manifesto for the English counterculture. But perhaps more significantly for our arguments is its critical and political tenor. As he emphasizes a few pages later, discussing the Frankfurt School philosopher Ludwig Marcuse's book on pessimism, *Pessimismus. Ein Stadium der Reife* (1953),[180] Marcuse, "was on to something there: that pessimism is the best. Optimism is bland, pessimism is the best. Thus humanity only comes into the foreground when you're a pessimist."[181] Given that Eisler was living in the GDR and that these interviews were broadcast on GDR state radio this is extraordinary, but there again, this is not so far from the temper of Brecht's revolutionary realism. And this is why we should emphasize how differently expressed these feelings are musicologically by Eisler compared to Adorno. Like Adorno, Eisler is working through some of the class-based ethnographic problems attached to "use" music that also preoccupy the early rock and pop critics of the folk revival in England. Like Adorno, Eisler in these interviews has little time for the clichés of commitment

---

178 Ibid, p139

179 Ibid, p14

180 Ludwig Marcuse, *Pessimismus. Ein Stadium der Reife*, Rowohlt Verlag, Berlin, 1953

181 Hanns Eisler, *Brecht, Music and Culture,* op cit, p18

in music; they serve only to link partisanship to aesthetic reaction, and to pre-modernist organicist fantasies and tonal banalities. But these reservations – and his refusal of political-musical vanguardism ("Over-politicizing in the arts leads to aesthetic barbarism,")[182] – possess a different kind of moral authority to that of Adorno, given that they are spoken *within* a movementist framework. They appear as the outcome of struggle and praxis as opposed to abstract rationalization, the result of an *engaged* rather than an academic post-ethnographic aesthetics. Consequently, this allows his reflections on the popular to live critically *inside* modernism, as opposed to facing it or hovering on its borders.

There is a sense therefore, that Eisler sees the song-form and the song cycle in particular, as the Ur-form of music's dialectical encounter with its limits and possibilities and with the poetic. In this spirit he quotes Friedrich Hölderlin's magnificent line, as a defining motif for the social function of words and music: "Although our songs are frail, they belong to the life we want."[183] And maybe this is why Eisler was so impressed by Brecht's "huge musicality"[184] as much as by his poetry. He saw Brecht as someone who contributed more than simply words to his songs. He contributed a particular *musical tone* through the words. And perhaps, in turn, this has something to do with Brecht's guitar playing! Extraordinarily for an amateur German musician in the 1930s Brecht played the guitar, when guitar playing was a rarity, even in professional jazz circles. But then again it almost makes sense: it provides another connection to the vernacular and the voice, to the ballad and lament that shape the pathos of his and Weill's early musical-theatre. It also conjures up an image of the great setter-of-other-words to music composing a few lines to a poem by his beloved Villon, and playing it to Eisler, in exile in London, in Eisler's flat on Abbey Road, trying to make sense of frailty and defeat – the frailty of songs written and sung out of defeat. Yes, that Abbey Road! Eisler lived there in 1934, as if reconnoitering the place for what was to come, as if – as he says himself twenty-five years later, oblivious to the massive changes that are to overtake popular music – he was the "messenger who has to deliver something that endures."[185]

---

182 Ibid, p140

183 Ibid, p203

184 Ibid, p21

185 Hanns Eisler, *Brecht, Music and Culture*, op cit, p178

So, when I say that the late English counterculture moves of Henry Cow re-configure the 'mass songs' of Weill and Eisler, they draw on more than an extant political aesthetics. They give the dying embers of the counter-culture a glimpse of where the musicological struggles of the remaking of the popular and the avant-garde come from. In the musicology of Eisler the song-form is the ballast of any dialectical encounter between the pop-ular and the immanent-aesthetic; and Henry Cow at least acknowledged this in *In Praise of Learning* (a Brecht title of course).

That this re-functioning of the mass song created little intellectual curi-osity in England in 1975 in the counterculture, however, is not surpris-ing, given how rarely performed Brecht and Eisler, and Brecht and Weill were during this period, although *The Threepenny Opera* was staged at the Prince of Wales Theatre in February 1972, with Vanessa Redgrave and Barbara Windsor, directed by Tony Richardson, in a translation by Hugh MacDiarmid. Brecht's influence on new English theatre was certainly palpable and long overdue in these years, after John Osborne's petty-bourgeois self-lacerations: Edward Bond, John Arden, Howard Brenton, Howard Barker, and Caryl Churchill, are all indebted to the interrogatory demands of Brecht's dramaturgy. Yet the untying of old assumptions and expectations seemed short-lived and largely divorced from the wider questions about cultural transformation that the rapidly retreating counterculture had enabled. Thus, most of the innovative the-oretical work on Brecht's dramaturgy and philosophy of drama and the popular was actually being done far away from the Royal Court and oth-er would-be 'centres of excellence,' in film theory (*Screen*), where there was an active culture of reception for an interdisciplinary theatre, and the political willingness to dismantle the restorative tendencies of liberal English high culture. But this does not mean that Henry Cow's opening up of progressive rock to movementist song-forms did not produce any ideological after-effects at all, or failed to reorient some musicians and listeners to find points of connection beyond the obvious. Thus, as the populist rock revival gathers force in 1975 to mutate into punk, one of the key shifts out of the last days of progressive rock is a newly attuned sensitivity to the song of ironized and cynical social reflection and to the song of experience and solidarity, that the old movementist folk singers took for granted. The idea of the song-form as a vehicle for extended vocal and instrumentation exchange is in retreat, to be replaced by the revival of a punchy miniaturism – the three-minute rock song – which is also reflected in the shift in reggae from the formal innovations of dub to Bob Marley's stately songs of liberation. One singer who transitions between the end of the old counterculture and the new song-forms, with some élan, and a sense of the new is Robert Wyatt.

Wyatt is one of the few musicians who exits the end days of the counterculture, with his achievements intact as a basis for new serious work, as if at some point, his attachment to the song-form finally began to make sense to him, in a situation where the larger scenic shifts of the counterculture began to fall apart. In 1971 he leaves Soft Machine in order to start new and varied projects, but after breaking his back and being confined to a wheelchair in 1973, and as such unable to drum except in the most perfunctory of ways, he has to rethink his options. As such he turns extensively to song composition and home recording. *Rock Bottom* (1974), the first album of songs he records after his accident, defines this moment of transition out of progressive rock and the late counterculture. Still very much attached to the heterodox possibilities of the song-form, nevertheless, the album also looks for a way of opening up a post-progressive rock space for the non-traditional song. In this respect the songs draw on all those techniques of vocal indeterminacy and de-masculinized drift he developed in Soft Machine; but subjects them for the first time to the structure and discipline of the song sequence – if not exactly the song cycle. But if these are songs of experience – love and commitment, alcoholism, depression and self-harm – remodeled, through a stripped-down progressive rock instrumentation (Wyatt is backed, either by Richard Sinclair or Hugh Hopper on bass and Fred Frith on viola on 'Little Red Robin Hood Hit the Road') they still retain a connection to the familiar threnodic tone of the early days. One might say, then, that the disparate effects of threnody are given an integrated form. This is mostly due to Wyatt's dissolving each song into the next and the systematic use of drone-patterns and multitracked organ on some songs ('Little Red Robin Hit the Road'), that parallel and underwrite his soft, sopranic, sung-spoken voice. The result is a kind of aquatic, melancholic undulation that runs across the album, as if Wyatt's voice is being carried slowly along by the stream of the instrumentation, for example in his singing against Hopper's high-register bass on 'Alifib,' creating, overall, a raga or trance-like quality. Supposedly influenced by the vocal flows of *Astral Weeks,* the album shows what had been incubated in Soft Machine and his previous collaborations. As Wyatt was to say: *Rock Bottom* "isn't rock 'n' roll, it isn't jazz, it isn't modern classical music, it isn't folk music. It doesn't exist as a genre."[186] Yet, nevertheless the album is a showcase for the kind of

---

186 O'Dair, *Different Every Time*, op cit, p203

song that the indisciplinarity and hybridity of the English counterculture made possible, and that Wyatt himself contributed to with Soft Machine. In this, *Rock Bottom* resists the growing pressure to miniaturise the song and return it to a stable set of conventional rock markers, reconfirming the song-form as a continuing site of subjective-expressive possibility.

This is also reflected in his next album *Ruth is Stranger Than Richard* (1975), on which he collaborates with Frith on a number of songs (*Muddy Mouse,* a b, and c, and *Muddy Mouth*). Less distinctive than *Rock Bottom* – possibly because Wyatt is not the sole composer of any tracks, with the exception of 'Solar Flares,' which he had written two years previously – nonetheless, it reworks his familiar threnodic and langorous style (on 'Side Richard'), only this time without the multilayered sonic textures of *Rock Bottom*; piano and voice alone predominate, with intermittent backing from Bill MacCormick on bass and Gary Windo on bass clarinet and tenor/alto sax. Yet if both albums sustain a heterodox engagement with the post-generic song-form opened up by the counterculture, Wyatt, also begins to commit himself to a refunctioning of the Weillian 'mass song' and the contemporary pop song in a spirit of surrealist *détournement,* whilst, at the same time, recovering the song of solidarity and protest for a new rock audience, via the aesthetics of the readymade of Viv Stanshall and *Sgt. Pepper*. This 'interpretative' political-archival work doesn't overtake his primary commitment to composition and new song-forms, but forms a parallel activity that highlights the contemporary possibilities of the 'mass song,' particularly after Margaret Thatcher comes to power. In this he is less interested in bridging these approaches to create a new modernist 'mass song' as such – in the manner of Henry Cow – than in acting as a kind of political tribune and poetic/bardic vector through which the songs are ideologically re-functioned. In the case of the highly familiar pop songs, Neil Diamond's/The Monkees 'I'm a Believer' and Chic's 'At Last I'm Free,' he takes the upbeat gloss and self-assertion of the Monkees, and Chic's slow soul ballad, to reveal a 'hidden' melancholy, that, in a chiasmic displacement (in the context of his political commitments) becomes a sober approbation of revolutionary hope, much in the spirit of Eisler's 'pessimism is the best.' His gorgeous version of Nile Rodgers 'At Last I'm Free' (ostensibly a love song), from 1982 opens up a wonderfully rich, semantic content in which 'I,' emancipatory struggle and historical defeat obliquely collide. "At last I am free. I can hardly see in front of me. I can hardly see in front...of... me," (words that Rodgers wrote apparently when he was a Black Panther, after being attacked by police in Central Park in New York). In the case of the canonic communist songs of commitment – the 'Internationale,' the 'Red Flag,' 'Stalin Wasn't Stallin' – he reinvests their deflated capacity for solidarity (outside of the communist movement) – their 'dead Stalinist semantics' – with a reflective longing.

This reinvestment here in these still ideologically rich (latent) song-forms has a precise political provenance for Wyatt, who at the time was a member of the Communist Party of Great Britain, joining in 1979: that is, his treatment of these canonic songs faces two ways simultaneously. On the one hand, they display an obvious commitment to the political 'mass song' canon – and its incorporation in a global tradition of the popular song – but on the other, they are the work of a dissident communist tradition inside the Communist party after the 1970s, in which after the mass exoduses of the 1950s and 1960s, communist practice becomes expressly anti-Stalinist. Or more precisely: Stalin and the Soviet peoples' heroic struggle against fascism during WWII, is separated from Stalinism as a bureaucratic system and oppressive politics, and Stalinism, in turn, is separated from communism as a workers' internationalism. The primary task was still to defend the Soviet Union as socialist bulwark against American imperialism, but to disarticulate its present and future from the crimes of Stalinism. This obviously presented a number of irresolvable tensions on the ground: the post-revolutionary achievements of Soviet communism were hardly and rarely distinguishable from the practices of Stalinism. Yet, it points to one of the forces that drove Communist party politics in the West and Africa in this period as they became increasingly uncoupled from 'Sovietism': a return to the popular front cultural politics of the 1930s and early 1940s in the USA, that had continued to have considerable cultural success in those Western Parties where Sovietism was irrelevant to local histories and struggles, such as Italy in the 1960s, and South Africa in the 1970s. The party that Wyatt joined in 1979 was certainly tired, even de-fanged, but it had this rich range of cultural precedents to draw on, that enabled Wyatt and many other musicians and cultural workers to link their own heterogenous interests and commitments to a new movementism – however tenuous it actually was – as Thatcher and Ronald Reagan came to power.

One might say, therefore, that Wyatt's involvement with the CPGB was certainly *contraire*, given his recent countercultural past, and given the growing post-Stalinist crisis of Soviet Communism, yet it in its very perverse steadfastness, it throws into relief, a deepening political crisis – or crisis of the political – that had already swallowed the counterculture and its own revolutionary hopes, and that was now in the process of completely swallowing the old left itself. It also echoes more prosaically the Dadaist Tristan Tzara's decision to join the French Communist Party in 1936 during the Soviet purges, in order to get 'his hands dirty' (although he left in 1956). So, when you hear Wyatt singing 'At Last I'm Free,' in 1982 on *Nothing Can Stop Us*, at the beginning of the Thatcher government's attack on the old industrial working class heartlands of Britain, you can also hear his own willingly embraced predicament; freed from the impossible expectations of the counterculture revolution into the concrete struggles of party politics, he nevertheless "can hardly see in front" of himself. If it is possible for one person alone to concretize the contradictions of a cultural moment or conjuncture, then Wyatt's exit from the late English counterculture, armed with a new commitment to the song-form, would come pretty close.

Wyatt's musical trajectory from the late 1960s to the mid-1970s and into the early years of Thatcherism follows the indisciplinary challenges and expectations of the period, always sensitive to the demands of the popular and avant-garde in irresolvable tension. And this is why the 'songs of defeat' on the ironically titled *Nothing Can Stop Us*, produce a historical conspectus that shows how long in the making and remaking Hölderlin's songs of 'frailty' have been, and continue to be. These songs move back fifty years to melancholically embrace Brecht and Eisler on Abbey Road. Yet, if they are songs of defeat, as uplifting acts of *détournement* they are also songs that resist the historical reification of meaning. And this is why the defining character of Wyatt's music over and above the reworked hit songs and mass songs, is his continuing commitment to what the counterculture articulated and enabled more defiantly. The songs on *Rock Bottom* and *Ruth is Stranger than Richard* take up a range of indisciplinary techniques and spatiotemporal innovations (voice-instrumental drift), which are indivisible from the achievements of the counterculture and the great modernist transformation of the song-form after 1965. In this respect the frailty of these songs that "belong to the life we want," has to be set against the extraordinary changes in the song-form and the social relations of popular music during the counterculture.

Progressive rock may have been, in the end, an unstable solution to the conflict between the popular (song) and the demands of an immanent-aesthetic, but in its assimilation and reflection on the formal-cultural conflicts and contradictions of the period, it asked of the popular and the avant-garde a number of questions, that fundamentally shifted the 'cognitive economy' of popular music. Rejecting what was conventionally expected by 'use' music as a whole, it produced an unprecedented reordering of the spatial-temporal dynamics of words and music, defying the ethnographic limits of both the conventional 'song of struggle' and of the capacity of the young 'untrained' consumer for attentive-listening. Indeed, in its re-functioning and re-assemblage of the attenuated sonic spaces of free jazz and post-1950s atonal and environmental music, within the framework of the song-form and music-theatre, progressive rock arrested the cognitive regression and depoliticization of popular music, whilst drawing on rock music's formidable libidinal and collective energies. The spatiotemporal extension of the reception of popular music is, then, a determining factor in the music's cognitive and collective impact. As Todd Gitlin recalls:

> the afternoons and evenings seemed to stretch, the present liquidly filling all time past and time future, not just the words but the spaces between notes saturated by significance, the instruments sounding in the ear more distinctly than could have been imagined before. The songs drifted on, and on, leisurely, taking their sweet time; no longer were they written for efficient two-minute jabs on AM radio.[187]

This is why words such as attenuation, stretching, drift, that I have used repeatedly in my analysis of the music of the period, are more than the formal attributes of the new song-form and progressive rock, they define a mode of production and as such a corresponding set of conditions of reception. In line with jazz, post-50s atonal music and the new sonic environmentalism, listening to popular music is separated from the immediate needs of dancing, atmospheric distraction, and subcultural identification. Consequently, the extended song-form and the extended conditions of production and reception of progressive rock have an extra-musical significance here: they are the means by which musicians and listeners were able to secure the requisite cognitive distance from traditional popular culture as the basis for a different set of social attachments and investments in making and listening to music.

---

187 Todd Gitlin, *The Sixties: Years of Hope, Days of Rage* [1987], Bantam, New York, 1993, p202

In this sense the de-temporalizing social form of the counterculture – its commitment to dissolving the structures of incorporation into segmented work time and leisure time – find its musical correlation in the extended form and conditions of reception of the music of the period. The resistance of the lived social relations of the counterculture to 'segmented time' and the resistance of the new popular music to the segmented constraints of the old popular culture, co-define each other. There is an important, sense, therefore, that for the first time under industrial capitalism the 'time' of popular music is out of sync with the drive to segmentation and repetition. As such there is a material-technical dynamic to this transformation. The success of this spatial shift would not have happened if musicians had not readily taken the opportunity that was presented to them by the new recording technologies and techniques in the wake of the music industry's development of the 33rpm album in the early 1950s (first introduced in 1948). With the development of the 33rpm LP the music industry was able to record on to vinyl music to high standards of fidelity for around 45 minutes in duration, enabling popular musicians to compose material and improvise beyond standard lengths. Moreover, it enabled musicians to think of the 33rpm vinyl album as an extended finite space for the production of one complete work, or a number of works within an extended sequence – for example the song cycle – that invited the listener at home to listen to the whole album in one sitting, as opposed to listening to a single or singles or, distractedly to tracks on the radio. Duration does not produce attentiveness in and of itself, but it does condition the listener – in Adorno's sense – to follow the immanent changes in the structure of the music, and therefore allow the space to 'think' the relationship between its parts. This meant that listening to three-minute singles alone, for a new generation of record buyers, felt like a diminished or incomplete experience given the concert and recording possibilities opening up to the new music. Furthermore, the extended duration of popular music enabled by LPs also coincided with a new economy of scale in the music industry in the 1960s, as a result of the willingness of small record companies and some larger companies, to allow the new musics to define new audiences as opposed to the record companies imposing what appeared most saleable about the new music on new audiences (which of course eventually happened).

> The period of 1965 to 1970 was one of "turbulence" for the record industry. It was struggling to absorb a strange new style, rock; record company executives were often unsure as to what would sell, and how to

best market records for specific record-buying pub-
lics. This situation encouraged a healthy competition
among the large labels, as well as musical experimentation on the part of musicians. The economic
vitality of the late 1960s and early 1970s made such
experimentation a commercially viable proposi-
tion for large and midsized record labels alike. As a
result, musicians had unprecedented leverage with
the record companies in terms of what they were
allowed to release; they were often encouraged in
their eclecticism and experimentation by sympathetic record company figures. Furthermore, they were
given a control of the recorded product in terms of
production, graphics and album cover art, packing,
etc., that earlier popular musicians could have only
dreamed about.[188]

But if changes in recording technology and studio production and the
willingness of record companies keen to 'wait and see,' provided the necessary conditions for the new music, they were not sufficient conditions.
The new record companies were responding to forces that initially they
had little influence over, insofar as the new music was not simply a transformation in taste – that the companies could channel and finesse in
their own interests – but a manifestation of widespread changes in cultural allegiances and class-cognitive sensitivities, that bypassed the usual
music industry demographics and manipulations. If the major companies or 'independent' companies had ignored the music or insisted that
albums were only for compilations, this would of course have blunted
the music's distribution, but the counterculture and its revolution in sensibility would have rolled on regardless, eventually bringing the companies in line.

The new young listeners, therefore, were not produced as listeners
through access to the new technologies of production alone. On the contrary, they were led to the music, live and recorded, as a consequence of
their desire to see a different kind of music come into being and flourish,
and as such, the desire for a new culture that was greater than the sum
of its individual musical parts. The culture created the expectations for
a new music. This is why Edward Macan's reflection on record company

---

188 Edward Macan, *Rocking the Classics*, op cit, p190

pragmatics above – as if the counterculture was simply a happy and fortuitous encounter between shifts in adolescent taste and the new techniques of recording – fails to address how the changes in technological re-
production at the time, converge with, and are *shaped by*, the techniques
of indisciplinarity released by the changes in the class relations of popular
music's production and reception. The extension of the song-form and
reworking of the song cycle under progressive rock is not simply about
the *filling up* of the newly available recording space, or an opportunity
for musicians to 'express' themselves outside of the usual constraints, but
a way of re-functioning the cognitive boundaries of popular music and,
therefore, a way of redefining the ideological priorities and subjective
conditions of the popular. And it was not just the musicians who did this,
but also, importantly, the audience. It was the demand of those listeners
who wanted a different stake in a different kind of culture – a culture
distinguishable from compulsive repetition – that enabled musicians to
continue to demand formal control over what they wrote and recorded. And this is why the extended song-form and spatiality of progressive
rock, demonstrates a reflexiveness that is no different from free-form jazz
and new classical music; the popular music of the counterculture, the
avant-garde and new classical music, all identify the temporal compres-
sions of commercial popular music as being oppressive. But, for the best
of the new music in England in the late 1960s and early 1970s, securing
the new popular music's distance from these constraints was not simply
about imitating the immanent-aesthetic duration of 'serious' music, but
of resisting pre-judgements about what the popular should do or could
not do. The new conditions of production and reception were never
about exiting the popular, the diatonic, and the libidinal energy of rock
as such. Allowing extensity to play its part in this was therefore, crucial;
but extensity and complexity alone could not guarantee attentiveness or
even interest. Crucially the fundamental issue of the expanded spatiality
and hybridity of popular music in the counterculture was *control*; control
over how and to what ends musicians were able to work through the contradictions of making new music for the market. Extensity of form and
a defiant musicianship and the creation of a new generation of listeners
were expressions of this. That the music industry after 1976 clawed back
some of this autonomy, for fear of musicians and trained listeners 'taking
over' popular music, so to speak, does not diminish its ambitions, or its
after-effects, certainly in the wake of punk and the great expansion of
the heterodox popular song in the early 1980s, if not the expansion the
song-*form* as such.

CONCLUSION

IN 1965 BEFORE THE AMERICAN COUNTERCULTURE HAD HARDLY COM-
mitted its first extended guitar solo to disc, Frank Zappa wrote a snide,
typically cynical song about the Watts Riots in LA, 'Trouble Every Day,'
which was included on the Mothers of Invention's *Freak Out!* (1966). A
churning New Orleans, swamp-rock song about the violence and loot-
ing, it did nothing to hide its distaste for the rioters as much as the police,
with a mocking glee that he was watching it all unfold on TV, and pre-
sumably not in his back yard. The music is tedious and the sentiments are
outré and emotionally disconnected – as is most of the album – as if there
was nothing there on the streets in Watts, no black bodies and lives destroyed by a grinding racism, and that a musician notionally attached to
a radical culture unfolding coast to coast could not use, with some understanding. But that would have been illicit to Zappa, a failure of nerve for
the musician, who should know better than sing about a world oblivious
to the entreaties of musicians with ideas and ideals. 'Nothing to see here'
and 'nothing to hold on to' could have been Zappa's mantras in the late
sixties and early seventies. Thus, even before the counterculture in the
US had a chance to feel and assess its own losses, failings, and false turns,
Zappa was attacking it unremittingly in his songs and public statements,

as if the counterculture was personally responsible for post-war monopoly capitalism. Indeed, in a hypertrophic reading of 'mass culture' as a totalizing system of control, Zappa, talks about the counterculture as if all its musical ambitions, social relations and critical values were an elaborate fraud, an unstable Potemkin-like structure of monetized self-delusion or political naivety. Thus, for those who don't want to look too closely at the counterculture Zappa's cynicism seems to hit the mark; a dose of righteous realism in a sea of irreality and West Coast 'blah.' And his position didn't change much. In a 1969 interview he bewailed:

> So there's a bunch of youthful British leftists who take the same leftist view the world over. It's like belonging to a car club...Basing their principles on Marxist doctrine this or Mao Tse-Tung that... It's really depressing to sit in front of a large number of people and have them all be that stupid, all at once.[189]

And in the 1990s looking back on the sixties: "most of [the music] was manufactured, the goal was to make money and not create an anthem for a generation."[190]

The critique of 'mass culture' then is barely cognizant of what can oppose it. In fact, whatever kind of critical values might be attachable to Zappa at various points in his career (*Hot Rats*) – when his music is most threatened by conservative forces – most of the time, and certainly at the high point of the counterculture, he sounds like a roustabout Spiro Agnew – a Spiro Agnew, that is, who had been given a wig and costume and lucrative contract, and told to get on and make mischief. And much mischief *was* made, but to little avail musically – although, with a sprawling, misplaced energy and hubris. Zappa's early albums (*Freak Out!*, *Cruising With Ruben & the Jets* [1968], and *We're Only in it for the Money* [1968]), are bewildering in the ornate efforts they go to pastiche popular song-forms and pursue their doctrinaire anti-countercultural

---

189 Frank Zappa interviewed by Larry Kart, 'Zappa: The Mother in Us All,' *Down Beat*, October 30, 1969, quoted in Doyle Green, *Rock, Counterculture and the Avant-Garde, 1966-1970: How the Beatles, Frank Zappa and the Velvet Underground Defined an Era*, McFarland & Company, Jefferson, North Carolina, 2016.

190 David Wragg, 'Or Any Art at All? Frank Zappa Meets Critical Theory,' *Popular Music*, Vol 20, No 2, 2001

invective. Turning immanent critique into a programmatic career move Zappa is nothing short of dogged in his dismay at the counterculture, playing everyone for fools: the punters and fans (particularly women), the countercultural radicals, drug-heads, freak-out musos, politicians and music executives. Spiro Agnew sound-alikes in a wig and costume are pretty thin on the ground in the US counterculture in the late 1960s, particularly those who have turned their cynicism into writing songs that are momentously indifferent to the transformations taking place in popular music. Not even deep-undercover FBI officers in the SDS and West Coast communes thought of this, or imagined it as a possible strategy of ideological 'de-programming.' So, to make a counterculture career out of the intellectual demolition of the counterculture (or a particular emancipatory reading of it), *from its very beginnings*, is unprecedented at the time and extraordinarily perverse. But even more perverse, given Zappa's own avant-garde musical credentials and ambitions, is his preference for the ironization of rock-blues song-forms, rather than their actual transformation and extension; indeed, in the majority of his work he uses irony to block off the modernist refunctioning of the popular song, and as such disrupt the lines of connection between the emancipatory dialectic of the song-form and the formal possibilities opened up by the counterculture, so central to the English counterculture (as in, his album *apostrophe (')*, from 1974). The songs are written in a grey spirit of: this is all mercantile culture deserves, that is, *nothing less than utter gratuitousness* – a position, which despite emerging from a critique of mass culture ends up sounding like the common sense and bottom-line accounting of Tin Pan Alley. Pastiche for the Bonzo Dog Doo-Dah Band and the Beatles, for instance, was always integral to the critique of what the counterculture had thankfully left behind. And this, in many ways, is the root cause of Zappa's and Beefheart's falling out. Beefheart felt he could never fully trust Zappa in supporting his critical claims on the popular song-form, certainly in relation to Zappa's involvement with *Trout Mask Replica*. Even Zappa's invitation to Beefheart to contribute vocals to 'Willie the Pimp' on *Hot Rats*, felt according to Beefheart, as if it was grudging.[191] But for all Zappa's misplaced disaffection here, his position does point to the heightened, and therefore qualitatively different, social and political conditions under which these kinds of judgement were being made in mid-to-late 1960s America. And this has a significant impact on how we read the musicological and literary-scenic achievements of the English

---

191 See, Mark Barnes, *Captain Beefheart: The Biography*, Omnibus Press, London, 2011

music counterculture, and certainly its techniques of indisciplinarity, as we will discuss further below.

Zappa's 'realistic' ironization and redaction of the content of the song-form is the result of the confluence of four sets of social, cultural and political forces, that indisputably raised the temperature of *all* debates on the popular, music, politics and the counterculture in the US during the period. The martial trauma of the Vietnam war and the US's vaulting imperialist South East Asian intervention against Soviet and Chinese communism; the vast penetration of racist oppression and assumptions in everyday life, that reached levels of absolute degradation in the big city ghettoes; the scale, density and hegemony of American mass culture, which, as regards popular music, accounted for 80% of all sales globally; and the retreat and fractiousness of the Old left in the wake of the anti-communist purges during the 1950s, that created a post-party alliance of critical liberal forces and the new left (seeded by the Beats), that began to prioritize a *spiritual* and *cultural* critique of American capitalism above all else – an actionist critique, in fact, that refused to postpone its own emancipatory possibilities to the future and the external 'working out' of the dialectic. All these forces, all absolutely intertwined, produce a social topography, that in its growing tension between its deep structural impediments, and emerging fault lines, doesn't just release a huge outpouring of critical and libidinal energy – as the fault lines widen – but correspondingly produces a centrifugal breakdown in the class, race and sexual relations and social forms of American bourgeois culture. The flight of working class, lower middle class and middle class youth from the suburbs – the 'footsoldiers' of the counterculture – the mass opposition to the Vietnam war, the emergence of revolutionary black struggle, the nascent women's liberation movement, the rise in drug culture, the adaptation of new forms of communal living and non-monogamous sexuality, all work, in a growing vortex of resistance, to reject an overwhelming sense of social and cultural immiseration. Immiseration being a condition of wealth and leisure and high culture as much as of poverty, cultural exclusion, and exploitation, and as such granular in its totalizing extension and penetration, across work place, family and public life. Shifting this immiseration, therefore, could not be accomplished simply through the standard mixture of critique, petition and wage struggles, but through a vast re-appropriation of everyday experience, in all its particularities, in order to break the link between reality and reason. And this meant, of necessity a reordering of what political action as opposed to cultural activity meant in conditions where the fundamental struggle was seen as being against the cultural and spiritual degradation of capitalism itself. The 'right here, right now' actionism of the US counterculture, consequently, was driven by the exemplary and disruptive act, whether on a mass scale – the huge mobilizations against the war – or on the local scale by neo-Dada and Yippie negations of routine or oppressive realities. 'Doing'-as-'undoing' to great effect or small or incidental effect was equally important and equally destabilizing of common sense and instrumental thinking.

Of course, disordering on this scale needs to be *organized*. And the US counterculture was no different from its allies and critics on the movementist and Party left as seeing its success in terms of how well it strategized and gave collective purposes to the disruptions and anti-war and anti-bourgeois spectacles. One of the myths about the US counterculture is that its leading participants and advocates were intellectually indifferent to systematic thinking. They were not, at least before the collapse of the West coast counterculture into New Age life-stylism; what they were indifferent to was taking for granted the notion that critical reason alone guaranteed emancipatory transformation. Yet, in the end, it is the question of how you organize *after* the intensity of here and now actionism and the avant-gardism of the will has passed – indeed has been suppressed or assimilated – that is crucial to the future of any revolution in cultural values and sensibility; how you go on after 'clearing up' so to speak; how you produce historical testimony as practice. All revolutions in sensibility and lived relations divorced from the structural negation of capital, will, of course fail as systemic transformations. But knowing this before the doing of it is no answer, for the doing itself is the 'answer.' This is why the organized old left was undoubtedly correct about the counterculture's increasing drift away from the necessity of building 'non-cultural' alliances with labour. But the revolutionary dynamic of the American counterculture had already *exceeded* the demands of labour itself, making the prospect of labour leaders 'correcting' or 'adjusting' the avant-garde and cultural demands of the counterculture in the end regressive. In other words, this excess of the counterculture had already dispossessed class struggle of its traditional (ethnographic) coordinates and horizons. This is why the US counterculture demonstrates an anomic and unmanageable dynamic, which is unprecedented during this period of radical global upsurge. As Todd Gitlin declares: the counterculture,

> whatever it was, was beyond our control [the left
> that is], and we must have sensed that the disciplines

of politics (including our own) were in danger of being overwhelmed.... That all these uprisings should
have materialized in the first place from anesthetized
America was altogether astounding.[192]

It is no surprise, therefore, that the new music becomes key to this diffu-
sion in the US. As a series of intense points of mediation and symbolic
amplification of this actionism and dissonance and revolt it makes the
collective use values of the rock music central to the social impact of these
wider struggles and disruptions, that is: rock makes the direct transformation in values and sensibility legible and functional on an *everyday basis*. And this is why mass culture's shaping of the US counterculture from
the beginning is so influential: it produces a *heightening* effect that is very
different to England and elsewhere, because of the sheer scale and integrated texture of its impact. Given the extensive geographical distances
coast to coast, America's large population and disparate communities and
weak shared cultural reference points, it is the mass distribution of the
music in tandem with the increased impact of image culture via TV, that
gives the music a hegemonic reach and vast social compass dispropor-
tionate to the influence of the number of those young people actually
involved in the production of the music and the counterculture on the
ground. Accordingly, as a consequence of the huge sales of popular music, and given popular music's powers of collectivization, the stakes of
music for the counterculture become very high indeed, as high, in fact,
as the politics of the counterculture itself. This is because popular music
in this period concretizes and sensitizes listeners to the possibilities and
limitations of mass culture as mediation of collective experience in new
and intense ways.

Thus, around the same time Zappa was writing 'Trouble Every Day' and
denigrating the new music as no more than a money-making machine
– and as such failing to learn from the counter-hegemonic demands of
the moment – in August 1965 Barry McGuire went to the top of the
American charts with his anti-nuclear anthem 'Eve of Destruction' (written by the 19 years old, P.F. Sloan), the first loosely movementist song of
the period to do so. What is extraordinary is that McGuire achieved this
with very little mainstream airplay, as the state and radio owners found
ways of excluding the song on grounds of Cold War patriotism and moral propriety, increasing the sense for those who bought the record and

---

192 Todd Gitlin, *The Sixties*, op cit, p212 & p221

identified with it that this was a real breakthrough. As a result, the press and guardians of public order lost no time in attacking it for its subversion and countercultural recalcitrance. Indeed, for those who saw its 'dark humanism' as anti-patriotic it became, a "surrender to atheistic international Communism."[193] One doesn't have to like the song at all to realize that its rise to prominence represents a fundamental shift in cultural and political expectations, over and above simplistic notions of music business opportunism. Not even Woody Guthrie could have dreamt about writing a song that successfully linked popular democratic sentiments to a dissonant rejection of US foreign policy. No wonder conservative record companies were roped into replying and encouraged to release patriotic spoilers – which all sold poorly – because at this particular point, prior to the Beatles own dissonant entry into the counterculture, the impact of such a song felt like pop music could unnerve as well as raise the temperature of teenagers on the dance floor. So, when *Freak Out!* is released, Zappa's ice-cold pastiche and irony looks more like bad faith than canny critique: an evasion of the contradictions of music's commodity form. But then, again, one can see how easily the totalizing critique of American mass culture, and the totalizing (Cold War) critique of the legacy of left movementism go hand in hand in the growing libertarian masculine attachment to rock in the US counterculture, and therefore, how Zappa's cynicism feeds into the celebration of rock as such.

As a 'third move' the libertarian ideology of US rock in the late 1960s establishes its non-conformity through the rejection of both the would-be passivity of the mass cultural song and the perceived inertia of popular music's attachment to the political collective. Zappa's 'realism' is therefore an early version of this. For by 1967 it is rock *itself* in the US – even, in Zappa's alt-capitalist, pastiche version – that provides the countercultural uplift, and as such defines the counterculture's symbolic release from the Moloch of 'straight' culture. In other words, rock and libertarian ideology get overwhelmingly entangled in the US as a consequence of the massive social and political forces that subtend the critical formation of the counterculture, producing a romantic notion of the rock musician as an outrider to bourgeois conformities, and, therefore, attaching rock's successes and failures, omissions and commissions, to a familiar narrative of betrayal and redemption. This is the heightened ideological effect of the US counterculture of which I speak; and, as a consequence, there is a

---

193 Gitlin, *The Sixties*, op cit, p195

constant desire at this time to renew rock's intensities, as if these alone are the measure of the counterculture's transformative power.

Consequently, one can see why the libidinal drive of rock in the US counterculture appeared so enthralling, yet so, overbearing to some English ears in the 1960s, given that rock didn't seem to carry the same sense of disorder and profound collective force in an English culture only just dissociating itself from Empire, and still barely conversant with the intense modernism that had driven so much of the US counterculture's dissonant literary rebellions. By 1965, Dylan had been absorbed as the link between folk past and rock future, but there was no obvious transmission belt between the realities of a US counterculture, borne of massive social struggles, that had, affected all generations and all classes (sympathetic or violently opposed) and the staid rituals, dreary platitudes and tawdry confinements of a post-1950s English bourgeois culture in decline. There is a sense, then, that the US counterculture is far bigger in its reach than its musical dynamic, even if it is the music that sustains much of its social and collective impetus. The counterculture in England is likewise bigger in its reach than its musical achievements, but it is precisely *music* that is decisive in the class transformations that occur in the English counterculture. This is because the English counterculture's mediation of social and cultural crisis is not politically systemic in the way that the American counterculture is. Social, cultural and political struggles, do not reach the same level of intense interconnection as they do in America, given the counterculture's reliance on, or recovery of, a pre-industrial pastoralism and paganism and local plebeian traditions. This is why we might say that the English counterculture in the mid-sixties, is *deflationary and disaffirmative* as opposed to revolutionary, and as such, its musical achievements are defined and enabled not by the mass exodus of workers and the lower middle class from the suburbs into the cultural hubs of the metropolis, but with a negotiated rejection of class expectations locally, in small towns and cities, on the terrain of popular participation in, and consumption of, music itself and the creation of new cultural values; hence, the importance of the South East of England to the development of progressive rock. Thus, in these terms what distinguishes the US counterculture and its heightening of sensibility is the *abandonment* of class as a defining category of struggle. This abandonment is a condition of the rejection of bourgeois culture and the entry of young workers, the lower middle class and middle class into the counterculture. In England there is no general and utopian dissolution of class relations in this sense – a generalized 'leaving' of class as a rejection of wage-labour and parental and state control – but an uncertain meeting of working class, lower middle class and middle class, as they come to define an egalitarian place for themselves as other than wage-labourers – particularly through music – on the terrain of the new culture.

One can see, therefore, why the varied and innovative techniques of indisciplinarity are definitional of the English counterculture in the 1960s and early 1970s: they are linked to a counter-hegemonic project that takes its distance from Empire, English high culture and traditional popular culture, and those forms of American popular music – particularly rock – that seemed irrelevant or a hindrance to making music of distinction, under very different conditions to that of the US. This doesn't mean that the music of the English counterculture defines itself against the music of the American counterculture. But it does mean that American popular culture and American rock culture – even in their countercultural forms – are subject to critical scrutiny, and, therefore, to judgements about what is useful and amenable to the remaking of English popular music and what is not. This is why the mythos of American rebel-rock has very little hold over the best of the new English popular music between 1965-1975; it seems to run counter to what is required of culture seeking to re-define its local identity and critical horizons in the wake of the increasing penetration of American mass culture, and its commercial exploitation and musical narrowing of the counterculture globally. Thus, much of the most significant English music of the period is self-consciously concerned with disentangling the link between libertarian ideology and traditional rock, given the ease with which rock's supposed freedoms were becoming identifiable with those of the American free market. This does not make Zappa's presentiments about the US counterculture correct. Rather it reveals that notions of 'freedom' and 'countercultural resistance' were in the end something other than outriderism, and therefore irreducible to the libidinal affects and energy of rock music, whatever its merits. In other words – for musicians at least – to defend the emancipatory spirit of the counterculture was to resist its increasingly reified masculine images of rebellion and transcendence as a condition of 'going on' musically. It was therefore, imperative – as a matter of musical development and survival – to defend and extend the modernist possibilities of popular music that the counterculture had decisively opened up after 1965. This is why, despite the belatedness of the English counterculture and its relative distance from the heightened intensities of its American counterpart, it allowed space for English musicians to reflect on rock culture itself, in a kind of critical continuity with the wider modernist revaluations of

English culture in the mid-to-late 1960s. As a result, in much the same way British post-bebop and free form jazz in the early-to-mid 1960s was concerned to detach itself from the long arm of American influence,[194] the English counterculture wanted to remake rock culture outside of an egregious Americanism, even if American popular music was seen as the cornerstone of countercultural values. This explains the very different formal and literary content and musicological concerns of English popular music in this period. The 'new folk-thinking,' bardic uplift, post-atonal atmospherics, and song-voice extensities of progressive rock, all rework rock culture from within in a localized rejection of a rock parochialism that was beginning to shape the commercial imperatives of the international, American-led music industry. In these terms what distinguishes the musical transformations of the English counterculture is their greater sensitivity to the contradictions of making music for the market, and, therefore, a greater willingness to resist its centrifugal dynamic, even if this centrifugal dynamic was accompanied by liberationist rhetoric.

But this is not a story about English perspicacity as against American indulgencies, and therefore not a narrative about how English pragmatism wins over American libertarian transcendentalism. But, rather, how a number of English and England-based musicians, given the fluid conditions of production and reception of popular music in the UK in the late 1960s and early 1970s were not blind-sided by rock culture alone as the answer to the condescensions of high culture, and the depredations of mass culture. US rock music seemed too caught up in defining its rebel credentials to notice, firstly, how the axis of popular music had shifted away from the blues – placing different demands on rock – and how rock itself was now utterly congruent with the interests of the music industry and mass culture, aligning conventional American rock/blues – despite its protestations – with a hegemonic Americanism. As such, the US counterculture's assumption that libidinal energy was sufficient to elevate music above these constraints began to look tainted and a conservative limitation on the heterodox possibilities opened up by the modernist innovations of the counterculture. Remember the American counterculture was also the time of the popular success of Grand Funk Railroad, Mountain, The Allman Brothers Band, Country Joe and the Fish, and the Grateful Dead, bands that confused louche blues repetition with extensity. Indeed, Beefheart may have been lauded, but it was bands

---

194 See George McKay, *Circular Breathing: The Cultural Politics of Jazz in Britain*, Duke University Press, Durham, North Carolina, 2005

like these that benefited disproportionately from the US counterculture and codified its 'rebel' images. This is why the English counterculture's response to the insidious entanglements of rebel rock with a narrowing of the musical exigencies of the counterculture, is inseparable from a reflection on Americanism, for good and bad. Americanism is thus both the thing that the English counterculture absorbs and admires for its elementalism and transgressions, and the thing to be dismantled or deflected in the interests of sustaining what is productive in American music (particularly jazz, and the contribution of black modernist jazz musicians), and what is necessary and useable in English and modern European music. Consequently, the music of the English counterculture is historically determined and self-reflexive in ways that are quite different to the music being produced in the US; richer even. And this is why the fixation on 'rock' and outriderism, of transgression and 'selling out' (in Zappa's terms), misses the widespread changes in the class relations of the production and reception of popular music, particularly in England.

In England the late 1960s popular music is both the confirmation of an empty adolescent working class and lower-middle class rebellion – sold back as the countercultural spirit of the times – and the destabilizing exit point into new musics, in which the working class and lower middle class participate in the production of new values, irreconcilable with the expectations of the old bourgeois culture; hence the singular importance methodologically of attaching these new values to the production of techniques of indisciplinarity. For this moves us away from an unmediated notion of resistance, to resistance *as* creativity, or more specifically to a notion of working class and lower middle creativity that exceeds its pregiven (ethnographic) limits. Thus it is important to see the production of the English counterculture not as the spontaneous irruption of the newly waged – the result of a bit of extra money in the pockets of adolescents – but as the determined and determinate desire on the part of working class and lower middle musicians and listeners, to make a new place for themselves out of the constraints of post-war high culture and the old popular culture: a radical remaking of the popular that sweeps along all those who see and want to defend its egalitarian *and* musically expanded possibilities. The production of techniques of indisciplinarity is driven by the desire, accordingly, to create new forms and relations that redefine and re-function the very meaning of the making of popular music. That this occurs with the richness and complexity it does in England between 1965 and 1975 is the result of a unique conjunction of social and cultural forces that, as I have outlined, form an overlapping constellationality: the

1944 Education Act and the impact of the English art school system on the lives of those with little chance of a higher education; the defence of a postwar anti-imperialism and anti-martial plebeianism; the radical reconnection to utopian visions of the pastoral as a critique of waged labour and city living; the popular opening up of public culture to a belated modernism (Dadaism, Surrealism, prophetic bardism, post-1950s European atonal new musics), and the de-masculinization of rock as a localized, ('new folk-thinking') English distancing from Americanism. If this is not a revolutionary mix in any obvious sense – that is if it lacks the incendiary political context to turn cultural politics into politics – it nevertheless provided the requisite resources to open up a gap between the old culture and the new counterculture, that creates an unprecedented breach of the postwar deference between ruled and rulers. But how big was this gap, and consequently how extensive was its subaltern reach? What did the English counterculture actually achieve 'from below'?

For those critical of the radical claims of the English counterculture, the participation of working class and lower middle class musicians in the production of the new music of the 1960s has always been exaggerated or deemed incidental. Indeed, participation in the most exacting and innovative of the new music was, it is claimed, minimal. Progressive rock only confirms this; its involvement of working class musicians was rare given its fundamental exclusion of the 'untrained.' Moreover, the personnel of the bands who shaped this milieu were remarkably small and geographically limited; musicians moving from one band to another, in a kind of an extended shape-shifting groupuscule, as if each band was a version of another (Egg, Soft Machine, Gong, The Whole World, Matching Mole, Hatfield and the North, King Crimson, Henry Cow, Slapp Happy, National Health). Some of this is true but it also distorts that which enables the innovative work to flourish. The music I discuss in this book is the 'end point,' or concretion, of a long and extensive and uneven process of cultural and musical de-habitation, in which shifts in class relations and identities open up the space for new musical techniques and new modes of attention, that, *all* can learn from. Applying crude demographics and head counting to the English counterculture – in a way similar to the way popular music's multiple use values are easily excised through the fetishisation of commodity fetishism itself – is therefore, secondary to the new horizons and points of heterodox inclusion provided by those (innovative) working class and lower middle class musicians, who reshaped the new music from the ground up, bringing new listeners with them. Consequently, the actuality of the shift in class boundaries of producing and listening does not stand or fall according to the abstract grounds of mass participation; an impossibility under the alienated conditions of waged labour. Obviously, there can be no mass working class participation in a process – such as the radical counter-culture – that runs counter to workers' own perceived needs and place within the hierarchies of official culture. However, there can be a size-able fraction of the class, particularly the young, and particularly through their collaboration with those outside of their class, which, through the transformation of their own needs, shifts – through their own production and commitments – the expectations and perceptions of the class as a whole. In this respect, the significance of the event of the counterculture is not reducible to a sociological (even Adornian) account of its failure to carry through its techniques of indisciplinarity into the heartlands of bourgeois power. On the contrary, the techniques of indisciplinarity in their very doing and answer to what was absent and unformed before, changes the terms of 'going on'; things may go on in the same way before the changes occurred but they can't go on to the *same effect, with the same degree of surety*. Hence, for example, the very act of thinking of the rock 'band' as a place where 'untrained' musicians might give themselves over to 'research' changes how the band-form is thought about forever. All dismissals of the English counterculture of the 1960s as largely a middle class phenomenon – and a mere fluctuation in taste – does a distinct injustice, then, to how techniques of indisciplinarity from below in this way challenged the prevailing postwar class settlement, in which the last thing that workers and the lower-middle class were supposed to produce was meaning. And this is why popular music is fundamental to this reset-tlement; the production of popular music has the heightened capacity to channel 'untrained' creativity.

Thus, we need to be clear: the counterculture was a training ground for this 'untrained' creativity, over and above what it provided as a respite from bourgeois culture, or – for its detractors – what it provided by way of comfort for the music industry. As I have stressed, the fact that the counterculture allowed young workers and the lower-middle class an identity other than that of wage labourers is a determining factor in giv-ing young working class musicians the confidence to create another place for themselves in the culture. Hence the spiritual, transcendental and an-tibourgeois ideologies of the counterculture are residual when compared to the actual transformative technical/cognitive shifts it put in place. Or, rather, such ideologies would have no valence and material manifestation without their connection to, and shaping by, the demands of indisciplinary technique.

But if this challenges the familiar countercultural topography of dupes and rebels, beautiful souls and wayward cynics, we should, however, not lose sight of the fact that counter-hegemonic struggle for new (unalienated) experiences of belonging and attentive-listening, cannot, in themselves, dissolve the wider authoritarian function of music under capitalism; that is, to capture the listener for the pleasures of repetition and standardization and the consolations of the diatonic, and therefore narrow music's extra-musical use values. Indeed, there is no single music out there, past present or future that can achieve this, for music itself cannot do this by itself, which means that the majoritarian fantasies of the mass song – in all its forms – and the minoritarian rigours of the immanent-aesthetic method are equally constrained. Eisler is right in this respect: the pursuit of a singular immanent-aesthetic method, or the reliance on the movementist popular song alone as a source of counter-hegemonic use values, are both delimited in their powers of praxis and 'disalienation.' Yet, music and social transformation happens all the time. This is because the use values of music are social through and through. Music is not the cognitive background to our social world, but the medium through which ideas are imagined and made socially active. In other words, music is not a model for praxis *for* other realms, whose powers of cognition then need to be defended in an ideal form against the standardizations and regressions of mass culture – as in Adorno – but the conflicted and aporetic and unfolding practice of finding a place in this world, here and now. There is therefore no 'emancipation' in one kind of song-form, or objectifiable critical mode of listening; there are only the multiplicities of use in a multiplicity of settings, across a multiplicity of needs. But if this levels off the cognitive value of the popular song-form and immanent-aesthetic method, nevertheless this doesn't answer the collective and affective function of the song-form itself. And this is why although the song-form doesn't have any particular historical and cognitive *privileges*, it does however, have a defining relationship to music as social medium, through its literary and scenic hybridity, that outweighs non-vocal music, given, its rich and extensive range of use values – as I have repeatedly argued in this book. In other words, *the song-form is where the social use values of music are both complexified and extended.* To defend the song-form's possibilities against those who would diminish its musicological value – or limit it instrumentally to the vanguard of politics, in Eisler's sense – was, as we can see clearly now, one of the historical tasks of the English counterculture confronted with that unprecedented space for formal manoeuvre that its modernist cultural belatedness briefly provided. Thus, despite the limitations of Adorno's critique of the popular song, we are back with Adorno here in at least one way.

What is at stake in relation to the conditions of a 'capitalist regression in listening' and, conversely, in relation to popular music's commitment to techniques of indisciplinarity is a modernist responsibility to the song-form itself. If the song-form is to survive as other than repetition, then it has to be subject above all else to the subject-expressive demands of those who being 'untrained' or excluded from the professional domains of music making, would make it their own, or, in collaboration with those who see the collective and transformative value in this. The English counterculture between 1965-1975 understood and practiced something of this in its combined and uncertain traversing and disassembling of the song-form inherited from bourgeois, radical-movementist, and modernist and avant-garde musical traditions. This defines its historical singularity, and its extensive formal achievements, from Robin Williamson and Van Morrison's vocal sonorities, Peter Hammill and Van Der Graaf Generator's literary-scenic song-cycles, and Nick Drake's stark modernist subjectivity, to Robert Wyatt's lamentations and Henry Cow and Dagmar Krause's avant-garde movementism. Consequently, the minoritarian character of this music's engagement with the song-form at the radical height of the counterculture reveals its own distinct moral economy: a commitment to the song as the unfinished work of *poiesis*.

Lightning Source UK Ltd.
Milton Keynes UK
UKHW041008290620
365747UK00001B/32